D1120450

Tara Taylor Quinn

IT HAPPENED ON MAPLE STREET

LIFE . . . ROMANTICIZED

Tara Taylor Quinn

IT HAPPENED ON MAPLE STREET

Health Communications, Inc.
Deerfield Beach, Florida

www.hcibooks.com

Library of Congress Cataloging-in-Publication Data

Quinn, Tara Taylor.
    It happened on Maple Street / Tara Taylor Quinn.
      p. cm.
    ISBN-13: 978-0-7573-1568-8
    ISBN-10: 0-7573-1568-2
    ISBN-13: 978-0-7573-9184-2 (ebk.)
    ISBN-10: 0-7573-9184-2 (ebk.)
    I. Title.
    PS3617.U586I7 2011
    813'.6–dc22

                                                            2011002605

Publisher: Health Communications, Inc.
3201 S.W. 15th Street
Deerfield Beach, FL 33442–8190

TRUE VOWS Series Developer: Olivia Rupprecht
Cover photo ©iStockphoto
Cover design by Larissa Hise Henoch
Interior design by Lawna Patterson Oldfield
Interior formatting by Dawn Von Strolley Grove

For our parents,

Robert Barney, Joyce Barney, and Walter Wright Gumser,

who didn't live to see this day, but who, we believe,

are smiling with us; and Agnes Mary Gumser,

who we know is smiling with us.

And for Mike Barney and Chum Gumser,

the brothers who had such profound impacts

on our lives and left us far too early.

Acknowledgments

THE PARTS OF THIS BOOK THAT TELL OUR LOVE STORY are completely true. The tragedy is completely true. We fictionalized other aspects.

But our true story can't be told without acknowledging the three people who are a result of our having lived:

Rachel Marie Reames
Mindy Jo Barney
Chelsea Lee Barney

Our daughters are by far our greatest accomplishments, and we love them more than life.

We'd also like to thank Lynda Kachurek and Wright State University for their help and support with thirty-year-old photos and documents as we reconstructed our lives.

Dear Reader

YOU ARE HOLDING A ONE-OF-A-KIND STORY. I can say that because I wrote it, and I know that I am never ever going to write another one like it. This is a once-in-a-lifetime kind of book about a once-in-a-lifetime kind of love.

As a naïve and sheltered twenty-year-old, I trusted a man of God. And when he mistreated me, and told me the fault was mine, I believed him. For almost thirty years, I carried the secret of what that man had done to me. . . until my true love came back into my life with the determination *to set me free.*

This book, a romance novel unlike any other, is a tribute to a love that is stronger than time. Stronger than tragedy and human frailties. And it is a coming out. My family and friends will be hearing my story for the first time, right along with the rest of the world. I hope and pray that in its telling, other women will find the courage and conviction that I did not have; the trust and faith, to speak up when they are wronged, to tell someone . . . anyone.

And this book is a tribute to my husband, Tim Barney. He is proof positive that the love I write about, the love that is strong enough to survive anything, really does exist. I am Tara Taylor Quinn, *USA Today* bestselling author of fifty-five romance and suspense novels. And this is my true love story.

To find out more about True Vows, to join our mailing list, and receive occasional giveaways, visit, http://vows.hcibooks.com.

To find out more about Tim and me, including exclusive letters and photos, visit, www.maplestreetbook.com.

And to visit with me or find any of my other novels, please stop by www.tarataylorquinn.com.

Tara Taylor Q

One

I'D NEVER HAD A BOYFRIEND. Never even been on a date. I didn't go to homecoming. Or prom. I'd never been to the movies with a guy. Or anywhere else alone with one, either, unless you counted my brothers and father, which I didn't. I was eighteen years old, almost a sophomore in college. And I'd never been kissed.

There you have it. Right up front. I wasn't one of the popular girls. I read books. All the time. In between classes. During study hall. After school, before dinner, after work and studying, before bed, I read. On weekends, I read. I went babysitting. And I read. Romances. Always romances. Harlequin romances.

I had one in my purse when I drove to Wright State University in Dayton, Ohio, as a very determined, five–foot-two, 100-pound blonde who was certain I was ten feet tall and had strength equal to any challenge.

I started college with a lot to learn, but I knew very clearly what I wanted out of life. On that I didn't waver. At all. I had two goals. I was going to write for Harlequin. And, some day, I was going to find and marry my own Harlequin hero.

I was actually almost in my second year at Wright State because I'd done my first year attending part-time while still in my senior year of high school. I was in college because my father expected me to go to college, and I wanted to get it over as quickly as possible. I didn't argue with my father. Ever.

I was also in college because I absolutely adored learning. It was the writer in me. I could never know enough.

As I parked my new little blue Opel Manta, a month-old eighteenth birthday gift from my parents, in the student parking lot at Wright State University, I knew I was different from everyone else arriving for the first day of classes. I wasn't there to learn a career. I wasn't going to be a nurse or a teacher or anything else the education I was there to receive would provide for me. I'd happily get a degree, but, as a career, I was going to write romances for Harlequin Books. There was no Harlequin major in college. There wasn't a class that studied, or even mentioned, romance novels. There were writing classes, though— more if I majored in English. That semester, I'd signed up for the one writing class I was permitted to take. And I was taking literature, too. Fantasy. I was going to be reading *Voyage of the Dawn Treader*. I was going to learn from the greats.

And because an English major required a science class—something else I'd managed to graduate high school without—I took geology. Blood and guts weren't for me. They'd keep me up nights.

Rocks were innocuous. They'd put me to sleep just fine.

So there I was sitting in a geology lecture hall filled with a hundred strangers who were mostly my age—all of them having been kissed, I was certain—during my first full-time college semester.

Dressed in my favorite pair of faded, hip hugger bell bottom jeans— the ones that I'd cut from the ankle to just below the knee to insert the piece of white and blue flowered cotton fabric—I might look like the other kids. But I wasn't like them. I gripped my pencil, my college-ruled paper blank before me, waiting to take notes.

I'd already decided I'd have to take notes to remain conscious.

I looked around. After having been in class with the same kids for four long years, I still felt a little weird being in a classroom where I didn't know a single soul. Weird and kind of free, too. No one knew I was Tara Gumser, daughter of the Wayne Township school-board president. Daughter of the Rotary Club president. Daughter of the best singer in the church choir. Daughter of the best bridge player in Huber Heights, Ohio. No one knew I hadn't been asked to my proms. Either of them. No one knew I'd never been asked on any kind of date. Ever.

The room buzzed with energy. Freshman energy. After all, life was just beginning. The future was more question than answer—resting largely on the success or failure of the next four years in classrooms just like that one.

Did I stand out?

I didn't have to be there to obtain a future.

I had my future planned. I knew what I wanted and I wasn't going to be swayed.

It was the fall of 1977. I had my whole life before me . . .

~

I saw his hair first. I wasn't a hair person. I was very definitely an eye person. My one close high-school friend and I had talked about it. When I saw a guy, I always looked at his eyes first. And last, too. I didn't care about a man's outer image. Heroes weren't judged by their book covers. What I cared about was a man's heart. His soul. You could only get there through his eyes.

And there was this hair. I saw it walk in the door. Move toward the steps. Move up the steps. The rest of the room really did fade away, just like I'd read about in my books. I mean, the people were there. I still had peripheral vision. I was still aware of the buzz of conversation. But the focus on them faded away. I didn't notice them at all. I watched that head of hair instead.

It was dark. Really dark. Not as harsh as black, but darker than brown. It was thick. And long enough to curl up at the collar. It was parted in the middle and feathered down past his ears. My hair was feathered, too. His feathering was much better.

All I could think about—me, who'd never so much as held a guy's hand in a man/woman way—all I could think about was running my fingers through that hair. I could almost feel the rough silkiness sliding over my hands, tickling the tender joining between my fingers.

And somehow I was lying with him. His arms were around me. How else could I get to that glorious hair?

The body attached to the hair walked close. And then passed me by. Just like that. My great-hair guy was heading up the steps to the back of the room. To sit somewhere else. Near someone else.

But not before I'd caught a glimpse of his eyes.

They were brown. And there was something about them, a depth, that disturbed me.

For the first time in my life I'd come in contact with a real-life guy who intrigued me. Really intrigued me. Enough to make thoughts of my Harlequin heroes fade into the shadows.

More than anything in the world, I wanted to meet that great-hair guy.

I didn't meet him. How could I? It's not like I was going to go speak to him. And say what? *Do you mind if I run my fingers through your hair?*

Or, maybe, *you're the first real, flesh and blood breathing guy I've ever seen who made me feel "things"?*

Of course not—I was Tara Gumser. Walt Gumser's girl-child. I lived with my nose in books. And furthermore, why would I think for one second that a guy as gorgeous as that would have any interest in me, when not one of the 400 boys I'd graduated with had ever asked me out?

Class started. I took notes. And felt "him" behind me the entire time. The back of my neck was warm. My palms were moist.

Through the entire lecture I had one thought on my mind: what went up had to come down. If I busied myself after class, I'd still be standing there when he came back down the steps and left the room. And if I just happened to be leaving my row at the exact time . . .

I had it all planned. I wouldn't say anything to him. I couldn't be that obvious. Nice girls "didn't." My father, who had a temper that scared the bejeezus out of me even though he'd never laid a hand on me, had made it very clear to me that his daughter behaved with modesty and decorum.

Period.

Nice girls didn't talk to boys first. They didn't call boys. They didn't ask a boy out. They didn't let boys know they liked them unless the boy proclaimed his feelings first. And they didn't let boys even so much as smell the cow before he owned the barn. Legally. And had a license as proof.

Class ended. I busied myself closing my notebook very slowly. Conversation buzzed around me. Someone stepped on my foot, in a hurry to vacate the premises. Probably to drop the class.

My entire back burned. My senses were tuned. I had to time my exit just right. And I had to be legitimately occupied until then or I'd appear forward. Like, maybe I was interested or something.

I'd blow it before it had ever begun.

My notebook was closed. My pencil was back in my denim purse. I checked my schedule. Yep, I had a break after that class just like I'd known I did. I stacked my other books up on top of my notebook.

I made sure that my romance novel didn't show out of a corner of my purse. And I turned.

Just in time to see him exit out the other side of his row and trot down the steps on the other side of the room.

I wasn't surprised.

I wasn't like other girls.

I didn't meet guys.

I read books.

⌒

I was a writer. And that was exactly what I wanted to be. What I had to be. I was seventeen when I got my first job as a professional writer.

Seventeen when I received my first paycheck for writing.

It wasn't much. Twenty-five dollars. But on the line that read Pay to the Order of . . . the words typed right there beside them read Tara Gumser. That was me.

And in the upper-left corner, the identifier of the payee, it read, *Dayton Daily News.*

I was a stringer for the largest newspaper in the area. My beat was the Vandalia City council. Vandalia was a small city on the outskirts of Dayton. Once a month I went to their city council meetings, determined what of interest happened, and wrote a story about it.

I was a respected professional and on my way to writing for Harlequin.

I had my whole life in front of me. A whole lot of time to meet my Harlequin hero.

After I'd become somebody he'd want to meet.

I had myself firmly in check two days later when the next geology class rolled around. I'd thought of my great-hair guy far too much. All the time. Even when I was reading. One night, late, I'd been lying in bed reading and somehow my hero had great hair. Dark hair. Longish. Not at all as it looked on the cover of the book. He had brown eyes, too. And legs that looked . . . mmm . . . in jeans as they'd climbed steps.

So I was done. Over the nonsense.

I got to class early. I took my seat. I told myself to look at my literature book. I'd been busy with my real life's work—reading a Harlequin—and hadn't quite finished the reading required for my college literature class.

I couldn't concentrate. I couldn't breathe. I couldn't help glancing toward the door every two seconds.

I couldn't help being disappointed when my great-hair guy arrived and walked past my row without noticing that I was sitting there needing to meet him.

That was it. I was over him.

Over the next weeks, geology class got in my way. I was not interested in the subject, which left me entirely too much time to notice Great-Hair Guy. I'd get bored with the lecture and next thing I knew, class was ending and I'd spent the entire time fantasizing about *him*.

Was there any chance the guy was ever going to say hello to me?

Great-Hair Guy didn't say hello to me. At all. September traveled on. Leaves changed colors and fell to the ground. Some days my feelings felt like those leaves. Like I'd had a glorious moment of colorful possibility and then . . . nothing.

My great-hair guy—I secretly continued to think of him as mine as my thoughts didn't hurt anyone—came to class regularly. That impressed me. He participated, too, like he really knew what was going on.

Igneous, sedimentary, and metamorphic—I remembered the names of the types of rocks but I couldn't distinguish between them. I liked the words. What they represented were all rocks to me.

But I remembered all kinds of details about Great-Hair Guy. Like I was some besotted girl. You know, the kind that irritated me. Like she had no worth on her own but, rather, was judged by how cute her boyfriend was.

Great-Hair Guy had changed me. He'd impacted my life in a way I would not forget. I felt "things" whenever he was anywhere close to me. And I promised myself that I was the only one who'd ever know what he did to me. It was my embarrassing and shameful secret.

I knew I'd be the only one who ever knew that Great-Hair Guy gave me feelings down below as surely as I knew that I was going to write for Harlequin some day. As surely as I knew that I would find my Harlequin hero. Out there. When I was ready.

Just like all the boys in high school, Great-Hair Guy didn't seek me out. Didn't even notice me. The only difference was, this time I cared.

And just to make my life more miserable, there was a geology lab that I was required to attend if I wanted to fulfill my science credit and graduate from college. Lab classes started several weeks later than lecture and had fewer students per class.

Would Great-Hair Guy be in my lab?

I tried so hard not to worry about whether or not my hair stayed flipped under at the ends, whether or not my feathers winged. I tried not to picture myself in a pair of male eyes when I chose the tight jeans and the shirt that hugged my breasts. The shiny blue shadow I smeared on my eyelids might bring out the blue in my eyes—my best feature—but who was going to notice?

The chances of my great-hair guy being in the same lab I was in were minimal. The idea that he might actually notice me was ludicrous. And if I thought for one second he would ever speak to me I really was living in fantasy land.

I tried so hard not to care.

And my heart beat such a rapid tattoo against my chest when *he* walked in the door of lab I was afraid he'd notice. And think I was some kind of freak.

He didn't notice. My heart rate. Or me.

I was Tara Gumser. I read books.

And I hated geology.

But boy oh boy, did I like my great-hair guy.

I knew where he was every second during lab. It was like I was connected to him. I could feel when he moved. Hear when he talked. It was me I didn't recognize. What was the matter with me?

I was focused. Determined.

I didn't waste time on childish endeavors.

The teacher had papers to hand out. Who cared?

What? Wait! My great-hair guy was handing them out. He was coming my way. Handing a sheet to the guy in front of me. I was going to be next. I was going to make a fool of myself.

I couldn't look at him.

I saw the bottoms of his jeans. Saw the sheet of paper coming toward me.

I looked up.

And saw him.

He saw me, too.

I couldn't breathe. Couldn't be cool and nonchalant. Had no hope whatsoever of sexy.

And he moved on.

I was going to die.

I wanted to die.

And I had to get out of that class so I could relive the encounter, analyze every second again and again. Had I made a fool of myself? Had he noticed me even a little bit? Would he remember that second our eyes had met?

"His name's Tim." I turned to see Ann, a girl I sometimes carpooled with, coming up beside me as I walked down the hall after leaving the lab. I knew Ann from high school. And she knew I had a thing for Great-Hair Guy.

"I saw his notebook," Ann said. She was in lab, too. And she knew I'd never dated.

Tim.

Ann got a kick out of my newly painful state. In a compassionate kind of way.

"Don't look now, but your Tim is behind us," she continued as we walked toward the door of the building.

I didn't look. But I could feel him there.

My Tim.

Two

THERE WAS A TRADITION at Wright State University. A fall party on campus—a welcome to students. October Daze. It was held outside in the field next to the Rathskeller—a pizza-and-beer place on campus. There were booths with food and club paraphernalia. Live bands and lots of beer.

It was exactly the kind of gathering I avoided. I'd made it all the way through high school without attending a single party. Not one. I didn't drink outside of my home, where my dad would occasionally share a sip of his very smooth and expensive scotch whiskey with me because I was the only one in the family besides him who liked it, or my mom would allow me a taste or two from her glass of wine.

"Come on, Tara," Ann said the first Friday afternoon in October— the day after our first geology lab. I was huddled in my raincoat, the bottoms of my jeans dragging on the wet ground, and telling her I wanted to go home. The drizzling had stopped for the moment, but I had a romance novel burning a hole in my purse. I'd had a hard day at school, gotten a paper back in my writing class that the teacher hadn't absolutely loved, and I just wanted to crawl into a story and stay there.

"We *have* to go," Ann was saying. She was trying to talk me into going to October Daze. Because she wanted to go. She wanted to meet up with some guys she knew. "What if he's there?" she continued haranguing me about Great-Hair Guy. "You don't want him to find some other girl without you even having a chance, do you?"

Of course I didn't. "I don't even like beer."

"Have you ever had it?"

"Well . . . no, but I know I don't like it." I liked smooth, expensive scotch. My dad did not drink beer. And I was his drinking buddy. Me with my sip or two on the occasions when he actually had a drink.

"It doesn't matter if you like it or not," Ann laughed and hooked her arm in mine, dragging me down the hill away from my little blue Manta and the school books that she'd ordered we leave there. "You just drink it," she explained.

I let her pull me along. And I laughed, too. I didn't know why. I just did.

I was changing. Life was changing. Anything could happen.

The day was cool, overcast, and misting rain. A typical early October day in Ohio. He was barely eighteen and a bit overwhelmed, but no one was going to know that. He'd made it out of high school. Out of the small town where he'd grown up—even if only during the day. He'd made it to college and to a college party. He was going to enjoy himself.

Even so, the smell of wet grass on the cool air took him back to earlier days of football and playing in the mud. Back to a time when getting dirty was funny—the dirtier the funnier.

When had he left those days behind? When had being respectable become important?

And earning a degree even more important?

He made his way to the twenty-five-cent beer wagons and placed his order. His first college beer, and it was out of a plastic cup.

Silently toasting the college life, he drank. Stroh's had never tasted so good. Looking out over the hundreds of students huddled together, listening to the hippie-looking guys up on stage, he chuckled to himself.

He was a long way from his home on Maple Street. His brothers would be proud.

Two of the band members were hopping around, one on electric guitar, the other dragging a mic stand with him. The third guy was beating on drums as though he could somehow change the world with those sticks.

And all the while, the college students laughed and drank their beer as fast as they could pour it down. It was so different from the small town he'd grown up in.

A different universe.

In Eaton, he knew everyone. Or at least knew someone who knew everyone. Here he didn't know a single person. He was out of place.

But he was staying.

The youngest of five boys—three of whom were at least a full generation older than he, two old enough to be his parent—he'd learned early that he had to tackle life and wrestle from it what he wanted.

His mother, widowed when he was only five, had sacrificed much to get him there. He wasn't going to forget that.

He was going to succeed. Graduate. Make something of his life. He wasn't going to spend his entire life as he'd spent much of his youth, eating well enough at the beginning of the month and being grateful for the beans that were on the table by month's end.

He was going to own a home. And a washing machine.

He sipped his beer—feeling rich just being there—being welcome to the cheap beer and entertainment. They were for him as much as for any other person filling up the expanse of grass and food booths.

He'd had his first geology lab the day before. Held in a rectangular room made of cement block, with a long table in the center of the room, he'd entered slowly. Of the twenty-five seats, there had only been one that he wanted because the desk was strategically placed in direct view of the windows leading to the outside. If lab was boring, he wouldn't be completely cut off from the world.

He'd staked his claim, adjusted his belongings, and noticed the two girls sitting across the aisle.

They were both blonde. Slim. One was blue-eyed. Sweet looking. The other, a made-up and hair-sprayed rendition of the girlfriend every guy wanted.

The sweet looking one had looked out of place.

He'd wanted to meet her.

Thinking about it now, he cringed and took another big gulp of beer.

Lab had begun and the professor had asked for a volunteer to pass out the syllabus. Tim had seen his chance immediately and raised his hand. Passing out the papers would give him a chance to strut his stuff past the blonde—the one who was different. She'd captured his attention.

He'd approached her, smiled his best smile.

And got . . . next to nothing. She'd taken the paper he'd handed her.

Humbled, he'd taken his seat.

He was still thinking about her, though, while he consumed his first college beer, so that when he turned on the grass and saw her, at first he thought he was conjuring her up.

He wouldn't have created the shivering. Or the blue raincoat. But those jeans . . .

He was cold too, but only because he hadn't pulled his sweater on over his T-shirt. Soon the beer would be warming him up just fine. He'd been drinking it since he was a kid.

He'd done his share of cigarette smoking, too. But he was done with that nonsense.

He watched the girl. She was standing with some other people. The made-up girl from geology lab, who was speaking with a couple of guys. If he had his guess, he'd say the blonde in the blue raincoat wasn't hearing a word they were saying. She was looking off over the crowd.

He could approach her. It was a party. People did that.

But he'd tried his charms on her once. And wasn't eager for another . . . nothing.

The made-up blonde wandered off with the two guys. Baseball players, if he had his guess.

He'd made the tennis team. An individual sport. Which suited him just fine. Besides, he was good at it. Had played for his high school, too.

He waited for the girl in the blue raincoat to move along with the rest of her small crowd.

She didn't.

With another sip of beer for courage, he edged his way toward her.

"Hi."

"Hi." She looked straight at him. Like she knew him, or something.

"You look cold." He stood there in his T-shirt, beer in hand, looking warm. He hoped.

"Yeah. I am."

"Aren't you in my geology lab?" He was aiming for casual.

"I don't know, maybe."

"You were sitting with that girl in the blue sweater, right?"

She glanced off in the crowd. "Ann? Yeah." Then she was looking straight at him again with those beautiful blue eyes. She had a grin on her face. And a half-full plastic beer cup in her right hand. Her left arm was folded across her chest, her free hand firmly clinched to her right arm about the elbow, as though hugging away the chill.

"I'm Tim."

She nodded. "I'm Tara."

"You from around here?"

"Huber Heights. How about you?"

"Eaton."

"Where's that?"

"Close to the Indiana border."

"Is it in Ohio?"

He'd been asked before. "Yeah."

"How long does it take you to get here?"

"Forty-five minutes."

"You drive back and forth every day?"

"Yeah, or I catch a ride."

"Wow. I thought my twenty minutes was far."

"It's not so bad." But then, he'd only been at it for a few weeks.

"Is this your first year here?"

"Yeah, I graduated in May."

"I did, too."

She was his age. Good.

Tim didn't want to leave her, but he couldn't think of anything else to say, either.

"Well, I gotta go," he said before things turned bad.

"Yeah, me, too. I'm freezing out here." She didn't move, though.

"Okay, well see you around."

"Okay."

He walked away, feeling as though he was caught in some time warp. Had that really happened? Had he actually just met the girl that he'd noticed in lab?

And that grin she'd given him—stuff like that didn't happen. Especially not to him.

She was cute. Quiet. And she seemed so sweet. Not the type to play with a guy's head, or jump from guy to guy. Tara was the type of young woman mothers approved of.

I didn't tell Ann I'd met him. I didn't tell anyone. Tim was my secret. I didn't want anyone else giving me their opinions about him. He hadn't asked for my phone number. Which I knew would be the first question out of Ann's mouth, and her prognosis, upon hearing the answer, would not be good.

I couldn't bear Ann's sympathy.

Besides, he'd said "See you around," and that could mean that he wanted to see me again. Couldn't it?

I hoped so.

God, I hoped so.

Because thoughts of Tara popped up randomly over the weekend while he was at home on Maple Street, Tim looked for her on campus all day Monday, but she seemed to have dropped off the face of the earth. Then Tuesday morning he turned the corner outside the library and there she was not more than twenty yards away and heading straight toward him.

That girl, Ann, was with her, but he wasn't going to lose his chance.

"Hi," he said.

"Hi." Even he couldn't miss the welcoming smile on her face. She was glad to see him. It was all the encouragement he needed.

"Hey, you want to wait for me before geology lecture today and we can sit together?"

He could feel Ann's stare, but he ignored her.

"Sure."

Score.

Tim was standing in the hallway outside the lecture room, early for a change, when Tara walked up an hour later.

"Hi."

"Hi."

They had that down. It was about all they seemed to say to each other.

"Ready to go in?"

"Yeah."

He held the door open and she walked off with purpose ahead of him, stopping at a seat a lot closer to the front than he would have chosen. Saying nothing, he sat.

She took notes in class. He hadn't expected that, either. There were more important things at hand to talk about. Who cared about rocks?

The more he sat there, taking in her deep powdery smell, the less he wanted to be sitting in class. He had to get out of there before he embarrassed himself. Jeans didn't leave room to hide pertinent evidence.

Class ended and Tara was gathering up her stuff like she had someplace to be. He had to make his move.

She turned, looked him straight in the eye, and he forgot what he'd been about to say.

"You want to sit together on Thursday?" he asked.

"Okay." Her smile had him going all over again.

Kids were leaving around them. Some guy knocked into him. "You busy after class on Thursday?" he blurted next, not quite the way he'd planned.

"No."

"You want to hang out?"

"Okay."

"I don't have a car." He had to tell her. She'd find out soon enough, anyway. "I'm getting one, but I don't have it yet."

"How do you get to and from school?"

"A friend of mine. We graduated together."

"He lives in Eaton, too?" They were walking down the steps of the lecture hall, Tara in front of him, and she turned to look at him.

"Yeah."

"So what's your friend going to do if we hang out after class?"

"He works on Thursdays. I usually just wait around here for him."

"That's no fun. You want to come to my house? You can meet my mom and we can hang out there."

Hell yes, he wanted that. But . . . "I have to be here to meet my friend when he gets off work."

"What time is that?"

"Five."

"I can have you back by then."

She was offering him a piece of heaven. And hell, too. What guy wanted a girl driving him back and forth places? Especially on a first date?

Still, his mom hadn't raised a stupid son. "You sure you don't mind?"

"Of course not."

"Okay then."

"Okay." They were outside class, and Ann was a few steps away, waiting for Tara.

"See you Thursday."

"Okay."

He watched her walk away, noticing how hot her butt looked in her jeans. And then he realized he was grinning.

He'd only been in college for a month and he had a date.

Three

THE TWO DAYS UNTIL THURSDAY WERE INTERMINABLE.
Everyone I knew—my family, Ann, and Rebecca, my closest friend
from high school—knew I had a date. In my world, this was almost as
big as graduation.

And yet I wanted everyone to act, I wanted me to act, as though the
occasion was no big deal.

A boy was coming over. It happened to girls all the time.

I was a nervous wreck all through class, and excited, too, and didn't
hear a single word of the lecture. Tim looked fabulous in his jeans and
sweater.

And on a completely different wavelength, I couldn't wait for my
mom to meet him.

By the time we were in my car, I was shaking. Didn't know what to
do with my hands. Or any other part of me. I was a foreigner in my
own land. Sitting in my own car. Alone with a boy. A man.

I was outside myself, watching me. I had a man in my car. And I was
driving.

Who was this girl?

And how in the hell had the world spun so completely on its axis? In
the space of a week I'd transformed from the bookish girl who no one
noticed, to sitting alone with the man of my dreams. My Tim.

I had no idea what to say.

I knew about romance novels. About dukes and earls and worldly businessmen who flew their own jets and ate girls like me for their afternoon snacks.

And . . .

I knew boys. Of course I did. I lived every day of my life with two of them. They liked sports. And I was the best darn Little League scorekeeper I knew.

"You sure your mom's not going to care that you're bringing me home?"

"Yes." I was positive about that. My parents had despaired over my lack of interest in dating. I'd heard "Get your nose out of that book" so often, I'd started hiding out in the bathroom to read when my parents were still up. Didn't seem to matter how long I took in there, they never bothered me.

And that was not something I was going to tell the man sitting next to me. He was not going to hear about me using the restroom. Ever.

Or about my penchant for romance novels, either. After years of living with my brother's ribbing about them, I knew better than to confess my life's plan.

The fact that I'd never had a date, that this was my first-ever date, fell in that same category.

What guy would want a girl no other guy wanted?

I drove. Hoping I didn't do something stupid.

"Don't worry about my dad," I told the man sitting next to me. "He won't be home when we get there." Dad was on duty at his real estate office and wouldn't be home until after Tim had to leave. Mom and I had made certain of that.

"My older brother isn't there, either," I chattered away, making turns, driving too fast, slowing down too quickly when I came to lights. "He's away at college," I said. "I miss him like crazy. He and I are only thirteen months apart, and last year when he left for Armstrong was the first time in my whole life that we've been separated, and I hate it."

Tim nodded. I caught the motion out of the corner of my eye, and stole a full glance at him. He smiled.

Oh, God. That smile.

He seemed interested in what I was saying. So I kept talking.

"He's a musician. So's my dad. They play by ear. But Chum, that's my brother," I said, embarrassed, as I always was when I first told people my older brother's name. It wasn't his given name, but it's all I'd ever known him by. "Chum plays guitar. He's really good. I play, too, but only for me. I'm not good like he is."

I talked fast. Always had. My brother had teased me about being an auctioneer when I grew up because I talked so fast. Could I help it that I had so many thoughts that they had to race themselves out of my brain?

Another nod. And I said, "Chum's real name is Walter, like my dad and grandfather. When he was born my grandmother was changing him and said that there were too many Walters and told him that he'd always be her little chum. The nickname stuck. None of us ever called him Walt."

I was rambling. Free thinking. It was better than panicking. Or worrying about everything that could go wrong. "I remember when we took him to school a year ago August. The whole family went. It was horrible leaving him there. And on the way home, we were in this podunk place in Alabama, where Armstrong University is, and my dad made a wrong turn and we had to stop at this farmhouse out in the middle of nowhere to ask directions, and the old farmer guy, he looked at us and shook his head and in all seriousness told us we couldn't get there from here. Can you believe it? Like, what, we could never go home because we were there? I mean really . . ."

We were getting closer to my house. Closer to Tim meeting my mother. She just had to like him. I was going to die if she didn't like him.

I was afraid of my father, but next to my childhood soul mate,

Jeanine, who lived with her folks in Wisconsin, my mom was my best friend.

And I was bringing home a person who I would gladly leave my mother's house to be with.

How crazy was that? I barely knew him.

And how could I walk in my house feeling the things that Tim made me feel? I was tingling in places a good girl didn't tingle. Would it show? My mother knew me so well. Would she be able to tell?

Would the neighbors see me pull up with Tim? Would my little brother be home? Was the sky still blue and the grass still green?

I was Tara Gumser.

And I was bringing a man home with me.

"Do you have brothers and sisters?" I asked, because I wanted to know everything about this guy. And because I didn't want to freak myself out about the coming meeting.

"Brothers, no sisters."

He wasn't the most talkative person I'd ever met. But that was okay. I could talk a lot. When I liked the person I was with. I had thoughts about everything.

"How many brothers?"

"Four."

We were stopped, and I stared at him. "Four?"

"Yeah."

"Older or younger?"

"Older."

"You're the youngest of five boys?" My incredulity showed. I wasn't savvy enough to stop myself.

"Yes." He turned and looked out the window. He was shy, and I'd made him uncomfortable.

Calm down, I admonished myself. *You're going to lose him.*

"What about your parents?"

"What about them?"

"Do you live with them?"

"With my mom."

"They're divorced?" I didn't know anyone closely who'd been through a divorce. Or whose parents were divorced.

"No."

"But your dad doesn't live with you?"

"He died when I was five."

Oh my God. My heart bled. All over the car. My dear, sweet, great-haired Tim had pain in his life. I wanted to make it all better right then and there.

"I have a friend—she actually lived with me and my family last year during our senior year of high school—her dad died when she was five, too. He was a teacher. And a football coach. Our high-school football field is named after him and his twin brother, too, who was our tennis coach and athletic director. Heidkamp Field."

He nodded.

"What did your dad do?"

"He was a teacher." And he was done talking.

I wanted to take his pain away.

I was falling in love.

And no one was going to believe that. No one. Not in a million years. But I knew. I recognized the truth as surely as I knew I had to breathe to stay alive. It settled upon me with a certainty that didn't leave room for doubt.

So the secret was mine. To cherish. And to keep hidden away where no one could do it damage.

He sat in the blue Opal Manta watching Tara drive. Not only was she beautiful—so much so that he kept wondering about the abundance of assets hidden behind that soft white top and the tight-fitting blue jeans—she was also an impressive driver.

Her car was a stick shift.

What girl drove a standard-shift car?

Tara did.

Every time she stopped and had to start again, they started moving smoothly, first gear into second, then third, and finally fourth without so much as a hitch. No hopping. He had friends who could still only drive automatics.

Before he knew it, they were in Huber Heights, a newly incorporated city that was a hub of Dayton and swarming with people. So she was a big-city girl and he was a small-town guy—he could hold his own with the best of them.

When she turned off from State Route 201, one of the main roads through Huber Heights, onto Brandt Visa, the suburb's ritziest street, he started to get uncomfortable. He lived in a rented house on Maple Street, with grey exterior shingles. It was nothing compared to the huge brick homes on landscaped acre lots that they were passing by now.

Hopefully they were simply passing all these elegant places to get to a house in the country.

He'd barely finished the thought when Tara made a right turn and then an immediate left into the driveway of a trilevel, Tudor-style house, one of only two homes on Drywood Place. One of two elegant brick custom homes.

"Come on in and meet my mom," she said, turning off the car and grabbing her denim purse.

He was in way over his head.

The front door of the house he'd grown up in was a single piece of wood with a handle that swung open and shut and locked at night. You opened it and walked in one person at a time. Tara approached a set of double doors inlaid with etched glass, put her key in a deadbolt lock, and then pushed gently on one of the pull-style door handles and stood back for him to enter. They could easily have gone in together.

He stepped into a foyer that was as big as the kitchen at home. From there he could see Tara's kitchen, twice the size of the one on Maple Street, and part of a family room off to his left, a formal living room straight ahead, and stairs to the lower level off to his right.

Tara walked toward the kitchen area and, nervous as hell, he followed her. Her mom was standing there in a gray dress and slightly oversized glasses. The only other thing he noticed was her smile.

"Hi, Tim. Welcome," she said.

"Nice to meet you, Mrs. Gumser." He held out his hand. It always felt strange and somewhat confusing to him to meet his friends' parents. They were always about half his mother's age. Tara's mom was no different. She looked to be about the age of his oldest brother.

"It's nice to meet you," she said, taking his hand. Her grip was soft, but sure. Tim liked her. "Tara's talked about you . . ."

"Come on," Tara interrupted, turning back the way they'd come. "I'll show you the rest of the house."

He saw the living room. Her dad's organ. A formal dining room. Some stairs that led, she said, to three bedrooms, including hers, and a couple of bathrooms. She showed him a bedroom on the main level, a laundry room, and another full bathroom. Tim could barely take it all in, and she was heading for the stairs he'd seen off the foyer when they'd come in.

The first thing he saw on the lower level of that house was of a pool table, and he relaxed just a bit for the first time since she'd pulled her little blue car onto Brandt Vista Drive. People with a pool table couldn't be all that uptight.

There was a small office down there, too, but he really liked the room with the wet bar, a full-size working pinball machine, Atari video games, and a poker table. Definitely a man's refuge.

Even the furniture was guy-like—the bottoms of the table and the couches were all made out of beer barrels. There were two couches, black leather with some kind of color design along the back.

"What do you want to do?" she asked. "We can play pinball. Or pool. Or . . ."

He hadn't meant to do it, but she was so damn cute and driving him crazy, and before he had a single thought about the advisability of grabbing a beautiful girl in her home on their first date, Tim pulled Tara to him and pressed his lips against hers.

Just like that. They'd never even held hands and he was kissing her.

He could have ended up in jail.

The kiss would have been worth the trip. Her lips were so soft.

Tara's arms were around him and the kiss deepened. They fell down to the couch and he didn't have enough blood supply to his brain to conjure up any thoughts. Involuntary actions took control.

Until he opened his mouth and Tara did the same. He moved his tongue, lightly probing her lips—and her tongue touched his, too. It was like a dance: everything he did, she followed expertly. His tongue entered her mouth fully and she not only accepted him, she entered him as well.

He'd never in his life been kissed like that. Or kissed someone like that. Instead of relieving some of the pressure he'd been feeling over the past few days every time he thought about this girl, the feelings only intensified. His entire body was on fire.

Lying down with her, feeling her body along the length of his, just seemed natural. He'd never had sex, had no intention of having sex right then—he just had to be closer to her. And, as if their brains and bodies were already communicating, as if the dance merely continued, she moved with him until she was flat on her back and he was lying on his right side, half on top of her. Their lips had never broken contact.

Slowly, he edged himself closer to her until his crotch was firmly pushed up against her left leg. She didn't protest.

He had experience. Knew exactly how to touch a girl, and he didn't fumble as his right hand made its way under Tara's shirt. Her stomach was bare to his touch and he stroked it a few times before sliding his hand along the outline of her rib cage. He couldn't stop himself. Didn't think. He just moved instinctively, touching her everywhere. She wasn't telling him no. And his hand just kept exploring. Her breast was only a breath away, teasing the edge of his finger, and he moved again and covered the roundness.

The desire burning through him drove him. The way she moved her hips when he touched her mound drove him further. Her bra was in the way so he went under it. Her bare breast seemed to welcome his touch, reaching into his palm, fitting as though it belonged there.

Her kisses were as hot as the rest of her body, her lips moving on his in ways he'd never imagined lips could move. She was a power he couldn't resist. And he continued his exploration of her body.

Over to her other breast and the nipple that was already hard. He stayed there for a while before his hand started to roam again, back down across her stomach to the button on her jeans. He didn't even attempt to unfasten the closure, but he didn't let it stop their adventure, either. Sliding his fingers beneath the waistband of her jeans, Tim touched her pubic hair.

And he had to stop. His penis was ready to explode and that imminent danger finally brought him to his senses.

What in the hell was he doing? It wasn't like he'd never touched between a girl's legs before, but this was a first date. And her mother was right upstairs.

He pulled back, and looking down at Tara he could hardly believe he was living his own life. She was so beautiful she made him ache. Her lips were swollen, and she had a look of awe in her eyes.

"We have to stop or we're going to be in trouble."

She nodded. And reached up to kiss him one more time. He kissed her back and would have been lost to all rational thought if she hadn't broken the contact. She moved slowly, trying to sit up, and Tim moved too, reluctantly getting off her.

They didn't say anything as they put themselves together, but he took her hand as they climbed the stairs.

Her mother was still in the kitchen.

"Mom, I'm leaving to take Tim back."

"Okay." Mrs. Gumser came around the corner, drying her hands on a towel. And Tim realized the enormity of what he'd just done.

Tara's hair was messed up. Her makeup mostly rubbed off. He felt like his jeans were stretched two sizes out of shape.

"It was nice to meet you," he said. "Thanks for having me over."

Mrs. Gumser had to know that they'd just spent more than an hour alone in the basement, but she didn't seem the least bit suspicious about what they'd been doing.

"You're welcome," she said. "Please come back. Anytime."

Tara was quiet on the drive back to Wright State, and Tim didn't have any idea what to say to her. The way things had happened so quickly was embarrassing.

She pulled up to the curb at Wright State and he opened his door.

"I had a good time," she said.

"Yeah, me, too."

He got out of the car and heard her say, "If your friend's working next Thursday, too, you can come over again."

"Okay."

He shut the door.

She drove off.

Four

I COULDN'T BELIEVE WHAT I'D DONE. I was no longer untouched. Just like that. In the space of hours I went from never been kissed to experienced.

Mom served dinner like it was any other night. Pork chops and scalloped potatoes and peas.

I ate. I left the table. I couldn't sit there. Not with Tim's kisses still tingling against my lips. Not with those disturbing feelings between my legs.

I couldn't stop thinking about him.

Couldn't stop wanting him.

My father would say it was wrong. That I wasn't a nice girl.

I didn't answer to my father any more. I answered to Tim. I was his.

"So?" They weren't even out of the Wright State parking lot before Steve, Tim's closest buddy from high school, started in on him.

"What?"

"How'd it go?"

"It was nice." The fields and trees were there, just like always. The bridge and the water below. And nothing was the same.

"Nice."

"Yeah."

"What's nice?" Huddled over the steering wheel in a jean jacket that couldn't possibly ward off the cold, Steve scoffed at him.

"Just nice."

"Come on, man," Steve chided. "What was she like?"

"She was nice." Tim stared out the window, wishing Steve would just shut the hell up and step on the gas.

"Nice, how? Did you kiss her?"

"Shut up."

Grinning, Steve turned onto the highway, sat back and said, "You did, didn't you? You kissed her."

"I was at her house. Her mom was there."

"So did you like her?"

"She's nice."

Eventually Steve shut up.

Saturday morning, I woke up early. And sick to my stomach. What in the heck had I done? I wasn't a good girl anymore. I'd let a boy touch me in places no one had ever, ever touched me before.

Worse, I'd liked it.

And he wasn't there with me. He was working, in the meat department of the grocery store in the small town where he lived.

Forty-five minutes away from me.

I did my house chores. I had to dust. The most boring occupation known to womankind. Until now. Now as I dusted, I thought about Tim. I felt him. Dusting gave me the freedom to let my mind wander wherever it wanted to go without interruption. Dusting freed me from having to explain my silence. I went downstairs and sat on the couch where Tim and I had sat.

And wondered if he'd ever talk to me again.

Had I been a total fool? Letting a guy use me, just like I'd been warned they'd do? I'd been too easy. Loose. All of the horrible things I'd heard about "those" girls.

And I'd done it all on a first date.

But, oh, it had been good. Better than good. That hour with Tim had been what most girls only dream about. The magic. The emotions that had consumed us with mindless need . . .

By that afternoon I was a mass of confusion. Excited and ecstatic in one moment. Despairing the next.

What had he thought?

Did he want the cow even though it had peeked its head out of the barn?

Had he really liked me to begin with?

I wished my big brother was home from college. And I was glad that he wasn't there to witness my humiliation. He called, though.

"What's up?" He asked when Mom told me to pick up the phone.

"Nothing."

"That's not what I hear."

"What? I got an A on a paper this week. I wrote about Angel and Cherie." Cherie was the family's toy poodle. Angel was mine.

"Mom said you have a boyfriend." He didn't give a darn about my school work. Never had.

My face burned. I didn't want to know what Mom had told him. Was I in trouble? Or going to be teased?

"I guess."

"What's his name?"

Like Mom hadn't told him.

"Tim." And don't you dare say anything bad about him. Don't criticize. And for God's sake, don't tease.

The silence was excruciating. I adored my big brother. And I'd never had a boyfriend. What would this new territory bring between Chum and me?

"He plays tennis," I blurted. Chum had played on the high-school team. He didn't play at college though. He bowled there.

Did that make Tim better than Chum? Because he was playing collegiate tennis?

Had I just put my big brother down?

"You like him," Chum said.

"Yeah."

"A lot."

"Yeah."

"Just make sure he treats you right."

The knots in my chest let go. I started to breathe. "He does. I promise, Chum. He's the sweetest guy I've ever known."

At least I hoped he was.

"I'll have to meet him."

"I know."

"Just tell him that."

"Okay." I would. Maybe not exactly like my brother had ordered. I'd lose the warning tone. But I'd tell Tim that Chum wanted to meet him. If I ever heard from Tim again.

I waited all weekend for him to call. He did not. By Sunday night, I wished I'd never met him, never brought him home. My first foray into dating and I'd screwed it up horribly. I'd given Tim things I couldn't take back, ever. I'd given him my first taste. My first touch.

And I'd done it right there in my own home. I'd betrayed my parents. I started to take the long way around to the kitchen so I could avoid the basement door.

I was angry. At him. And mostly at me. I knew better. My father had taught me better. My church had taught me better. And the first time a guy showed interest in me, I threw all of my morals, my convictions to the wind. I was nothing but a cheap loser.

He didn't have to know that, though. I went to geology class on Tuesday with one thought in mind. Act like I didn't care.

I managed to pull it off, too. Right up until I walked down the hall toward the lecture hall and saw him standing out there. He had on a green striped sweater with a button-up shirt under it. The shirt's collar, also green, lay neatly on top of the sweater. His jeans looked new. And that belt buckle . . .

It was big. Metal. And I remembered the cold hard chill of it against the bare skin of my stomach.

Leaning one shoulder against the wall, he was watching kids come around the corner. Like he was waiting for someone.

If I'd known a way to back up and unshow my face from around that corner, I'd have done so. My heart was beating so fast it was interrupting my breathing. My stomach was churning.

He looked right at me. And pushed away from the wall. He smiled. Walked closer.

"Hi."

"Hi."

He reached his hand out toward me, looking me in the eye. My hand moved, before I could form a single thought. And with our fingers entwined we walked into class.

He *had* been waiting for someone.

Me.

The following Thursday, Tim sat with Tara in class, playing with the palm of her hand. Her left hand. She was taking notes with her right hand.

"Think about what we're going to be doing this afternoon," he leaned over to whisper. He couldn't think of anything else.

Him and Tara. Downstairs on that couch.

Every time he looked at the tightly ribbed blue-striped sweater she had on with her jeans, he thought about the soft skin and breasts that he knew were underneath it. Kept thinking about touching them.

"My lips on your lips." He leaned over again.

"Sssshh."

Not quite the response he'd been looking for.

And neither was the welcome they received that afternoon when they finally got to Drywood Place. Tara had asked him if he wanted to drive this time, and he pulled into the driveway next to a shiny new blue Cadillac.

"My dad's home."

There was reservation in her voice, which transferred to him, doubling in intensity on the way from the passenger seat.

The front door opened as they approached and a man who was more his mother's age than Tara's mother's age stood there in a dark blue suit, white shirt, and red tie. His shoes were the kind you saw in fine stores with high-dollar price tags.

His hair was almost as long as Tim's. And his glasses were tinted.

"Dad, this is Tim."

They weren't even in the house yet. Tim stuck out his hand.

"Nice to meet you, Mr. Gumser," he said.

The older man's grip was crushing, but Tim held his own. Tara's dad said something, probably "Nice to meet you," or "Welcome," or maybe "You touch my daughter again and I'll kill you." What Tim heard coming back at him was, "Ugh."

They finally made it in the door, and Tara's mom was there.

"Hi, Mrs. Gumser. Nice to see you again," Tim said, relieved to see the familiar and friendly face.

"Come on in, Tim. Would you kids like something to drink?"

"Pepsi," Tara said, when he was going to decline and hopefully guide her toward the basement.

"Tim?" All three of them stood there looking at him.

"I'll have a Pepsi, too," he said, sweating beneath the striped sweater he'd pulled on that morning, hoping she'd like it—imagining her fingers underneath it.

They all sat at the table. Mr. Gumser didn't like him, but he was classy about it. Tara and her mom did all the talking, except when Mr.

Gumser was inserting questions for Tim—all of which Tim managed to answer.

"My wife tells me you go to Wright State."

"Yes, sir. I'm a freshman."

"Tim's majoring in geology," Tara inserted quickly, and then turned to her mom. "I got my pebble paper back today."

Tim knew about that already. She'd had to do a five-hundred-word essay describing something, and Tara had described a pebble.

Tim figured he'd have gotten ten words out of that one, if he'd been lucky.

"I got an A," Tara told her mom.

And so it continued. Tara and her mom talking, Tara's dad interrogating.

The man was looking out for his daughter. Tim understood that. And all in all he was happy to be there—even if they weren't in the basement, yet.

They didn't make it there later that day either. Tara surprised him yet again when, shortly after her father left the table she stood up and said, "You want to see my room?" She just blurted it out. Right in front of her mother. And then she looked at her mom. "It's okay, isn't it?"

"Of course," Mrs. Gumser said, clearing their glasses from the table. She was making something in the kitchen—dinner, he supposed, though it was still a little early in the day for that.

"Sure, I'd like to see it," Tim said, wondering what kind of family he'd walked into. Either Tara's parents were the most trusting adults he'd ever met, or the most open-minded. Judging by the inquisition he'd just been through, and the girl he was getting to know, he figured it was the former.

Her parents trusted her. Enough to let her take a boy to her bedroom.

The room was . . . girlish. Brown carpet. Yellow walls. A big bed with some drape thing over the top of it, like a princess in a Disney flick. The rest of the furniture was kind of white with some gold on it. And there was a gold velvet-looking chair in a corner by the window. It had a lamp and marble table sitting next to it. Not one thing was out of place or just laying around.

There was nothing in the room that he could relate to, until he saw the instrument leaning in another corner.

He headed straight for it—keeping his gaze off the bed.

"Is this your guitar?"

"Yeah."

"Do you play it?"

"For me, only. Like I told you, my dad and brother are the musicians in this family. You should hear Chum play the guitar. He's good enough to be a professional. We actually had a band for a while in high school, but I didn't play guitar. I just played the tambourine. And sang."

"Your band ever play anywhere?"

"A couple of school gigs, a party someone hired us to do. And then Chum formed a band with some older guys, and they played some parties and things until he left for college."

He still held the guitar. The frets were well worn. The rest of the instrument gleamed like it was brand new.

And expensive. It was a Yamaha FG-75—he read the sticker on the inside of the case.

"What can you play?"

She shrugged. "Lots of things. But I only play for me. I'm not, you know, good or anything."

"What kind of stuff do you play?" he asked again.

"John Denver stuff. I don't know, other things."

She stood there at the end of the bed, looking happy and worried at the same time. And he couldn't help thinking about her there at night, all alone, without her clothes on . . .

He handed her the guitar. "Play something for me."

"No, really, I'm not that good."

"I don't care. I just want to hear you. Please?" He looked her straight in the eye, and it was like something happened. Like they said something without using any words. Weird.

What in the hell was going on?

Whatever it was, Tara took the guitar and climbed up on the bed. Her jeans stretched across her thighs as she crossed her legs Indian style and settled the guitar across her lap.

She strummed a couple of times, staring down at the strings, and then started to play strings individually.

"There is . . . a house. . . ." When she started to sing "The House of the Rising Sun," he didn't move a muscle. He couldn't look away, either. She played like someone who was plugged in to a different place, like no one was in the room with her.

She'd lied.

"That was really good," he said a couple of seconds after the room fell silent.

"Thanks." She didn't look at him, putting the guitar back where it belonged.

He'd been planning to kiss her, had been fantasizing about it on and off all day, but he didn't. They hardly made out that day at all.

He was still glad he'd gone.

Five

I'D NEVER BEEN HAPPIER. NOT EVER.

Nothing in life—not summers with my best friend in all of the world, not horse camp when I was twelve, or the trip to Disneyworld when I was fifteen, not even coming home from work to find a new car waiting for me in the driveway all wrapped up in ribbons and bows—compared to being Tim's girlfriend.

I wasn't Tara Gumser anymore. I was part of a couple.

I kept reminding myself of that fact the Saturday night after Tim had met my dad. I was sitting in the car Tim had borrowed from his twelve-years-older-than-him—and married—brother.

The Ford station wagon wasn't like anything I'd ever been in. It was pretty new, like Mom's car, but my folks only drove GM products.

The car smelled like cigarettes. My folks had quit smoking forever ago.

We were on our way to Tim's house on Maple Street. He was going to show me his weights. I was going to watch him work out.

"You sure you want to do this?" Tim asked, taking his gaze from the road long enough to look at me. He had on a black jacket and blue jeans and just looking at him made those feelings come back between my legs.

"Yeah, of course I do."

It felt so right, sitting there with him in a family car. Like we were a couple who were going to have kids to fill up those backseats.

"We could do something else if you want."

"I want to see your house. And watch you work out." I got a little hot saying that, but I was going to be really disappointed if he changed his mind. I thought about him all day and all night and I didn't even know where he lived. Where he slept.

Besides, I'd spent my whole life watching guys do their sports. If not in person, then on television. The male domination in my household insisted, collectively, that a sporting event, *any* sporting event, took precedence over any other show being broadcast on television.

I was actually looking forward to the weight-lifting part.

The reason I was tense enough to split in half, which he must have picked up on, was because I was going to meet Tim's mom. She wasn't going to like me. I just had this feeling.

I was too sure of my opinion. I said what I thought.

Yeah, not good.

And when I wasn't saying what I was thinking, I didn't say anything at all.

I just wasn't good at social pleasantries. Mostly because I thought they were duplicitous and a waste of time. I'd tried to make casual conversation a time or two, but the words just sounded dumb and I'd embarrassed myself.

Tim's mom was going to hate me.

"Have you ever seen the *Rhoda* show?" We were driving forever. Really far from home. Out into the country. There were no towns around. Not a fast-food hamburger joint anywhere for miles.

I was completely out of my element.

And I wanted to be with him so badly. I focused on his hands on the steering wheel. They made me feel safe.

And excited me at the same time.

"Yeah," he said. He was excited, too? Had I said that out loud?

And then I remembered the *Rhoda* question. That was so me, having three different conversations going on in my head at one time.

"With Valerie Harper?" I asked. The *Rhoda* question came from my earlier thoughts about sports reigning supreme in my house.

Watching Tim lift weights sounded . . . erotic . . . but I did not want to saddle myself with a guy who thought life revolved around sports.

What I did want to do was saddle myself with Tim. I knew that already. I was thinking about a future with him. Wanting a future with him. A lifetime's worth of future.

I might not have dated before, but I knew what I wanted. I'd always been that way. And I was generally right—about what I wanted.

"Yeah, *Rhoda* with Valerie Harper."

"Really?" I asked.

"Yeah."

"Rhoda, as on *Mary Tyler* . . "

"*Moore*," he finished, sitting back with the ease of a man comfortable with the powerful machine he controlled.

"You watched *Mary Tyler Moore*?"

"On Saturday nights."

So had I. Every single Saturday night all through high school. Whether I was babysitting or at home.

"Did you see the one where Rhoda's mom stayed with Mary?" The episode had aired in the first season back in '70 or '71.

"Ida? Because Rhoda wouldn't see her? Yep."

He really knew the show. And why was I surprised? He was my perfect mate.

"Rhoda was always my favorite character," I felt free to share now. "I was thrilled when I heard she was getting her own show. I couldn't believe it. I looked forward to that show all week. I didn't plan anything that whole night because I wasn't taking any chances that I'd have to miss that first episode."

He nodded, like he'd done the same.

"So the night for the season opener comes, and I'm there at the TV fifteen minutes early with the channel on, ready to watch, and my dad comes in and turns the station. It was *Monday Night Football*. There would be no *Rhoda*."

"Did he know you'd been waiting to see the show?"

"Yeah. But it was *Monday Night Football*."

"So after all that you missed the show?"

"No, my mom got the little television in the basement to work well enough for me to see it down there. It just had lines going through it the whole time. But what really made me mad was that my dad slept through the football game that was on the big color TV upstairs."

"That's not right."

That's what I thought.

And Tim had just passed my test.

We'd also passed all the miles between my house and his. We were on Maple Street, and he was pulling up beside a lovely wood-sided home that was historic and antebellum in feeling. It had character, unlike the identical brick homes that had overpopulated the town where I lived.

And panic set in. This was where I was going to fail the Mom test.

⁓

"Tim? Is that you?"

The voice struck a chord of fear through my already shaking body.

"Yeah, Mom. We're here." Holding my hand, Tim pulled me inside the kitchen door, through the dining room, and into the living room where his mother sat. There was an end table beside her. It had a lamp on it. She was a lot older than my mom.

"Mom, this is Tara. Tara, this is my mom."

I smiled. "Hi."

"It's nice to meet you. Tim says you're from Huber Heights." I didn't know if that was a good thing or a bad thing.

"Yes, ma'am." At least being Walt Gumser's daughter meant I'd had manners drilled into me.

She nodded and looked like she was going to say more.

I was just thinking I might do okay when Tim pulled at the hand that was still attached to his and I was turning my back on his mother.

He was making me rude when I was trying so hard to be perfect.

"We're going to lift weights," Tim told his mom.

Before I could say more, we were heading back the way we'd come.

He didn't stop pulling until we were in his room. It was on the first floor in the middle of the house and was long and kind of narrow. A stereo and turntable were on the left side of the door next to a desk. The weights were across from the desk. Behind all of that was his bed.

And his mother was out in the living room. She knew we were in Tim's room. With his bed.

And the erotic weights.

Suddenly, I was mortified. I opened my mouth to tell him so. But didn't get the chance.

The second the door was closed Tim pulled me to him. He was like a starved man, clutching me so tightly I couldn't think of anything but him. Being as close to him as possible.

His hunger mirrored mine, and I didn't feel any shame at all.

I was burning up. Nothing else mattered but his lips pressing against mine, opening mine. I had no idea what to do, but I needn't have worried about what I didn't know. Loving Tim was natural. My tongue knew how to mate with his.

Or he was just an incredibly good teacher.

I couldn't get enough—didn't ever want the moments to end. He stepped backward and with his hand pressed against the back of my thigh, took me with him. My body was an extension of his. Connected to his.

I needed more.

I knew it was wrong when he laid me back against the bed. We were there to lift weights. His mother was just feet away. Good girls became bad girls when they lay on beds with boys. And I couldn't stop him. My brain and my heart were at war, and my brain was not going to win.

"You're so good at that." His voice was husky. He was lying on top of me, cradling me with his arms, staring down at me with those brown eyes that I recognized from another lifetime. Another realm.

"At what?" The words stuck in my throat.

"Kissing."

He was kidding, right? I had no idea what I was doing. No experience except with him.

"I want to kiss you again."

"Okay."

My answer wasn't necessary.

I couldn't stop him from kissing me, but I would stop him after that. He wouldn't get to second base again. My bra was going to stay in place. He was not going to touch my breasts. And certainly not my nipples. The way that made me feel was just plain wrong.

I was a good girl.

But he could kiss me for the rest of the night. The rest of my life.

Tim's tongue was playing with mine, touching, withdrawing, exploring. I loved it. Was consumed by his musky cologne. The half groans he was making ignited me.

His hand was at my side. Under my shirt. But that was okay. It was only my side. He was not going to touch my breasts again.

He moved, his hips rubbing against my pelvic bone.

I moved, too, opening my legs just a little bit. And he rubbed. He was big beneath his jeans. And hard. Like a rock.

I was fascinated by this part of him that touched me and grew. I wanted to see it. To watch it. To feel it.

And his hand slid up, touching my ribs.

That was okay. It was just ribs. He was not going to touch my breasts. I opened my mouth wider.

And I moaned.

This was wrong. And so right. I needed him.

His hand slid over my breast. It stopped on top of it. Cupping it. It was time to tell him to stop. And I was going to. As soon as he tried to get underneath my bra. He could touch my bra. He could not touch my breasts.

My breath came in gasps, my whole body straining for something that was just out of reach. Something I'd never experienced before. I didn't know what would happen. But I knew that I'd sell my soul to let it happen. I yearned to find what was there. I had to fly. And to fall.

Tim unclipped my bra and covered my naked breast with his bare hand. He touched my nipple and then held it between his fingers.

And my hips were reaching up to meet his. To seek his. To push against his hardness.

Oh, God. Help me. Forgive me. I was not being a good girl.

⌒

That night on the way home, I nestled up to Tim in the car, lethargic and in love. I'd probably hate myself in the morning—again—but at that moment, in the dark, private world in the car, I was happy. The radio was playing softly in the background and, as a song came on, I listened to the words, traveling along with them, until I realized I could have written the song. Every single word was true.

It can't be wrong . . . The woman crooned, and followed the words with something about it feeling right.

"I love that song. I broke the silence that had fallen when we'd hit the highway. "Every word of it is true."

"'You Light Up My Life,'" Tim named the song. And then said, "You do mine, too."

He smiled down at me and hugged me close.

⌒

Parking his brother's station wagon in the circular drive in front of Tara's house, Tim walked her to the door. It was late. After midnight.

He had to get home—had to be at work at the deli in the grocery store in town at 6:00 AM

But when she said, "Do you want to come in? Maybe have a Pepsi, some caffeine for the ride home?" he hesitated.

There was a light on in the foyer of the house. Everything else was dark.

"What about your parents?"

"I'm sure they're in bed. They won't care. They'd rather you have some caffeine than fall asleep on the way home."

He was in the door before she said another word. No way was he turning down a chance to have Tara in his arms again.

He wasn't sure what happened to the Pepsi idea. One second they were standing together in the family room, and the next they were in a bean bag in front of a fireplace that still smoldered with embers.

"My folks must've had a fire tonight," he heard Tara say, though he couldn't be sure of that either.

All he knew was that the woman of his dreams was in his arms and he couldn't get enough of her.

Ever.

The next thing he knew it was 4:00 AM.

Shit. He had to get Mike's car back and get to work. Neither Mike nor his wife cared that he borrowed the car, but they'd care if they needed it and he hadn't brought it back like he'd promised. They had little kids to take care of.

With a hurried goodbye, he started on the long drive that had very quickly become rote to him. So rote that by the time he hit his exit, still fifteen minutes from home, he was having a hard time keeping his eyes open.

"Just a few more miles," he said out loud, rolling down the window for a bit of fresh air.

And when, a couple of minutes later, he started to nod off, he said it again. "Just a few more miles."

More like ten. His voice fell flat in the car's lonely interior.

The next thing he heard was tires on gravel.

Jerking, he woke up and realized that he'd missed a curve and was heading straight for a telephone pole. Fast.

He slammed the brake pedal to the floor and turned the steering wheel sharply. The car spun around and he held on, dizzy, scared.

He was going to die.

Suddenly the car came to a complete stop. With his head feeling like he was still spinning, he looked around. He'd landed about ten feet from the telephone pole, still upright. He hadn't hit anything. Nothing was damaged.

Except his psyche.

Thank God. Mike would kill him if he wrecked his car. There'd be no forgiveness there.

Because it wasn't the first time Tim had been in a spinning car. Shaking, Tim was suddenly back a few years, thirteen years old again. He and his brother Jeff had been out with a couple of buddies late one night. Jeff, fourteen then, had been driving. A sign indicating a coming turn was blocked, and they'd taken the curve too fast. The car had rolled, and they'd ended up in a farmer's field.

When they'd made it out of the car and limped their way to a house, they'd called Mike. Their brother had come to get them and then spent the night in the emergency room while Tim's broken collarbone and various other injuries were tended to. Mike had let both of them know then that there better not be a second time.

Taking his foot off the brake, Tim eased the car forward slowly, a few feet at a time until he was back on the road. Wide awake now, he knew one thing. He couldn't risk his brother's wrath for his stupid choices. It was time for him to look for his own car.

Six

I DIDN'T READ ROMANCES ANYMORE. They paled in comparison to the real thing. I didn't need to imagine my Harlequin hero, or find him on pages of books written by women privy to all of the things I could only imagine. I didn't need to imagine anymore.

I had the real thing.

I just had no idea how to keep him for more than the moment. I loved our moments, but I needed a future. And I needed it fast.

Before I became something I would hate for the rest of my life. A loose woman. Harlequin heroines did not have sex before they were married. They married for convenience and a lot of other wrong reasons, but they didn't have sex without marriage.

If I was going to write for Harlequin, I had to be worthy of a Harlequin heroine. I had to be a Harlequin heroine.

Those women were my mentors.

My moral compass.

I had to live up to them.

And I was thinking of Tim no matter what activity I was engaged in.

"Run errands with me?" My friend, Rebecca, was staying with me again. She'd had a run in with her brother-in-law and didn't want to go home to her room in her sister's house.

Rebecca knew me. Better than most. And I'd been neglecting her.

"Sure," I said, jumping up from the gold chair in the corner of my bedroom, the room I'd been allowed to decorate myself, the room that I'd shared with Rebecca for most of our senior year.

Tim might call. I didn't want to miss him.

But Rebecca was lonely. She had issues. We'd been friends since the fourth grade.

And her father had died when she was five; he'd been a teacher, just like Tim's. She'd had a hard life. I cared about her. Before Tim, I'd been there for her 100 percent. What kind of person was I if I suddenly ditched her?

"Let's go," I said. "I'll drive."

We usually took Rebecca's car. It was bigger and she'd had her license longer, but I wanted to use my gas so she could save hers. I was going to miss Tim's call, but I was being a good person.

My heart wasn't appeased. It yearned for Tim.

Rebecca needed to stop at the card shop. I talked about Tim all the way there.

"He thinks President Kennedy's assassination was orchestrated by one of his own." I stated the virulent news where I knew it was safe.

"Wow, he was?"

"I don't know. Tim thinks so."

"Wow. I had no idea."

I had no idea, either. But I wondered if he was right. I'd heard the supposition before. But for the first time in my life, I was considering the possibility.

Tim was changing me.

And that scared me.

"I need a funny card for Kirby," Rebecca said as we walked together into our favorite card and gift shop. I was huddled in my jean jacket and still freezing.

"Has he called you?"

"No, but he and Kelly have been working out, getting ready for baseball."

Baseball was in the spring. This was the fall. And Kirby's twin brother, Kelly, didn't like Kirby hanging out with Rebecca.

They were rich boys.

Rebecca lived in a house with holes in the floors. And the walls. Not that Kirby or anyone else we associated with knew that.

"Maybe you should wait until he calls you," I said, looking at the racks of cards as we made our way down the aisle.

Romance.

I glanced. *For the Guy in My Life.* Did Tim see himself that way? Or would the possessive cramp him?

To My Lover. No. We needed no further encouragement in that area.

To the One I Love. There was a couple on the cover that reminded me of Tim and me. He had luscious dark hair and she was little and blonde. But what I liked most was the way the man was cradling the woman in his arms and looking at her as if she were all he'd need for the rest of his life. I opened the card.

You and me. Together forever. I wanted to buy the card. It was perfect. And I hoped Tim thought so, too. But he hadn't said so. He hadn't said anything about the future.

For the One and Only. I opened that one, too.

When I found you, I found the other half of myself. Exactly. But what if Tim only wanted sex?

"There you are." Rebecca came around the corner, and I turned red. I had no business looking at these cards. Tim and I weren't even going together.

"I've been looking all over for you," Rebecca said, glancing at the cards in front of me. Thankfully I didn't have one in my hand. I could, ostensibly, have been daydreaming. Or just walking by.

My pretty friend handed me a card. Charlie Brown and Snoopy were on the front. The message was about friends who belonged together. "What do you think?"

"It's good," I said, feeling sorry for her. Rebecca had had more boyfriends during high school than I'd had hamburgers in an entire year. But Kirby was the one. I'd never seen her so tied up in knots over a guy.

And I'd never seen one less interested in spending time with her, either.

"I was thinking I'd drive it over to his house and leave it in the mailbox."

Kirby lived forty-five minutes away—in the opposite direction from Tim. "What if he sees you?"

She shrugged, glanced at the card again. "I'm not sure about this one. Give me a sec to take one more look."

She could have all the time she wanted. I had my own dilemma: my own inner demon driving me to buy a card for a man I was desperately in love with who hadn't said a word about loving me back.

I moved on. Friendship.

Was that what Tim and I were? Friends? The first couple of cards I looked at I put back. They were clearly intended for friends like Rebecca and me.

Hey Dummy. The card caught my attention. Ziggy was on the front. I liked and respected him for his pithy insights.

The message was lighthearted, casual—nothing like the avowal of undying love I needed to impart. *Hey Dummy.* Like I didn't think he was perfect. Like I wasn't besotted. Irreverent, when I was bone-deep certain that Tim was the most intelligent man I'd ever known.

Glancing behind me to make certain that Rebecca wasn't anywhere close, I opened the card.

I think you're Great! The words were written in a large scrawl, on a slant.

And I knew I had to buy the card. Tim might think me forward, pushy. He might get cramped. Run in the opposite direction. But if he was going to do that because I was crazy about him, because I needed to tell him so, then it was best that I find out sooner rather than later.

And at least it wasn't an avowal of undying love.

I made a beeline for the register, hoping to pay for the card and hide it in my purse before Rebecca saw what I was doing.

I waited until the cashier was finishing with the last person at the counter and went forward.

"What'd you find?"

It was like Rebecca had been watching me, waiting, she appeared so quickly. Pounced so quickly was how it felt to me.

"A card."

"Can I see it?"

I handed it to her. And looked at the ground while she read. The carpet was grey. Commercial. Dirty and ugly.

"You're getting Tim a card." She handed it back to me. If she told my mom, in front of my dad, that I was buying Tim a card before he'd even said he liked me, I'd get a lecture for sure.

"Yeah." And if she thought it was the wrong thing to do, too, I was going to do it anyway. No matter how much her level of experience in the dating department outweighed mine.

Rebecca had liked a lot of guys. I was in love.

The words of wisdom I was expecting didn't come.

"What do you think?" I asked.

She nodded, her perfectly feathered bangs giving her that elfin look that all the guys went for. Her breasts were overly enviable in size, too. A fact that was further emphasized by her slim waist and the tight sweaters she always wore.

"You think I should give it to him?"

"Yeah, I do. You really like this guy."

"Yeah."

"Yeah, well, he needs to know that. And to do something about it if he hopes to keep you. Besides, it doesn't say anything about the L word, so it's not like it should scare him completely off."

Wow. I wasn't as backward as I'd thought.

He found his car at the first dealership he visited—a Pontiac LeMans Sport Coupe. It called out to him when he pulled on the lot. The second he saw the pristine exterior with the black landau roof and, inside, the leather seats and the shifter on the console, he knew the car had to be his.

He pictured Tara in the passenger seat. And in the backseat, too. She'd be impressed. She'd love it. How could she not?

He wasn't going to say anything to her about it, though. Not until he knew for sure it was his.

"Can I drive it?" he asked the salesman who approached him out on the lot.

"Yeah, you can take it overnight if you want, let your mother and brother have a look at it."

He was in Eaton where he'd lived all his life. Where everyone knew his family—and his business.

He didn't need anyone to have a look at it. He knew cars as well as anyone in his family. But he wasn't going to blow his chance to keep the car overnight.

And when his student loan came in a couple of days later he hurried back to the dealership, worried the whole way that the car would be gone.

It wasn't. It was as if the LeMans was just sitting there waiting for him to take it home.

The next day sitting with Tara in geology lecture, he was about to burst with his news.

"Ever make out in the backseat of a car?" he whispered about a quarter of the way through the lecture.

"Tim," her whisper was firm, a reprimand, not an invitation. She squeezed his hand, though. They were holding hands—his right to her left so she could take notes—as they did every class these days.

"I hear sex is great in cars," he tried again halfway through class.

"Sssshhh."

"Well then, I won't take you for a ride in my new car," he said.

At first, she seemed to think the threat was just more of his nonsense, and then her eyes widened and her face broke out into the grin he'd come to know, the one that stirred his blood every time.

She scooted down in her seat. "You got a car?" She was still facing forward, her hand up like she was playing with her mouth in some studious, mode of concentration.

"Yeah."

"When?"

"Last night."

She stared at the professor, like she was paying attention, except that he was talking to a student who'd had trouble finding a particular table in the textbook. A table he knew Tara had already found because she'd had her book open to it.

"What kind?"

"Pontiac LeMans Sport."

"What color is it?"

"Gold. Black leather interior."

"When can I see it?"

"As soon as class ends if you want to."

She turned toward him then, and the excitement in those blue eyes was everything he'd hoped it would be. "You have it here?"

"Yep."

"Can I drive it?"

He hadn't thought about that. A girl driving his prized possession. His first car.

But this wasn't any girl. This was Tara. "Of course," he said. He'd seen her handle a shift. She was a pro.

He didn't really regret the words when she was behind the wheel of his new car just hours after he'd purchased it. He did second-guess them, though. And squirm a bit. The shy girl he knew changed when she got behind the wheel of a sports car. Her shyness evaporated. And left a wild woman in her place.

Tara took his new machine from zero to seventy in about ten seconds—which was hard on the engine. He didn't want to criticize her, though. Or spoil her fun. He held on. And started to pray.

They made it to the expressway in one piece. They made it without so much as a single complaint from the car. She gunned the motor and, both hands on the wheel, grinned from ear to ear.

He was glad he'd made her so happy and saw the curve just ahead.

"Slow down." The words burst out of him.

"I was only going eighty and I was slowing down for that curve."

"Okay." If she said so.

He made it another two minutes. Just until he saw the next exit. "Hey, pull off here," he said.

She did, bringing the car to a smooth halt at the gas station just off the ramp.

"You want to drive?" she asked.

"Yeah."

Still smiling, she hopped out, came around the hood and settled into the passenger seat where he'd been picturing her when he'd bought the car. Her seat.

Where she belonged.

"The car's great, Tim. I love it."

And I love you, were the first words that sprang to his mind. To be quickly followed by, *But from now on I'm driving because this car's a lot more powerful than your Manta, little girl, and I don't want us to die before we have sex.*

"Come on, hurry," I said to Ann one day late in October. We'd just come from class, and I was supposed to meet Tim. I couldn't wait to see him. Didn't want to waste one second of the time I had with him.

"He'll wait for you."

"I don't want him to have to wait." I had a note to give him. And hoped he had one to give me, too. He was always asking me to write him notes.

I loved writing him notes. I'd seen my friends write notes in high school and now I finally had someone to write to.

Problem was, as much as Tim liked getting my notes, he wasn't as good about writing back to me.

And I needed him to write to me. I needed to know how he felt about me. I needed to be able to tell him how I felt about him, and a girl couldn't tell a guy first.

At least this girl couldn't. My father was a smart man, and if he was certain that a girl who proclaimed love first was only asking to be used, then I was certain, too.

I'd reached the student union where I was meeting Tim.

Our song was playing. "You Light Up My Life." We had a song already.

I'd bought the recording right after I'd heard it in Tim's car. It was about a girl who'd been all alone, who'd been adrift and sitting in her chair, looking out into the night, just as I'd done, sitting in my gold velour chair on the plush brown carpet I'd chosen, staring out the window of my upstairs bedroom those many Friday nights when Rebecca, and most of the girls we knew, were out on dates.

All those nights I'd sit alone, the light on the marble table beside me turned off, looking at the street below and dreaming about my Harlequin hero, the man who was out there someplace and who would take away my darkness.

The song really did tell my story word for word. Until it got to the part about filling up my nights. My nights, the parts where I went to bed and tried to sleep, were painfully empty.

And I wondered, as I stood waiting on one side of the swarming student union, if any of the hundred or so college kids lounging around me, talking, goofing off, eating, and studying knew that I wanted to go all the way with Tim Barney.

I felt guilty and on top of the world at the same time. But no matter how many moments of shame I put myself through, I wasn't sorry for what Tim and I had done at his house on Maple Street. He'd touched my clitoris. Every single time I thought about it, that excited tingle would start in my groin and spread.

It's all I thought about. Tim's hands on my skin. His arms around me. His mouth on mine. I relived the moments, and I lived for the next time I'd be alone with him. The next time he'd reach for me. Touch his lips to mine. Put his tongue in my mouth and . . .

"There he is," Ann said, pointing.

I looked. And melted. He was in jeans and that black jacket that I loved. His hair was as thick and long and wild as always and his eyes . . . those brown depths . . . they were focused on me. Really focused on me. Like I was the only person in the room. The only thing Tim saw.

My heart filled until I thought it would burst.

I reached out my hand when he walked up, and he took it like he owned it. He did own it.

And I had to talk to him. I couldn't be alone with him again. Not until we talked. Because I knew what would happen, and I couldn't let it. But I didn't trust myself not to let it.

I was a good girl. I didn't let anyone touch me like I'd let Tim touch me. I couldn't do it again. And I couldn't let it go any further until we'd talked. He had to promise that we had a future. That we were more than a hot and heavy college fling. I wanted to make love to him. I couldn't do that until I was married.

Period.

I wasn't stupid. I didn't expect him to ask me to marry him right then. But I needed to know that getting married was a possibility for our future. I needed to know that I was more than sex.

I slipped him the note I'd written. And thought about him reading it.

I'm glad you got the car. Things will be much easier. Now that he no longer had to come and go as his buddy dictated, we could spend more time together.

And then I got to the stuff that was really critical.

I think you're lying to me about your mom liking me. She only saw me for a second, and then we didn't give a very good impression by staying so late. Next time, we'll have to talk to her some more, and you'll have to get me home early!

I felt like such a bad girl. And I didn't like feeling that way. I'd spent my whole life being a good girl. I was a good girl.

There was a little more stuff about the movie we were planning to see on Sunday. And then came the most important part.

Love ya, Tara

I couldn't tell him I was in love with him. I couldn't even say I love you—out loud —though the words screamed themselves inside of me. He hadn't told me that he loved me. And I couldn't say that first. I couldn't be that forward. I couldn't let him know that he had me that completely.

Not if all he wanted from me was sex.

And to that end, I'd added the last line of the note. *P.S. Hey! I want to talk to you soon, okay?*

I'd told him several times that I needed to talk to him. He always said okay, or nodded, but anytime we had five seconds alone, we were too busy locking our lips together to be able to get words through them.

Seven

THE CARD SHE'D GIVEN HIM, TELLING HIM HE WAS GREAT, was tucked away in the little metal lockbox in his bedroom. Locked up for safekeeping, not for hiding. He still did double takes when he woke up in the morning, trying to believe that a girl as beautiful as Tara really saw enough worth in him to stick by him. Why should she? She could have any guy she wanted.

And it wouldn't be too hard for her to find a guy who had more to offer than he did. He couldn't buy her nice gifts. Hell, he could barely afford to take her out for a fast-food dinner.

On the last Thursday in October, just before he left for school, he looked at the note she'd given him the day before. She'd signed it "Love ya." What in the hell did that mean?

Did she have feelings for him? Maybe love feelings? Or was she just being casual and cute?

But what about that last line, about needing to talk. When someone says "We need to talk," what follows usually isn't good. The words were almost always a prelude to "Things aren't working out for me." Or "I want to date other people."

Not that he and Tara had talked about such things. He assumed she wasn't seeing anyone else, but she hadn't said. He hadn't asked. And neither had she. Before he left for school, he locked the letter in the box with the card.

She was waiting for him outside of geology.

"Hey," he took her hand as usual. "You want to go to a party in Eaton this weekend?"

"What party?" She was frowning.

"A Halloween party. It's at Steve's girlfriend's house." Steve had taken the news that they wouldn't be carpooling anymore pretty well.

"Who's going to be there?" She was frowning.

"Kids I hung out with in high school."

"Couples?"

"Mostly." Was that good or bad? If she didn't want to go, why didn't she just say so?

"And you want to take me?"

"Yeah." He'd asked, hadn't he?

Her serious expression broke into a smile, and she hooked her arm through his. "Okay, I'd like to go with you."

He'd been worried for nothing.

⁓

I was a nervous wreck on the way to Eaton on Saturday night. In my entire life I'd never been to a party of kids my own age. I'd heard wild stories, though, and had no idea what to expect. Huber Heights was four times the size of Eaton, and there was probably a lot more bad stuff that went on in Huber Heights, but what if Tim wanted to get drunk? Or they had pot there?

What if all the kids were cracking jokes? I wasn't funny. Most particularly not on the spot.

I wanted to meet his friends, to be a part of his life. I wanted him to be proud of me.

Eaton was really small. He'd had about a hundred kids in his graduating class. I'd had seven hundred in mine.

He'd know every single person there.

I was scared to death I was going to embarrass him.

I was also afraid I was going to find myself face-to-face with an ex-girlfriend. Maybe someone who meant more to Tim than I did. Someone who'd broken his heart who wanted him back.

Someone who was part of his small-town world and knew him a lot better than I did.

The only good news, as far as I was concerned, was that Tim had insisted that we just wear jeans and sweaters to the party. No costumes for us.

The party was in full swing when we arrived. Tim took hold of my hand at the car and didn't let go.

"Carol, this is Tara. Tara, Carol, Steve's girlfriend."

"Oh, hi!" I smiled and so did the other girl, but I felt like I was under a microscope.

"Hi," the girl said and then looked straight at Tim. "Barb's here."

Tim didn't so much as blink. I wasn't even sure he'd heard the girl.

During the next few minutes I met what seemed like a hundred people. Way too many for me to keep track of names. Besides, half the kids were in costume, so it wasn't like I would recognize them if I ever saw them again.

We made our way out to the garage and sat on a bale of hay.

"Who's Barb?"

"Barb who?"

"I don't know. Carol just told you Barb's here."

Tim glanced around, still keeping my hand firmly within his. "I'm not sure, but probably Barb Cottrill. I knew her in high school."

"Were you two an item?" I had to know.

"Heck, no."

I was still smiling when Carol's mom joined us, sitting down on a chair across from our bale of hay.

Tim introduced us. I squeezed his hand and said hello.

"Tim says you're from Huber Heights."

"Right."

The woman told me about someone she knew from the Heights. She sat and talked to us for a long time. She asked about my studies, my mom, and Tim's mom, too. She stayed long enough for me to feel welcome. To realize that I was actually enjoying myself.

I might even be able to go back into the crowd with Tim and, if miracles happened, find something to contribute to a conversation with people my own age so they would like me.

These were Tim's people. If I didn't pass muster, they'd tell him so. And their opinions might make a difference. After all, he'd known them all his whole life.

I was just gearing myself up to face the crowd when Tim stood, pulling me up with him.

"You ready to go?"

"Go?" Really? I wanted to be there with him. But I wasn't a partier. Still, I didn't want him to think I was a party pooper. "We can stay if you want to," I added.

"I want to go. I'd much rather have time with you at my house before I have to take you home." He looked me straight in the eye, those brown eyes of his glinting, and I melted.

No one was home when we got to Maple Street and Tim took me straight back to his room. Which was the only place in the world I wanted to be.

But I was scared, too. Scared of me. Of what I might do. I wasn't kidding myself anymore. I wasn't going to keep him away from my body, or out of my pants, but I had to keep his male body part away from my female body part.

My church had taught me well. I had to be a virgin when I got married. Anything else would be a lie.

And my father had taught me well. If I gave Tim everything now, he wouldn't ever need to marry me. Or even want to marry me.

I was so afraid of giving him everything.

I was also afraid of getting pregnant and being left to handle the next twenty or thirty years on my own.

And the second Tim touched me, as I'd known he'd do, I clung to him, giving him kiss for kiss, touch for touch. I loved his chest. The contours. The firmness. The way his nipples responded.

I loved his belly. It was different from mine. More coarse. Mysterious.

And below that—his penis. It embarrassed me even to think the word. But oh how the thing fascinated me. It grew. And hardened. I knew it did a lot more than that.

But whenever my Harlequin romances got to that point, the bedroom door closed in my face so I didn't know quite how that marvelous part of Tim did what it did. I had no idea how it all worked, practically speaking.

But I wanted to know.

An hour later, lying side by side with him on his bed, I was working up the courage to find out. The button on Tim's jeans was undone. His shirt was undone. My pants were undone and my sweater was up around my neck.

My fingers, moving along Tim's lower stomach, were inching their way downward.

"Tim?" The voice was just outside the door.

I jerked my hand back and flew off the bed.

"Yeah, Mom." He started to sit up. Slowly.

"Don't you think it's time you get that girl home?"

"Yeah. Okay."

We'd been caught, and right then, all I wanted to do was laugh.

Maybe hysterical laughter. Because life was so far out of control.

I was the first one put back together. I'd had my pants fastened before his mother had asked her question. Standing by the still-closed door, waiting for Tim to tuck his shirt back in, I glanced over at his dresser. Trying not to drown in a pool of embarrassment.

A class ring was sitting there.

A big one. His? I grabbed it up without thinking. Or rather, I was thinking, about him, his ring, his high school, the fact that he still had his ring. His mother knowing what we were doing. And blaming me because I was too easy. I wasn't thinking about how I might look, standing there gazing at his ring.

"You can have it if you want."

I swung around, the ring still between my fingers. "What?"

"That," he nodded toward the ring. "You can have it if you want."

Not quite the way I'd have envisioned being asked to go steady for the first time in my life. Who was I kidding? Like I hadn't fantasized the moment, with Tim, a hundred times in the past three weeks?

"Do you want me to have it?" I asked him, meeting that brown gaze head on.

"Yes."

He didn't look away. And my heart was his.

Completely.

Forever.

It wasn't an avowal of love, but, right there in his bedroom on Maple Street, he'd made a commitment to be tied to me.

Pocketing the ring, I took his hand and walked out to his car.

The morning after the Halloween party, Tim woke up and thought something was wrong with him. His lips were swollen to twice their normal size. Once he was fully conscious, and ran his tongue over his lips, he realized why they were swollen. He'd given them quite a workout.

He also noticed, when he went in to shave, that he had a bruise on his neck. And he remembered Tara's lips there, too, sucking on him. He wore his love scars proudly, the bruise under a turtleneck shirt. Tara had taken his class ring home with her last night. Who'd have believed that a hot college babe would commit to him?

He wanted to see her. To see his ring on her finger, but she had to work on Sunday—a job at Wendy's that she'd had since she was sixteen—and he had to work right after class on Monday, so it wasn't until Tuesday that he'd see Tara again. Until he could know that feeling of contentment that came from seeing your ring on a girl's finger, a girl who's telling the world, "Sorry, I'm taken."

She usually checked mail when she first got to school. Too impatient to wait to see her in class, he met her at the mailboxes. She had her back to him when he first saw her, and it dawned on him that she might not be wearing the ring.

"How's the ring fit?" he asked anyway, coming up behind her to nuzzle her neck.

She squirmed, which pushed her backside against his groin. Then she turned and held out her left hand, proudly displaying the large gold engraved setting with the purple stone in the center on a ring finger that was a quarter of the ring's size. The band, which he knew was gold, was covered in the pink yarn she'd wound around it. And around it. And around it.

"It fits great," she said, waving the finger that held the ring with that wad of yarn so big it inched down to her hand. "I love it."

He loved it, too, seeing his ring there on her finger. He also loved her, but it was too soon to admit that to her. They were just college kids exploring outside of high school, and he didn't want to seem too pushy and scare her away.

"I have something for you, too," she said then. Reaching into her purse, she pulled out a much smaller gold ring—this one with a green stone in it. "Will you wear it?" she asked, handing him her class ring.

Hell yes, he'd wear it.

"Yeah," he said, taking the ring and putting it on his pinky before grabbing her hand and walking with her into the student union. If he had his way they'd stay there all day, sitting around and drinking Pepsi.

He wanted everyone to see them together, to see that they were going steady. Hands off, guys, Tara was his.

⁂

They were together every second they could be, which wasn't nearly enough. Tim's job status changed at the end of October, requiring him to work at the deli of his hometown grocery store from 5:00 PM until 9:00 PM, five nights a week, which meant that he had to rush home every day after class. He worked on Saturdays, too, from 6:00 AM until 2:00 PM. The only part of the job he liked was the tapioca pudding he occasionally helped himself to while filling the containers at night. But that pudding wasn't nearly as hard to resist as Tara was. She was working, too, a few evenings a week and usually at least one weekend day for at least eight hours.

Geology class was the highlight of the week because he got to sit next to Tara for an hour, hold her hand.

He called her the first Friday night in November. He'd just come in from work and so had she.

"I can't talk long," he told her. He wasn't supposed to be talking to her at all, but he'd had to hear her voice. "Mom got the phone bill today. There was six dollars in long-distance charges to Huber Heights."

"Oh."

"Yeah."

"Was she mad?"

Hell, yeah, she'd been mad. Six dollars was a week's worth of groceries. "Not too bad."

"Do you have to pay her back?"

"Nah. But I can't run up any more bills."

He wanted to tell her he loved her. And that he missed her. Instead, they talked for another minute or so and said goodbye.

Their time together was more valuable than ever after the no-call rule. Tara was off work the second Saturday night in November, and they'd made plans to go see a movie. The plans were a mutually agreed upon attempt to be out around other people. To slow down the intensity of their physical relationship. Or at least, when Tara had said she thought it was a good idea, he'd agreed to go along with the idea because she wanted it that way. The last thing he wanted was to slow down the intensity of anything—most particularly their physical relationship.

Tim picked her up, wondering how long the movie was going to last, calculating how much time he'd have alone with her afterward. She answered her door, and when he saw her in those jeans and his favorite blue sweater, he felt a jab clear through him. He meant to smile and say hello, and he leaned forward and kissed her instead.

Her folks were out for the night, but Scott, her little brother, was there. Tara called out that she was leaving and they were off.

"The movie's at eight. You want something to eat first?" he asked, holding her hand as he drove, taking her hand with him when he had to use his hand to shift. She was so far away over there. Maybe bucket seats hadn't been such a great idea.

"I'm not that hungry," she said now. "But I'll have a little something if you are."

He wasn't hungry at all. Not for food.

"That leaves us an hour to kill before the movie. Anything you want to do?"

"No." She looked at him and smiled. "I missed you," she said. Her eyes went straight to his groin, and he started to grow.

"You want to go back to my place?"

"Is your mom home?"

"No. Neither is Jeff. They're both out for the evening."

"So we'd be alone?"

"Yeah."

"And miss the movie?"

"Unless you want to go. We can still do that, if you'd rather." They'd said they were going. He'd take her if that's what she wanted to do.

"But then we wouldn't be able to go to your house."

"That's okay . . . " It wasn't. He was burning for her. It had been two days since they'd seen each other and that had been at school. But for her . . .

"No it's not. I want to go to your house."

His house on Maple Street was the only place they'd ever been completely alone.

They were on fire for each other. There was just no sense fighting it.

When they got to his house, Tim thought about the last time they'd been there, the night of the Halloween party. His mother had come home, and he and Tara had had to stop what they were doing. He didn't want a repeat.

"Let's go upstairs," he said. There was a spare bedroom up there. It was way more secluded than his room in the middle of the house.

She didn't ask why they were going upstairs, or what was up there, or what they'd do there. She just held his hand as he led her. She didn't say a word as he walked her into the room that was seldom used, shut the door behind them and headed toward the one piece of furniture inside. A bed.

"Come here, Babe," he said, lying down on the bed and holding his arms out to her. With her arms reaching for him, she did as he asked, settling down on top of him. She lowered her head to his, and he started to come alive again.

It felt like it had been a year since he'd had her tongue in his mouth. He kissed her lips and then, rolling her over, kissed his way down her neck, stopping to leave his mark before moving further down, kissing the bit of her chest that the V-neck of her sweater allowed him access to.

"Mmm," she groaned, and he was hard enough to burst already. He straddled one of her legs, and she moved against him, the friction almost more than he could bear.

And he hadn't even gotten under her sweater yet.

But he did. He pulled the sweater up, letting him see her bra in the glow coming in the window from the streetlight outside. The bra was white. And he loved seeing it. Who'd have thought a bra would be as much of a turn-on as what was underneath it?

Running his hand along her stomach, he traced the edges of her bra, watching his hand touch her. And then he pushed his fingers up under the fabric. Tonight that wasn't enough. He wanted more. He wanted her bra off.

He reached behind her and fumbled for a minute or two because his fingers were shaky, but she was patient and he finally got the hooks undone. He didn't immediately lift the material free from her breasts. He looked for her instead, finding her expressive blue eyes in the near darkness.

"You okay?"

"Yeah." Her voice sounded a little odd, but she smiled at him. "I want to feel you . . . touch me."

It was all the invitation he needed. Practically salivating to see, to feel, Tim pushed her bra up under her sweater. He'd seen her nipples before, touched them, but he'd never had his mouth there. He lowered his mouth slowly, giving her time to stop him, but his lips met her breast without a hitch. He didn't suckle. He sure thought about it, though. He kissed her there. A lot.

And tonight, he couldn't stop. She was his. Wearing his ring. He hardly got to see her anymore. He had to do more and see more and touch more.

He reached for the button on her jeans. Slid it free. And then took down her zipper.

She wasn't stopping him. He was going to take off her pants. And then his. But he kissed her first. Her tongue darted in and out of his mouth, mimicking the act he needed.

He pushed her pants down enough, maybe an inch or two, to allow him easy access with his hand. Sliding inside her underwear, his fingers caressed her, touching her girl parts like he had on Halloween night. She moaned and moved and then that wasn't enough anymore either. And so he opened her and, as if it were the most natural thing in the world, he slid his fingers up inside her opening. She was wet and hot and perfect, and he was there. Inside her.

"Mmmm." Her moan made him wild, and he started to move his fingers slowly in and out of her, unable to think beyond her wetness on his fingers.

Tara's was the only body he'd ever been inside, and he couldn't get enough of her secrets. Not ever, not in a million lifetimes.

With his free hand on her breast and his fingers still inside her, he raised his head and looked her in the eye. "Let's make love."

Tara's eyes widened and closed, and the world stopped dead.

When she spoke, he didn't recognize her voice. "I will do anything you want, except that. I have to be married to do that."

She sounded like she was going to cry, and he pulled his fingers out of her.

"Come on," he pleaded, with his penis urging him on. "It'll be okay. I promise."

She shook her head. "I have to be a virgin when I get married, Tim."

Something had changed. And it wasn't him. She was serious. So serious she wasn't there with him, feeling the passion.

"Okay, Babe. It's okay. I won't pressure you."

"Promise me you won't ask me that again. I can't do that without marriage."

Looked like they were done in that room. "I'm sorry, babe," he said. "I didn't mean to push you or offend you. We don't have to do anything you're not comfortable with."

She tried to sit up, and he moved, letting her go.

She fixed her bra, righted her sweater. He adjusted his jeans, getting smaller by the second. She wasn't looking at him.

What the hell. He hadn't meant to upset her. And didn't want the night to just end. They still had a few hours they could spend together.

"You want to go get something to eat?"

"That sounds good."

At least she wasn't demanding that he take her home.

He got them to the only fast-food place in town before she could change her mind, ordering four tacos and a burrito.

Comfort food to take away the awkwardness that had fallen between them.

They ate in the car, still not saying much and, too soon, the food was gone.

Tara just sat there, and he had no idea what to say to her. He'd apologized. He'd promised never to ask again.

Not knowing what else to do, he put the car in gear and headed out to the country. He was driving toward the highway the back way, in the direction of Huber Heights, but got only as far as a deserted cove on a curve of road in the middle of nowhere before he pulled off.

Without saying a word, he leaned over the console and kissed Tara.

"I just want you to know that I respect your decision not to have sex until you're married, and I won't ask anymore," he said.

"Thank you." She didn't sound like his Tara at all. She also didn't sound any happier than he felt.

Starting to panic, Tim kissed her another time. And when she responded to that, he deepened the kiss. Her tongue met his, and he started to spin out of control all over again.

She was still his. And he wanted her more than ever.

"Let's move it to the back," he said, and then froze. Had that upset her?

The click as her seatbelt came undone almost made him laugh out loud, he was so relieved. He climbed into the seat behind them and helped her over the console, pulling her into his arms so tightly he had to tell himself to lighten up. She felt so good to him, he didn't want to let her go.

Kissing led to touching. It always did, no matter what he knew and thought and decided. They couldn't make love, but there were a lot of things they could do.

He unbuttoned Tara's jeans again, needing to be as close to her as he could be. Needing to be intimate with her. He pushed his hand down inside her jeans and she let him, spreading her legs as he caressed her between her thighs. He kissed her neck at the same time, and she started to moan, deeper than before. Like she was dying, too. His penis got tighter as her noises grew louder, and then she suddenly grabbed his hand and yanked it from her jeans.

"What's wrong?" he asked. Had he hurt her?

She was breathing heavily, almost gasping for air. "I . . . almost . . . lost my emotions."

His car smelled like sex, and he was hard as a rock. "What does that mean?"

"You know."

He was pretty sure he did know, but he wanted to hear her say the words.

"Why didn't you just let it happen?"

"No way. I would have been too embarrassed."

He'd brought her to the point of orgasm, and she didn't seem to know what to do with that. Which made him need to take her over the edge as soon as possible. He'd never had an orgasm with a girl, either, and he wanted to do that with her.

"Do you want to try once more?"

"No." Any other night, he might have pushed a little harder. But Tara wasn't herself. And one thing was for certain. He didn't want to scare his sweet girl away.

"It's getting late," he offered, hoping he sounded easy and non-threatening, and not as disappointed as he felt. "I should get you home."

There were other nights. Hopefully unending numbers of them. He'd get her to come.

Helping her into the front seat, Tim held her hand all the way back to Huber Heights.

Eight

I SPENT MOST OF THE DAYS OF NOVEMBER thinking about marriage. About marrying Tim. The guy hadn't even told me he loved me, and I was trying to figure out whether or not he'd ever marry me.

I didn't tell anyone. I knew what it looked like—like I was some pathetic girl who'd never had a date, was desperate, and was ready to jump into marriage with the first guy who showed her any attention at all. I also knew my own heart.

I'd waited for Tim to say something about our future when he'd asked me to make love and I'd told him I had to be married first. Just a few short words were all it would have taken. *I want to marry you. We're going to get married as soon as we're a little older. Will you marry me?*

He hadn't said anything. He'd just stopped what we were doing. As though he'd rather stop than talk about marriage.

And later, in his car, he'd said that he'd never ask again.

Did that mean that he had no intention of asking me to marry him? Ever? We were only eighteen. I understood that. We were young. In our first year of college. Neither of us could support ourselves, much less each other. We were both living at home. Tim had just bought his first car.

But he hadn't mentioned any of that. He hadn't talked about marriage at all.

And I'd almost slept with him anyway. I needed him so desperately. Morals didn't matter when I was with him. Love did.

~

"Thanksgiving's next week," Tim said one day after geology lab.

I knew the date. I'd been wondering if we were going to get to see each other at all over the holiday. I had no idea what his plans were and didn't want to impose. I was hoping that he'd at least stop by in the evening. Thanksgiving was a quiet day at my house. Just my brothers and parents, and football on TV all day. Other than when we were eating, the lights were out all day so that there was no glare on the television set.

"Will you come to Eaton and spend the day with me and my family? We all go over to my brother Mike's for the day. It's a lot of fun."

He not only wanted to see me, he wanted me to be part of his family celebration? My heart soared.

"Yes," I said, afraid I'd answered too quickly, sounded too eager. I hadn't even thought about it. Or asked my mother. After all, I would be spending my first holiday away from my family. But Tim had just handed me my dreams on a platter. I barely cared about the rest of it.

That was as it should be. A girl grew up to be a woman and left her home for her man. Tim was my man.

Thanksgiving arrived, and I was a nervous wreck trying to figure out what to wear and ended up with my normal jeans and a sweater. Orange with green and brown on it—like fall. I'd never met Mike—or anyone in Tim's family besides his mother and brother Jeff.

He picked me up at eleven.

"Who's all going to be there?" I asked as we drove from Huber Heights to Eaton. Chum was home for Thanksgiving. He'd just arrived early that morning. I'd wanted Tim to meet him, but after driving all night Chum had still been asleep.

"Everyone but Ed and Gary." Tim's two oldest brothers. I'd already met Jeff, Tim's one-year-older-than-him brother. The brother who still lived at home with him and their mother.

I was nervous about meeting Mike and Jane. About being in a houseful of people I didn't know. Afraid that they wouldn't approve of a city girl for their little country boy brother.

But more than being nervous, I was excited to be spending my first holiday with the man I loved. The first big holiday of my life as part of a couple. He was holding my hand, and I was grinning just because life felt so good.

And . . . his mother was going to be there. I hadn't seen her since Halloween.

"Does your mom know I'm coming?"

"Yes, of course."

"And she doesn't mind?"

"No. She likes you."

I wanted to believe him. But no matter what Tim said, his mother had to think I was a bad influence on her youngest son. I kept him out until 5:00 AM. And had been in his bedroom so late the night of the Halloween party that she'd had to kick me out.

I didn't see her when we first arrived at Mike and Jane's, either. She wasn't there yet.

But the house was full. Mike and Jane and their kids. Jane's parents. And siblings. Their spouses. Kids. In-laws and their kids. The kitchen was a flurry of activity. Noise and great smells and life. Nothing like the quiet Thanksgiving that I was used to, the one highlighted by naps in front of the football game—the one going on back at my house in Huber Heights.

Nothing about the day remotely resembled any Thanksgiving I'd ever had. Tim's mom arrived with a lot of food that she'd cooked at home. Jane announced when it was time to eat—but there was no table set. No seats designated. Just a long row of dishes filled with vegetable casseroles and potatoes and gravy and turkey and dressing and more food than I'd ever seen in one home at one time. People grabbed plates, went through the line, and sat anyplace that was available. A couch. A chair. A seat at the dining room table.

At my house there was one conversation at a time and you had to be polite and listen and speak only when you weren't covering up what someone else was saying. Tim's family dinner was filled with bustling conversations. Many of them. All over the house. All the time. And anyone could jump into any of the conversations any time.

I was mesmerized. Holding on to Tim for all I was worth. And in love.

I looked around, noticing Mike's wife in the middle of it all, and knew, then and there, that more than writing for Harlequin, more than anything else I'd ever wanted in my life, I wanted to be just like her—a Barney wife.

⁓

"Mom said to ask you in for dessert," Tara said when Tim took her home on Thanksgiving night. He was tired but accepted her invitation immediately, glad that the day wasn't ending yet. Maybe they'd have some time alone before he had to head back to Eaton.

Her dad was asleep on the couch in front of the television when they got there just a little past 9:00 PM.

"Walter," Mrs. Gumser said, "come and have some dessert with the kids."

Tara's dad grunted, but he got up and came over. He didn't seem nearly as intimidating with his hair sticking up on end. He was wearing an old-looking pair of brown slacks and a white T-shirt.

"What kind of pie do you want?" Mrs. Gumser asked Tim.

"Pumpkin," he said, though he really wasn't that hungry.

Tara chose pumpkin, too. And Pepsi. That girl and her Pepsi.

They all sat down to eat, and Mrs. Gumser asked about dinner. And seemed to really care as Tara described the day—and Tim's family—as though Tara really had loved it all. Tim hadn't been sure.

"Let me guess what you all did," Tara said when she'd finished describing his family to a T. "Watched football, right?"

"Of course."

"They had the game on there, too, but you almost didn't know it. Everyone moved around and talked and ate all day long."

Tara's dad hadn't said a word. His plate, filled with a strange concoction of apple pie and gravy topped with ice cream, was almost empty.

"Did the Lions win?" Tim asked him. He'd left his brother's house before the game ended.

"Bears. 31–14."

Whoops. Tara's dad was a Lions fan.

Before Tim could stick his foot any further down his throat, the front door opened and a tall, dark-haired guy wearing jeans and a brown shirt walked in.

Tim watched as his girlfriend jumped up out of her chair and threw her arms around the guy's neck. He squeezed her back.

And then she turned to him. "Tim, this is Chum. Chum, this is Tim."

He nodded. Said something that was probably okay, and waited for Tara to sit back down next to him. She did. And touched him, too.

"How was dinner, Sis?" Chum asked.

And Tara described the day a second time. Exactly as she had the first time. She must've really meant what she'd said to get it exactly the same both times. She made his ordinary family sound like something really special.

And then, still looking at her brother, she said, "Hey, get your guitar."

"Yeah," Mrs. Gumser added. "Go get your guitar."

Back with his guitar, Chum pulled out a chair and sat. "What do you want to hear?" he asked, looking straight at Tim, who had a feeling this sort of thing wasn't unusual in this house.

"What do you know?"

"Neil Diamond," Tara said.

"Neil Diamond." Her brother nodded, and with a few warm-up strums he started singing. Tim knew the song. "Hot August Night." Chum's voice was strong, and Tara hadn't exaggerated her brother's talent. But there was more than just ability at play here. Even an amateur like Tim could see how much the guy enjoyed music. He sat in the chair with his guitar perched on his knee and his head slightly tilted back, his eyes fully shut as he sang, and Tim would swear, if he closed his own eyes, that Neil Diamond was singing live right in front of him.

And the distance between him and Tara struck him in the gut. He was having a once-in-a-lifetime experience, at a concert that people should be paying money to hear, and Tara was sitting at home with her brother. Her life was so completely different from anything he'd ever known.

Tim and I made more dates. We were going hiking. And to movies. We made it to the state park to hike, once. But didn't make it to the trail. We were too busy touching and had to get back to his car. We didn't make it to any of the movies, either.

We made it into each other's arms and stayed that way. But he kept his word to me. He didn't ask me to make love with him.

He also didn't mention the future. I couldn't think of anything else. We were a walking time bomb. He might not ask for sex again, but I wasn't sure I wouldn't. And I knew if I did, he sure as heck wasn't going to say no.

Even though I knew it was stupid, I hoped that with Christmas coming I might get a ring. One that fit my finger. And had a little white stone on top.

And I bought him another card. One that told him how I felt without sounding too forward. After a week of angst, of worrying about whether I'd be pushing him away if I actually sent the card, I finally put it in the mail. It would be in the mailbox on Maple Street by the next day, and I thought about him reading it.

When we count our blessings at Christmas time we think of you.
Except I crossed out "we" and wrote "I."
Beneath the printed message I wrote my own.

Tim, I hope you have a super Christmas,
and that we can share many more. You have indeed
been a blessing to me. Thank you.
Lots of Love, Tara

My love was all over it if he wanted it. And if not, he knew that he had a friend who valued him hugely.

I didn't hear whether or not he got the card. What I did get, at school the next day, was an invitation to the Christmas party at Tim's work. It was an adult party being held at the Eaton Country Club.

He wanted to have me by his side at his party. Obviously, Tim liked me a lot.

~~~

He'd made it through his first semester of college. And the grades he had were actually decent, considering how much energy he'd spent on falling in love. The time off from class was great, but Tim was working more. And driving to Huber Heights more, too, now that he couldn't see Tara in class. On the Friday night before his Saturday night Christmas party he told himself he'd make it home at a decent time, to rest up for the next day and night. But Tara's arms had held him so tightly, the warmth of her body so comforting, he'd actually fallen asleep with her and barely made it home in time to shower before work. He'd clocked in late—for the third time. The girl was going to get him fired.

But in spite of the lack of sleep, he was raring to go when he clocked out at three that afternoon. He showered again. Took time with his hair and shaving, put on a brown leisure suit. the only suit he owned, He wore a white shirt with an oversize collar but no tie, and platform shoes. He'd borrowed Mike's brown beads and tied them around his neck, anticipating the night ahead.

Tara was upstairs when he got to her house and her mother called her down. She came bouncing down in a light blue dress that hung to just below her knees, and all he could think about was what was underneath it. She was smiling and had on Jontue perfume, her scent. It turned him on every time he caught a whiff of it.

She was so sexy. And with him. He felt lucky, as rich as anyone as he walked her into Eaton's country club an hour later.

"Hi, Tim. Who's this?" the greeter at the door of the party asked, writing with a red marker on Santa Claus and bunny name tag stickers. The woman already had his name written.

"This is Tara," he said, but everyone knew who she was. He talked about her nonstop. He could see all his coworkers checking her out.

He was a proud man as he moved around the room introducing Tara, and once he was certain everyone he knew had met his woman, he chose a small round table that was close to the bar and helped her to a seat.

"What do you think?"

She was grinning and beautiful and his heart was full of her. "They're nice," she said. "I'm glad we're here."

She glowed—nothing like the shy girl who'd trailed quietly beside him at the Halloween party.

"I am, too," he said, meaning it. "What do you want to drink?"

"I don't know. I've never had anything but my dad's scotch, and some wine."

"And beer," he said. "October Daze."

"Right. I didn't finish the one glass I had. I didn't like it."

"Come with me then."

They stepped up to the bar and ordered their first alcoholic drink together. Tom Collins. She loved it.

And he loved her.

* * *

Tim and I danced—something else I'd never done. We ate finger foods. And drank a couple of Tom Collinses. We stayed for a long time, and I had a blast.

Still, I was ready to be alone with him when we left to head back to Huber Heights. Maybe tonight we could talk. About us. Our future. Love.

We got to my house, sat in the beanbag chair, and Tim's hand started to slide up my leg. I was wearing panty hose. And the eroticism of his manly hand gliding on the nylon took me by surprise.

"I crave this," he whispered, his mouth at my neck. "I think about it—and you—all the time."

I started to shake. I'd had an "almost" avowal of love.

"I think about you all the time, too."

I loved him so much.

He kissed me then, and I kissed him back with all of my passion. He was finally starting to open up.

* * *

Tim worked on New Year's Eve day, but got home in time to shower and put on his best jeans and sweater before heading out to Huber Heights. He'd been there the night before, too. And had been late to work again that morning.

He didn't care. He and Tara were bringing in the New Year together.

When he got to Huber Heights, he couldn't make it anywhere near her house. Cars, expensive ones, were parked in every available space along both sides of the road and in her driveway. He pulled the Le

Mans into the closest spot he found. It was almost a block away.

Every window in the house on Drywood was lit up. He could hear voices and laughing from halfway up the drive. And music, too.

"Hi, Babe." Tara swung the door open as he walked up. Had she been watching for him? She looked as good as always, her blonde hair curled under at the ends, bangs feathered, and just a little bit of eye makeup on.

Her mom was there, too. "Tim," Mrs. Gumser said, smiling at him. "Please, come in. How was your drive over?"

"Fine. Long," he said and laughed, and she laughed with him.

And then she sobered. "You make sure you're careful tonight. There'll be crazies out on the road."

"I know," he assured her. "I will be."

She didn't look worried. She just looked like she cared. About him, too, maybe. Just a little bit.

But the best part was when Tara linked her arm through his and introduced him around to all of her parent's friends.

"This is my boyfriend, Tim," she said. Over and over. He could have listened to the words all night.

Even Mr. Gumser was friendly. He came walking up with a shot glass hanging on a chain around his neck, and Tim had to reassess his opinion of the man once again.

A guy couldn't be too uptight when he wore shot-glass jewelry.

They didn't stay long. They were stopping in at a party at his brother's house, too. But he hoped they wouldn't be there for long, either. The house on Maple Street was empty tonight. He wanted to bring in the New Year alone with Tara.

"You look great tonight, Babe," he said, holding Tara's hand as they drove.

"Thanks. You do, too."

"Your folks really know how to throw a party."

"They should. They have a million of them. Six this holiday season."

Why hadn't he known that?

"Does your dad always walk around with that shot glass?"

"No. Just sometimes. Mostly he plays the organ or piano all night."

He'd started just before they left. The man had been offered a job playing full time in a nightclub in Chicago or New York or someplace, and Tim could see why.

"People keep getting drinks for him, but I don't think he drinks them all. I've actually never seen him drunk."

"Listen, we can stay at Mike's if you want, but Mom and Jeff are both gone for the night, which means we'd have the whole house to ourselves all night long and I was thinking . . ."

"You want to go to Maple Street."

"Yeah." He wanted to be naked with her in the worst way. To start the New Year naked with her.

"Okay."

"You sure?"

"Yeah."

She smiled at him, and the world was good.

Nine

IT WAS FREEZING OUTSIDE, AND AS WE RAN FROM TIM'S car to the house on Maple Street later that night, I had a brief flash of our lives ahead—Tim and I married, going to family parties, and ending up at home alone.

I ached for that future.

And for him.

He did something with my coat when we got in the door and then came to stand toe-to-toe with me, pulling me into him, and opened his mouth over mine.

I'd worried about this night. Had even thought about calling Tim and canceling. He hadn't said another word about us or his feelings for me since the night of the Christmas party, and I needed to make love with him.

I was in serious danger of becoming a woman I wouldn't be able to live with.

And when he kissed me, I couldn't deny the love I felt for him. We were eighteen. Adults.

Consenting adults.

With his lips still touching mine, moving on mine, he walked me backward until my legs came up against a mattress. We were in the first bedroom we'd come to. Tim pulled down the covers. I was so on fire for him, I didn't really care.

He nudged me, and I went down, holding my arms up as he came to me. My lower belly was on fire, I was wet between my legs, and I throbbed in places I didn't know a woman throbbed.

I wasn't going to make love with him. I knew he wouldn't ask. But beyond that, I might not say no. I wanted to have limits. To say no.

Sort of.

I knew I should want to.

I wanted to be a good girl. A decent woman. A Harlequin heroine.

I wanted to let my emotions go with him. Like I almost had that night in his car. I wanted him to let go, too.

Tim kissed me, or I kissed him. I didn't recognize the woman in his arms. She pushed up his sweater and ran her hands along his chest. And as she touched him, as I touched him, I felt another pool of heat between my legs. I was empty there. I needed to be filled.

Tim pulled at my sweater and I sat up, letting him take it off me.

"You're sure we'll be alone all night?"

"Positive." He was unbuttoning my blouse. I wanted his sweater off him.

It joined my blouse wherever he let them go. He undid my bra, too. I lay back in the bed, the sheets cool, soft, against my bare skin—in direct contrast to Tim's heat as his bare chest met my bare chest for the first time.

I almost couldn't stand the pleasure. My hips came up off the bed, seeking—I wasn't really sure what. There was so much I didn't know. But my body knew. And it was pushing me toward a new world. One it had to have.

Tim unbuttoned my jeans. Unzipped them. He'd done that before. Many times. But that night, instead of sliding his hand down inside, he hooked his thumbs into the waistband and pushed them down. All the way down. I laid there in my panties and watched as he unfastened his own jeans and pushed them down, too.

His underwear still covered him, and they emphasized the huge bulge that I had to know more about it. I had to see it. Touch it. I had to know its power or die. Not because it was a male body, but because it was the essence of Tim.

I had to be a good girl. I had to go home to my father's house.

My conscience was at war with my heart, and I was going to be a casualty whichever way it went.

Up on his knees, Tim positioned himself between my thighs, between my pulled-down pants and my crotch. Bending toward me, he put his hands down on the bed on either side of my shoulders and lowered his hips to my crotch.

With my hands on his chest I could feel his heart pumping twice as fast as usual—and hard, too. His penis touched down on my soft area . . .

~

He hadn't plotted or rehearsed. He had no practice at going this far with a girl. Natural instincts took over, and Tim began to rub his penis back and forth on Tara's crotch. The feeling was so intense and great, and suddenly he knew what Tara had been talking about that night on the country road when she'd stopped him so suddenly.

He jumped off her, tightened up, holding back his emotions and fluids. And stepped out of his pants. He'd started to come.

"Where are you going?" Her voice sounded from far off. Her need called out to him.

"Nowhere, Babe. I heard the dog scratching. I need to get her away from the door before she ruins it."

It was a complete and total lie, but he couldn't let her see him in this shape. He didn't want to scare her. Or embarrass himself. He didn't want things to end so quickly.

He opened the door, stepped outside the bedroom, let the cold air hit him. He stood for a couple of minutes, leaning against the wall, and then turned back. . . .

I was glad he'd stopped. Saved me from myself. I should get up. Pull up my pants. Go outside and pet Mitzy, Tim's cocker spaniel. I'd met her several times before. I liked her.

I was still lying nearly naked on the bed when Tim came back, and I almost cried with relief when he lay back down with me. I touched his chest, my palms flat against his skin and then my hands moved lower. He was my man, and I needed to know all of him. When my hand reached his underwear, I paused. I couldn't take his underwear off. Couldn't be that forward.

But his hand was there, on top of mine, guiding mine. His underwear was wet. Together we got them down to his knees.

My breath came in gasps. The tension inside of me was so strong, guilt and desire built to the exploding point, I could hardly comprehend what was happening. He was lying beside me, kissing me, his hand on my breast, and I could feel his hardness against my hip. He was really wet. My hip was wet where he was touching me.

I moaned. Felt tears behind my closed eyelids. I was in the eye of the storm, helpless and frantic.

Tim pulled my underwear down to my ankles with my jeans. In some strange way, it had not seemed so bad to me, what I was doing, as long as I kept my pants on.

The cool sheet against my backside registered. I knew it was there. And that my bottom was naked.

He spread my knees and climbed between my legs, and I burned for him. He positioned himself so that the tip of his penis was pressing up against my opening.

"Let's make love" he said, violating the promise he'd made weeks before.

I didn't say anything. I couldn't say yes. And I couldn't say no, either. Tim moved against me, and I could feel my body accepting just the tip of him.

"Tara? Can I do it?"

He was leaving it up to me.

He pulled back and then put his tip in me again, still not pushing all the way inside me. I wished he'd just do it.

"Can I?"

If you let the cow out of the barn, there's no reason for him to buy the barn.

I knew where the words came from. I hated them.

And believed them.

I didn't just want Tim then, for that night, or that year. I wanted him forever.

"I can't do that until I'm married." The words hurt my throat. I started to cry, but held back the tears.

"Please, babe."

"Not that, Tim, but please don't stop touching me."

He pulled himself out of me and laid on top of me for a minute.

"Are you mad?"

"No."

He was disappointed, though. I could tell. And I didn't blame him.

A minute or two later he came back up to kiss me gently. To lay his chest against my breast. Eventually the passion started to burn again. He put his fingers inside of me that time.

But it wasn't enough.

It wasn't ever going to be enough.

⁓

January brought near-record cold and snow, and Tara was different, too. He didn't like to be paranoid, but it seemed like that night they'd spent naked in bed had changed her. He thought about asking her about it, but he didn't want to hear any bad news. He just held on, hoping that whatever it was would blow by.

One night in late January, a blizzard blew in while he was at Tara's house. They were lying in front of the fireplace. He'd been kissing her, touching her, and she'd been touching him, too. With clothes on, but only because they were at her house. Out in the open.

"You need to spend the night," she said sometime in the wee hours of the morning. "I'm worried about you driving home in this stuff."

Not quite the invitation to sleep with her he'd been fantasizing about.

"Don't you think you should ask your mother about that?"

"Mom already said it was okay before they went to bed. She told me if it didn't get any better outside to make sure you stayed. You can have my grandfather's room." It was the only bedroom on the main floor, down the hall past the laundry room.

Her grandfather had lived with them until his death less than a year before.

"Okay." He felt more than a bit uncomfortable but wasn't going to turn down the chance to spend the night at Tara's house.

He got harder just thinking about it. Pulling her close again, he nuzzled her neck and said, "I don't have anything to sleep in." He wore pj's at home.

Tara giggled. "I'm sure you'll think of something."

They lay there until the fire died and the room grew cold.

"We better get to bed before my folks get up," Tara said. She walked him down the hall to the room he'd be using. The place was fine. A queen-size bed, elegant cream décor. He didn't want to be there without her.

"Hey, babe, why don't you go upstairs and get ready for bed and sneak back down." Even if they didn't make love, just lying naked under the covers together, sleeping with Tara in his arms, would be heaven.

"I can't, Tim. Not in my parents' house. My dad would kill us both if he caught me down here."

"You sure?" They were in the doorway, he inside the room, she outside. Surely she wouldn't be able to resist. Not with him this close.

"Yeah."

"Okay then," he kissed her and started to close the door, hoping she'd push it open and join him. "If you change your mind you know where to find me."

She nodded. He held onto the door.

"Or if you need anything, you know what I mean . . ."

"I do, and forget it," she smiled, but her eyes weren't sparkling.

She was really going to leave him there alone. "Good night," he said.

"I'll see you in the morning, Babe," Tara smiled once more, and let the door close.

He climbed between sheets that smelled as though they'd been hanging outside on the line, and wondered what had happened between the family room and the bedroom to cause such a change in Tara. Out in the hall, as she'd said good night, she'd been distant, hesitant. Not at all the sexual tiger that he'd been making out with all night.

He went to sleep with a hard-on.

⁓

I didn't sleep that night. I tried, but the war inside of me was escalating to some kind of finale.

I'd missed my period and was scared to death that I was pregnant. Only Tim's tip had been inside of me, but he had released fluid. I'd asked some questions at school, done some reading. If I was at my fertile time of the month, what we'd done on New Year's Eve in the bed on Maple Street had been enough to impregnate me.

And the man I loved, the father of my possible child, was downstairs, sleeping in a bed that I belonged in, too. My father was next door, thinking I was a good girl.

Tim was eighteen and didn't have a lot of money. His mother wouldn't be able to help him, either. There was no way he could support a baby without giving up his whole life.

I wasn't sure he loved me enough to do that. I wasn't really sure he loved me at all.

He wanted me. I knew that. But if I'd let him go all the way in, if I let him have all the sex he wanted, would he tire of me and move on? Was I just keeping his interest because I was saying no?

He didn't talk about his feelings. I'd told him I needed to be married to do what I was doing with him. I'd asked him to talk to me. I'd written him notes, telling him we needed to talk. Nothing was working.

My stomach was a massive knot by the time I heard my folks getting up. Pulling on my yellow robe, I brushed my teeth and went downstairs, down the hall past the laundry room, the bathroom, and stood outside his room.

Would he be awake? Naked?

Was he a morning person? A grouch when he woke up?

My parents were talking upstairs. They'd be descending soon. I knocked.

"Who is it?" He didn't sound grouchy. He was groggy though, and I loved the sound. It made me want to crawl under the covers with him, leave the world and worries behind, and find peace and rest in the security of his arms.

"It's me," I said softly, debating whether or not to throw caution to the wind and follow my instincts. If I were pregnant, my parents were going to be disappointed in me soon enough anyway.

"Me who?"

"Tara," I said, getting frustrated. Maybe I was the grouch in the morning. Or maybe I'd just had too many sleepless, fear-filled nights.

How in the heck was I going to raise a child on my own? Or hold my head up at church? My parents would be so disappointed. Mortified. I'd be an embarrassment to them.

Yet I couldn't help but wonder what our would baby look like. Would it have Tim's brown eyes? And my blonde hair? Would it be a girl or a boy?

Would I ever have a husband and family? Or had I just ruined my whole life?

Tim was still under the covers when I opened the door. "You knew who it was."

"I didn't think my Tara would knock before coming in," he said, smiling.

I could melt in that smile. And lose myself in his dark gaze—no matter how bleak the future might be.

"That would be inappropriate," I said.

"Maybe so, but it's not like I'd complain. What time is it anyway?"

"Eight-thirty."

If I were pregnant, I could make love with him all I wanted. Until he was done with me.

And if he did stand by me in the beginning, how long would it be before he resented me? Blamed me? Started to hate me?

Left me at home with a child to raise while, driven by the need for freedom, he went out and found other things to do?

"Why are you up so early on a Sunday morning?"

"My parents are up, and I didn't want you down here alone with them up and around."

I was in the room, beside the bed, but I was afraid to sit down next to him. I fought the urge to open my robe and take him inside.

And I couldn't quit picturing him under those covers. His jeans were hung over a chair with a sweater. I couldn't see, without doing something obvious, like lifting the jeans, whether or not his underwear was with them or with him.

"Why are you acting like such a stranger? After all the things we've done, all the places I've touched your body, it's a little late for shyness, don't you think?"

I felt the heat rising up under my robe. And shrugged. If I told him I was afraid I was pregnant it would all be over.

He'd be scared. And tense. And it could all be for nothing. I might start that day. Or the next. It hadn't been a full month yet.

"Sit on the bed with me."

"I can't. You aren't dressed and my parents just came downstairs."

"What's that matter?"

"Nothing."

"Then why don't you want to be close to me?"

"I do. It's just . . . it would be too tempting."

I was starting to feel sick to my stomach and prayed that it was just a sleepless night. Nerves. Or even an ulcer.

I prayed I would start my period and that Tim would tell me that he couldn't live without me and ask me to marry him.

Ten

TARA SEEMED TO BE UNHAPPY A LOT. ANYTIME HE ASKED her if something was wrong, she'd tell him no, and he tried to believe that everything was fine. If she was getting tired of him, he wished she'd just say so.

Yet when she told him they had to talk, he clammed up, afraid she was going to break up with him.

"What are you doing tonight?" he asked her one Tuesday in early February. They were in the student union, staying warm by the fire.

"I've got the Vandalia city council meeting."

She went every month. He knew that. She covered the city's business for the *Dayton Daily News*. And in all the months they'd been going steady, he'd never shown any interest in that part of her life at all.

"Can I come with you? Drive you?"

"Sure."

She sounded so happy with the idea, he was happy, too, though even the thought of sitting through a city business meeting bored him to tears. Probably wouldn't be any windows there to escape through, either.

Still, he'd be with Tara and that was enough for him. More than enough for him.

I have to admit, I was proud as I walked into the Vandalia city building Tuesday night, knowing that I had the credentials to be there. I hoped Tim was impressed. I knew the room where the council met and headed toward it like I owned the place. Maybe he'd think I was important enough to marry.

I had my own seat. It was in the front. Inside the courtroom-like area, I made a beeline for my place, indicating that Tim should sit down next to me on the wooden bench. He sat close. His hip touching mine.

I wondered if the city manager would call the paper and complain. If someone would decide I was a kid who was inappropriate and not mature enough to handle the job of reporting city business to one of the state's major newspapers.

I didn't ask Tim to move. I took out my paper and pen and prepared to do the job I'd been hired to do.

"How long does this thing last?"

"Depends on the agenda. Anywhere from half an hour to all night."

It was a Tuesday night. We had school the next day. Tim had a long drive back to Eaton tonight.

"Let me have that." He took my pen and paper. And started writing my name. I loved how it looked in his penmanship. He was much more artistic than I was. He wrote his name. And our names.

I sat there and watched. Getting warm all over. And smiling.

And then I thought about the baby and felt all weighted down with dread again. I still hadn't started my period.

The city council filed in. A couple of members glanced at me as they took their seats. They smiled.

I hoped Tim had noticed. And that he'd see that I was good enough to marry.

The meeting was called to order. I took back my pad but gave Tim some paper and my extra pen. Roll was called. Minutes were read. Tim doodled. And leaned over and half licked, half blew on my ear.

I tried so hard not to notice. To pay attention to the business at hand. I jotted some notes.

The *Dayton Daily News* paid me for my writing.

Writing was going to be my career.

Tim kept tempting me with his breath. And whispering nutty things to me.

Eventually I ssshhh'd him. I'd done it in geology class all last semester, and every single time he'd just grinned and kept right on pestering me. That night he sat back, looking like I'd hurt his feelings.

The next item on the agenda was called.

And I wondered if they'd fire me from the paper if I turned up pregnant and unmarried at eighteen.

On the second Friday in February, I started my period. I was so relieved I sat in the bathroom and cried. For a long time. I cried for so long that I finally had to admit that the emotion pouring out of me wasn't relief. I was empty. Bereft.

Because I wasn't carrying Tim's child.

Which made no sense. I'd been physically sick worrying about a pregnancy. And when I found out there wasn't one, I was devastated. The war inside of me was taking a huge toll. If something didn't happen soon, I was going to lose my mind.

Tim had to give me his emotions as well as his passion, or . . . I didn't know what. I couldn't even think about living without him. But my stomach was in knots all the time. I wasn't sleeping.

I wasn't pregnant, but every single time I was alone with Tim that danger loomed. I loved him too much to resist him.

Driving to his house one night at the end of February, knowing what we'd end up doing when we got there—and needing it as badly as he did—I tried one more time.

"We need to talk."

I waited.

He sat there, saying nothing. Didn't he care about my feelings at all? How could he just ignore me?

His heart was there. It had to be. I just had to find a way inside.

"How old did you say you were when your dad died?"

"Five."

"What happened to him?"

"I don't know. He died. I was just a kid."

"Were you there?"

"No."

"Do you remember him?"

"Not much." He wasn't happy with me. Because of my constant pushing for talk, for more? Because I was unhappy?

Or because he was done with me?

❦

"My brother is coming home this weekend," Tara announced early in March. Sitting at the little phone table in the dining room on Maple Street, Tim listened to her with a growing feeling of dread. "He's coming home to see his girlfriend and his friend from college is coming home with him. Mom said he couldn't come home unless he could find someone to share the driving. It's twelve hours each way, and they're doing it in a weekend."

"That's cool." She was talking faster than usual. And she was unusually chipper.

"Chum wants me to go bowling with him and his girlfriend and his friend from college on Friday night. He wants time alone with his girlfriend and can't leave the friend with no one to talk to."

"What?" He'd known something was up, but he hadn't seen that coming. "He wants you to go out with another guy?"

"No! It's not like that! He just wants me to go so the guy won't be a third wheel."

"No way, Tara," he blurted. "I'm not letting you go out with another guy."

"You can't tell me what to do."

"I can't, can I? Just watch me. You aren't going on a date with another guy."

"You're right! I'm not! That's what I'm telling you. I'm doing my brother a favor. I don't even know the guy. Don't want to know the guy. I'm not going to be alone with him. I'm paying my own way."

"Call it what you want, it's a date."

"You can call it a date if you want to, but you're the only one who thinks so. I can't let my brother down, Tim. He doesn't ask me for much, and he really needs my help. It's the only way he can come home. He hasn't seen his girl since Christmas, and he thinks he wants to marry her. Besides, I really want to see Chum."

He didn't hear reason. Maybe he didn't want to. All he knew was that he was losing Tara, and the idea panicked him.

At the same time, he didn't want to be with a girl who didn't want to be with him.

"Fine. If you're going, then we're not seeing each other at all this weekend. I won't share you."

"Well, that's your choice."

She'd called his bluff.

I couldn't believe that Tim was being so obstinate. He knew Chum. And knew how much I adored my older brother. He knew that I'd walk through fire for Chum. And that I missed him a lot.

I'd walk through fire for Tim, too. I'd been sitting in it with him for months now. Most particularly those six weeks that I was afraid I was pregnant. But maybe he didn't want me walking through fire with him. Maybe he just wanted to make fire with me, burn us both up, and then move on.

I didn't hear from Tim at all on Friday night. I went bowling. I didn't do well. And I didn't care. I talked with my brother's friend. I got to spend a little time with my brother. His girlfriend didn't say a word all night—at least not to me.

And I went home. Chum left to take his girl to her house, and because my parents were already in bed, I brought his friend in to the family room, to sit with him until Chum got back and then the two guys were going to play pool or something.

I talked about Tim. About how much I loved him, and about how little of his inner feelings he shared with me.

The guy was nice. He listened. He told me that if Tim loved me, I deserved to have him say so. He warned me about guys who just wanted one thing from a girl. He said most guys just used girls. And that I had to be careful.

And then he leaned over to kiss me. His lips touched mine and I pulled back, my chest burning with guilt. I hadn't done anything but pull back and still I felt as though I'd betrayed my deepest heart.

But there was one thing I liked about that kiss. It didn't do a thing to me. Nothing. I didn't feel anything anywhere in my body—except shame.

No fire. Not even a spark. No feelings down below.

Nothing like I felt with Tim. I wasn't a bad girl. I wasn't loose or sexually crazed. I felt the things I felt with Tim because I was in love with him. He was my Tim. My soul mate.

My soul mate who didn't call me on Saturday. He'd said I wouldn't see him all weekend, but surely he hadn't meant that. He'd calm down. He'd see that he'd had nothing to fear. He'd call.

Even if he didn't see that he had nothing to fear—even, he believed the worst—he'd call just because it would drive him nuts not to. Because we didn't go all weekend without talking.

He didn't call.

My brother left Sunday morning, and I spent the entire day waiting for Tim to call. I tried to do homework. I tried to read. Nothing worked. I was heartsick. By Sunday afternoon I picked up the phone to call Tim, but I put it back down. I wasn't going to go chasing after him.

Maybe he'd been ready to get rid of me. Maybe this weekend, the thing with Chum, had just been an excuse for him to dump me.

Maybe he'd met someone else. Maybe he'd spent the night before making out with another girl in the bed on Maple Street. Or in the back of his car on a country road.

I'd see Tim at school the next day, and I was going to have to do something to get his attention. Something to find out once and for all if he had any feelings for me.

But I wasn't going to cause a scene. Or be one of those girls who hung on a guy after he was done with her.

I wasn't going to cry. Or beg.

His class ring pushed against my breastbone as I hugged my hands to my chest, and I knew what I had to do. If Tim had gone out on me because he'd determined that helping my brother meant I'd gone out on him . . .

I'd tell him I thought I needed my ring back. I'd put the seriousness of our situation right in his face. I'd force him to talk to me about us. I was taking a huge risk. I knew that. He could just call my bluff and give me my ring back. If he did, I'd have my answer once and for all.

But he wouldn't. I knew that. He'd ask me why I was asking for my ring back. And I was going to let him have it. I was going to tell him that I was in love with him and he better get on the stick and find a way to tell me how much I meant to him.

I wanted to talk about getting married someday.

And then I'd tell him I'd been afraid I was pregnant.

Or . . . he'd tell me that I needed to calm down, he'd tell me no, he wasn't giving me my ring back. He'd tell me that if I wanted it, I'd have to get it myself, which would mean getting physically entangled with him, and we both knew where that would lead.

Where we both wanted it to lead. In bed with each other.

Hugging his ring, with the yarn still firmly intact where it was going to stay, I went to bed early that night.

And cried in the dark.

⁓

It was Monday morning, March 14, 1978, and Tim stood outside of Tara's English class, waiting for her to appear. He was leaning up against the cement-block wall in the hallway thinking about what to say to her.

He'd missed her all weekend.

And he was still stinging over her date—favor or not.

She came around the corner, wearing her typical blue jeans and sweater. He tried to read her expression, to determine her mood as she came straight toward him. She wasn't smiling.

He didn't smile either. "Hi," he said, playing it cool.

"I think I need my ring back."

The words rang so loudly he felt like she'd shouted them. Like everyone around them, going to and from class, had heard what she'd just said.

He was shocked, taken back.

He was the one with the right to be mad. She was supposed to be apologizing.

Maybe he'd seen it coming. Maybe not. He'd expected her to break up with him someday.

He had no idea what to say.

But if he didn't get out of there, he was going to lose it. He had to do something quick.

"Okay." He pulled her tiny ring off his little finger and dropped it in the palm of her hand.

She stared at the ring. Just stared at it. And then, without another word she pulled his ring off her finger, yarn still in place, put it in his outstretched palm, turned around, and walked away.

He watched until she was out of sight.

I fell apart. There was just no pretty way to describe me after Tim. I tried to pretend I was okay, to keep up appearances. I was a Gumser, after all. There was protocol.

At some point my parents intervened. They'd determined that I had to get out—away from home. I was too much of a recluse. I spent way too much time with my nose in books. It wasn't healthy. I had to learn how to live in the world. Survive in the world.

But not too far out into the world. Not to begin with. It was decided, with Chum's help, that starting in the fall of 1979 I'd transfer to Armstrong University.

During his last years of high school Chum had joined a pretty strict church. One I'd never heard of. Before that he'd refused to go to church at all, so my parents, while disappointed that he wasn't going to church with the family, were glad that he was going. Armstrong was affiliated with his church—supported by it. Students attending the university were required to live on campus, to keep a strict curfew, to attend chapel every day, take a Bible class every semester, and go to church every Sunday morning, Sunday night, and Wednesday night. They were allowed only four absences a semester from any of those obligations.

Girls were required to wear dresses to class and to church, and dancing was prohibited. So was necking. Any girl exhibiting any impure behavior would be expelled.

If I went to Armstrong, I could be a good girl again. I'd fit right in with my need to be a virgin before I got married.

And maybe, if I worked hard enough, God would forgive me for my indiscretions with Tim.

I'd been singing in the adult choir at my church at home for years, the only kid in the choir. I was active in my youth group, had taught vacation Bible school the past couple of summers. Getting closer to

God appealed to me. Maybe He'd fill the gaping hole in my heart.

I agreed to go to Alabama with Chum.

Agreed to sell my little blue Manta.

I packed my things without complaint. The truth was I was glad to go. To find a new life. The old one hurt too much. Everywhere I looked were memories of Tim.

Of the things I'd done with him.

Obviously I'd romanticized the entire encounter. What to me had been acts of love had only been acts of sex for him.

He was what I'd been warned about—an eighteen-year-old hormonal boy whose pants ruled his heart and mind.

I didn't know whether I'd lost him because I wouldn't have sex with him, or because he'd grown tired of fooling around with my body. I just knew I'd lost him.

Armstrong wasn't what I expected—first and foremost because right before Chum and I left for school, he announced that he wasn't going back. He'd proposed marriage to his girlfriend—also a member of his church—and they were going to move to Columbus, Ohio. He was dropping out of college, but he promised my father that he'd enroll at Ohio State the following quarter.

I didn't want to miss a semester of school. I had no choice but to go to Alabama without him.

I was so homesick those first few months that I wanted to run away. The rules stifled me, made me feel as though I didn't fit in as I longed for the freedom I'd known at home.

But eventually, after attending daily chapel and going to Bible class, I started to draw closer to God. To understand how little my drama mattered in the big scheme of life. I volunteered at an orphanage. And joined a service club. I did jail ministry and sang in the school choir. I grew to like the strictness, made friends, had some fun times with girls in my dorm—and started to heal. Tim was still there. In my heart. In my thoughts. Even in my dreams at night.

But God was slowly starting to fill the emptiness deep inside me.

As Christmas drew near and I knew I was going to be near by Tim again, I sent him a card. Just a friendship card this time. But I wanted him to know I was thinking about him.

I wanted him to know my door was open.

I didn't hear back from him.

⁓

Tim picked up the card for the hundredth time. He'd put it in the box with the other cards and letters she'd sent him. Right next to the pink yarn he'd taken off his class ring. And the pair of glass-horse earrings she'd left in his bedroom one night.

I miss you. Tara had written, nine months after she'd devastated his life.

What did that mean? She missed him?

That she wanted to catch up for old times' sake?

That she cared?

That she wanted to get back together?

He'd met someone. A teacher. Emily wasn't Tara. But she was nice. And funny. Most important, she told Tim all the time how much she cared about him.

He looked back at the card, wondering what to do. He couldn't let his guard down, that was for sure.

He thought about writing her back. And then changed his mind.

But he didn't stop thinking about her. A couple of days after Christmas, when he figured Tara would be sure to be home on break from her fancy Alabama college, and with Emily's blessing, he drove to Huber Heights.

He had to see Tara. To find out what that card had meant.

He gave her no warning. And no chance to tell him not to come.

She'd said she missed him. Elation at the thought made him soar. Not that Emily knew that part.

Emily also didn't know that he'd get back together with Tara in a heartbeat if Tara wanted that.

But what if Tara didn't want to get back together with him?

And what about Emily? She was from Eaton. Was part of his world. They had a good time together. Cared for each other.

Tara must have seen him pull up. She was at the front door when he got there.

"Hey!" she said, standing there staring at him.

"What's going on?"

Her mouth was open. She looked kind of blank. He couldn't tell if it was a good blank or a bad blank.

"Are you going to invite me in?"

"Oh," she stepped back. "Sorry, come on in."

He did. She stood there, watching him until he felt like a bug under a microscope. And then she smiled. A huge smile that ripped at him.

She'd taken that smile away from him. Out of his life.

"It's really good to see you."

"Yeah, I know. I still look good." He was kind of proud of the smart-ass remark. And a bit sad about it, too. "How've you been?"

"Good. Okay. I like school. How about you?"

"I met someone," he said, putting it right out there. "I'm not sure about it yet, but it might turn into something."

"Does she know you're here?"

"Yeah."

Her face fell. Good. Maybe now she knew how he'd felt when she went off bowling without him.

"So what was that Christmas card about?" he asked. They were still standing in her foyer. She seemed to be home alone.

She shrugged. "I was feeling sentimental. Thinking about you. I couldn't let the holiday go by without saying Merry Christmas to you. I wanted to see how you're doing."

"Why?"

"Because I care."

"If you say so." His way of letting her know she wasn't going to hurt him again.

But then why was he there? All he'd had to do was ignore her card to let her know that he wasn't open to her anymore.

"So Tara, how're things down south? Sounds like you picked up a bit of an accent. Not turning into a briar like us Preble County folk, are you?" *Why was he doing this?*

She laughed. "You aren't a briar, Tim Barney. Not even a little bit."

She was killing him.

Why didn't he just ask her what he'd come there to find out? She cared for him. Great. As a friend, or something more? Was there still hope for them as a couple?

"You signed your card, "Lots of love." What did you mean by that?"

"It didn't mean anything specific. I was thinking about you and when I think about you, lots of love comes to mind."

What in the hell did that mean?

They moved into the kitchen. Sat down. He asked about her classes. She asked about his. He made the tennis team again and would be playing all spring. She told him about service projects.

"I didn't see your car in the driveway. Is it at school?" It had always been parked in the roundabout out front.

"No, we sold it when I left for Armstrong."

"Do you and Chum drive back and forth in his car?"

"Chum got married in September."

"That was quick! He wasn't even engaged!"

"I know. He just dropped it all on us in August. He married the girl he came home to see last March."

He listened to her responses but couldn't really focus on her answers. He wasn't asking the questions he really wanted to ask. So he wasn't getting the answers he needed.

But if he asked her if there was still a chance for them, she'd think that he needed her. That he wasn't over her. She'd feel sorry for him. And send more mixed messages. And he'd never get on with his life.

He shouldn't have come.

He stayed a couple of hours anyway. He and Tara probably talked more on that Christmas holiday night than they had in all the months they'd been together.

"It's weird, you know," she said at one point. "Everyone at Armstrong is always telling each other they love each other. It's a love-in-Christ-type thing—you know, we're all God's children, all brothers and sisters in Christ, but they just come right out and say "I love you," on a regular basis. My girlfriends tell me, even teachers will tell you, but I just can't do that. I try. But I don't tell anyone I love them except my family. That doesn't mean I don't feel the words, but I just . . . I don't know . . ."

Her words trailed off and Tim, whose heart had just about come unhitched from his body, spent the rest of the evening cutting up with her to avoid making a complete and utter fool of himself. Tara was too nice to hurt him on purpose. If he asked her for hope, she'd give it to him just because she was so nice. He didn't just want her to care about him. He wanted her to think there was no one on earth but him. And there was no way a girl like her, with her worldly future, would ever be content with someone like him. If she was as in love with him as he needed her to be, she'd have told him so when he'd asked what her card meant.

When he finally stood up to go she walked with him to the door.

"I have to ask you something," she said, standing with him in the darkened foyer.

"What?"

"What we did together, the physical stuff, did it mean anything to you?"

"Of course it did!"

"You weren't just a guy out for sex?"

"No!"

"Have you told . . . anyone . . . what we did?"

"No."

"Have you done anything like it since? Have you been as intimate as we were?"

Those blue eyes were gazing up at him, and they weren't part of his life anymore. "No."

"So we were special to you?"

What did it matter? "Yes."

The answer seemed to satisfy her.

And he was glad he'd stopped by.

Eleven

I WAS EIGHTEEN AGAIN—STARTING COLLEGE AT WRIGHT State and fantasizing about my great-hair guy. For the rest of Christmas break I thought about Tim. I kept watching for him to show up again. Every time I left the house, the first thing I did upon my return was ask my mom if there were any calls for me.

And just like in the past, I lay in my canopied bed—the one I'd once sat on to play guitar for Tim and cried myself to sleep the night before I headed back to college.

Tim hadn't contacted me again.

I told myself I was done with him, but I knew it wasn't true. During the long ride back to school—a ride that extended from the usual twelve hours to seventeen hours due to inclement weather—all I did was think about Tim. I analyzed everything he'd said.

And everything he didn't say.

He hadn't sounded all that excited about this Emily person. He'd been hesitant. He thought maybe there'd be more. What I knew was that if it were there, he'd already know it.

But what kept me going, what had me hooked, was the fact that he'd come by at all. He'd wanted to know about the card I'd sent. About the signature. He cared.

I couldn't wait to get back to school to my bunk in my dorm room and write to Tim. I had pen in hand before I'd even unpacked. Wrote for a bit, but I didn't sign off. I couldn't end my conversation with him.

> *Hello, Babe!*
>
> *I know this is strange, but I felt really super seeing you last week and I want to stay in touch. I'd love to have a place in your busy schedule.*

It was a long letter, a week in the writing, filled with every minute of my days. I tried to keep things light so I didn't cramp him or push him away. I described my room to him, the classes that were starting the following day. I talked about the pizza I'd eaten, meeting up with my roommates and friends again. I talked about the weather, the long drive back. I asked him how his classes were going. I told him that they'd announced that due to the cold, girls were going to be allowed to wear pants to class instead of dresses. I was most definitely not a dress person. And in between the news, I added the things I most needed to say.

Like,

> *Please be sure you're alone when you lift your weights.*

And,

> *I really wish that I'd met you now rather than last year, though I do have lots of fantastic memories that I'd like to keep!*

Toward the end, I got really serious.

> *What happened between us, especially physically, has never happened to me, before or since. Yes, you took a lot and I realize that it was partly my fault and I don't regret anything. I don't even know why I'm telling you. I sure didn't mean to. But I don't want you to harbor any doubt.*
>
> *I also hope that it was something special to you and that you are being honest when you said you'd not told anyone or done anything since. Otherwise it was a waste.*
>
> *I better shut up! This is probably the most I've ever let you know of what I think . . .*

*I'm very serious when I say that I'd love for you to write me.
By the way, if you're ever down by my house there's always
something waiting for you . . . a big kiss and hug.*

Tim wrote back, a pithy ditty telling me to move my fridge so I
didn't get fat. I didn't lose heart. I tried again ten days later. I wasn't so
emotional that time, though. Not until the end. Tim had noticed the
signature on my Christmas card.

It had intrigued him enough that he'd sought me out.

I signed my second letter, *Love Always, Tara*

I'd seen one of Chum's prior girlfriends sign a letter to him that way
once. It had touched me to the core. A vow of undying love. It meant
everything.

I wrote to Tim again on Valentine's Day. Not so much about my
daily life this time. Spring break was coming up, and I had really high
hopes that Tim and I would see each other then.

I'd made up my mind. If he agreed to see me, I was going to do
everything I could to get him into the backseat of his car and finish
what we'd started that night on Maple Street.

So I put my heart out there a little more. Not so much that I scared
him off. But enough for him to know that I wasn't playing around.

*I keep thinking back to last Valentine's Day—I was such an
ick—and you sent me that card.*

That was when I'd thought I was pregnant. And he hadn't told me
he loved me. I'd had such high hopes that I'd get a ring for Valentine's
Day . . .

*I'm really sorry for the hard times I've given you. I'm paying
for them now, though. I feel awful about it.*

Be a good boy.
Remember I love ya, Tara

He'd told himself that seeing Tara over Christmas break had been a good thing. Yes, she was his first love, and as such she'd always have a part of him, but he'd left her house and he hadn't fallen apart. He kept telling himself that all was good, that he'd moved on, as he wrote back to her over the next couple of months. They were friends. And that was fine.

He could tell himself anything. The truth hit him in the face when he got her Valentine's Day letter. Wearing his usual smile, his heart filled with "letter from Tara" lightheartedness, he opened the envelope.

His heart was pounding. His emotions churning. He was . . . outraged. Or something. It was the closing that got him. *Remember, I love ya.* My God, she said it, she wrote the words. Not just, *Love ya.* Or *Lots of Love.* She'd put the *I* there this time. Made it personal. He had evidence.

And then the nagging voice inside of him stopped him. This was Tara. Maybe she didn't really mean what he thought she wrote. A girl could love someone like a brother and not be *in* love with him. There was a big difference.

He added the letter to the others in his locked box. But those words at the bottom of that page caused him great angst.

They wouldn't let go of him.

What in the hell had she meant?

He was just going to have to be direct with her. There'd be no more cat and mouse. Too much was at stake.

February 20, 1979
Dear Tara,

   Hi, how are you? Received your letter today. Was glad to hear from you. I've had a lot on my mind. I'm still seeing Emily

*and I think it's safe to say that I love her more than last time I
wrote you. We're making plans together, maybe marriage in a
couple years.*

He wrote that deliberately. That should send a message to Tara.
Either tell me you're sorry you broke up with me and want me back or
let me go. But then he told her that Emily was still kind of hung up
on an ex-boyfriend, too. Before he messed up too badly, he got to the
point.

*Tara, I'm not sure how you meant that "I love ya" you wrote
at the end of your letter. It seems weird seeing it, because you
never did before. Let me ask you this. What was the extent of
your feelings for me? I just want to know if you really did care?
Please tell me honestly. Because I sometimes get the feeling no
one could really love me, that there's always something better.
Do you know what I mean?
I cared a lot for you. So much it almost hurt.*

This should get the answer that he needed.
And then he scribbled some more. Because he suddenly felt too
exposed. And because he needed her to negate his fears.

*But I guess it wasn't meant to be. Now all we can be is good
friends. Write back with some answers for me, please.
Love, Tim*

Four days later he had his answer.
He skimmed over the daily school crap and got right to the important
stuff.

*The extent of my feelings for you? That's a tough question to
answer, Tim. It's also unfair. However, I'll do the best I can. Yes,
I really did care, and I still do. You're a super person. There've
been a lot of times that I really wanted your arms around me,
bad! I don't know why it didn't work, but I've always cared.*

I told you when I was home why I never said I love you, and
I have still never said it—but that doesn't meant that I don't
feel it. I guess I wrote it because I didn't feel threatened. I just
wanted you to know that you're loved, and I'm here if you need
me—for whatever reason.

One week and four days till I'm home. I have to go to Wright
State the week I'm home. Maybe we can meet for lunch. I
promise not to eat you.
Love you, Tara.

He'd asked, and now he had his answer. She didn't say she was in love with him. He'd put it right out there and she'd talked in circles about caring and loving, but nothing intimate. She just wanted to be friends. Good friends, maybe.

At least now he knew for sure.

He wrote her back, telling her he'd meet her for lunch.

What could it hurt?

I was up before my alarm went off the morning I was due to meet Tim at Wright State. I showered. Did my hair. Put on eye makeup. I'd packed my blue sweater—the one he'd liked best—and my nicest pair of jeans, and when I put them on, when the fabric slid across my skin, I shivered. If things went as I hoped, Tim would be sliding his hands in place of that fabric before I was back in my bedroom.

I went to school early. Registered for the summer classes I needed to take to graduate from Armstrong the next spring. With the credits I'd taken during high school, I just needed a physical education requirement. I chose racquetball. Hard to believe I was already in my junior year.

And then I went to the student union to wait for Tim. Just like old times. Wright State wasn't on spring break yet, so the place was swarming. The feeling of homecoming was so sweet I thought about transferring back to finish my last year where I'd begun my college education.

Finding a seat closest to the fire, I read every word on my registration receipts. And then turned to the course catalog the guidance counselor had given me while, surreptitiously, I watched for Tim. I wanted to see him before he saw me. I wanted to be in his arms before he knew what hit him.

I'd hoped he cut class. Or leave early. He didn't.

His class ended at 11:00 AM. My nerves were at the screaming point by 11:05 AM.

At 11:15 AM I stood, started walking around the union, looking for him. He was probably sitting somewhere, waiting for me. But how could I have missed him? I'd had every entrance in sight.

I walked around until 11:30 AM. And then I sat again. I waited.

For my Tim.

At noon, I went outside, got in my car, and drove home.

⁓

I drove slowly. I had to face my mom. Tell her that Tim had stood me up. She'd pity me. And if I started to cry the tears weren't ever going to stop.

She was in the kitchen when I walked in the house.

"There's a message from Tim on the answering machine," she said before I got a word out.

My heart leapt. I knew it! Something had happened. His car broke down. He . . .

"He said that he was sorry but he wasn't going to make it."

"Did he say why?"

"No."

"Did he tell me to call him?"

"No."

"Did he say he'd call me?"

"No."

"Do you think he's okay? Maybe something bad happened."

"I think he changed his mind, Tara."

I thought so, too.

And for the second time in my life, Tim Barney had broken my heart.

The dorm room was the same. My twin bunk was still over there by the windows. The comforter was still beige and mauve with splashes of white. My two-foot-tall Raggedy Ann doll still graced the covers.

I was entirely different. The last time I'd slept in that bed I'd dreamed of Tim. Even before I'd fallen asleep. I'd poured out my heart to him from those covers as well during the two months I'd written to him.

We'd had our problems, but he was my Tim. We were destined to be together.

That's what I'd known the last time I'd been in that third-floor dorm room with the cold brick walls and commercially tiled floor.

Standing in the doorway, alone, the first one back to the suite after the break, I wasn't sure I could enter.

Tim was in that room.

Tim was no longer in my life.

It was really over. He'd made his choice, and it wasn't me.

I heard voices in the stairwell. Someone laughed. The sound was getting closer. I couldn't bear to be laughed at. Or find laughter to share, either.

I couldn't smile and say that spring break had been great. Or even okay.

I took a step. And then another. I closed the door behind me. I crumbled. I cried.

And the next week I signed up for every single social activity offered on the campus of Armstrong University. Someplace—among the people, God, the choices, the beliefs and studies and opportunities—I had to make a life for myself. I had to find a life.

Spring Sing was an annual event. An alumni weekend fund-raiser consisting of a theme and musical acts that followed the theme. All of the social clubs, Armstrong's answer to sororities and fraternities, competed with their attempts at musical theater and production. The show went on for two nights, Friday and Saturday, and was always, without fail, sold out.

Awards were given—top place was monetary. And the social-club members, who spent the money on service projects, really cared about winning.

My club, together with our brother club, had hired a choreographer and had been practicing every night for weeks.

"You ready?" The voice belonged to James, my social club's big brother—the male who attended all of our meetings to lead us in prayer. The tall, dark-haired man had brown eyes. And a mustache. He played tennis. If there was any resemblance to Tim in him, I chose not to see it.

"Yeah. My ribs are taped." My social club sisters said he liked me.

I probably liked him, too. In an innocuous sort of way. I was experienced now. My heart was no longer raw and open and available.

"You want to practice one more time?" He was whispering from our vantage point at the side of the stage. The other twenty kids in the same matching blue-silk skirts and slacks and tops stood around us in various curtain breaks in the wings.

"No," I said, biting back the irritation that was solely a result of prestage jitters. I was a member of a family of entertainers. I could do this.

"You want to go out for a soda afterward?"

"Sure." Everyone on my floor had dates. I didn't want to be alone. I didn't want to spend the next year dateless.

I was done being the undated girl in school.

James accompanied me to church the rest of that semester. We went to movies on campus and ate together sometimes on Sundays. We hung in the same groups.

And one night, when he walked me back to my dorm, he stopped just before we moved from the darkness of the shadows into the light shining above the front door of the all-girl habitat, and I knew what was coming.

This was it. The moment I'd been dreading. And yet . . . I liked him. He was kind. Nice looking. He really liked me. Enough not to choose someone else over me. And I didn't want to be alone.

The thoughts chased themselves around in my brain.

James didn't say a word. With his hands on my shoulders he pulled me closer until there was only a foot of distance between us. I saw him lower his head. Saw his lips coming closer. And I waited.

They were a little bit cold. We'd just had soda.

And then they were gone. With a smile on his face, James took my hand and walked me to the door.

I'd survived.

Twelve

I DIDN'T SEE OR TALK TO JAMES THAT SUMMER. I didn't see or hear from Tim, either. It was the summer of 1979. The worst summer of my life.

My father took exception to my newly formed allegiance with the church I'd joined. James's church, though I'd joined before I met James. It was Armstrong's church. The church where I'd found the God who'd filled my gaping heart.

My instructors at school had warned me that I'd probably get some resistance from my parents when I got home. They'd given me the mental and emotional tools to stay strong.

Scriptures. Words of love. Students from school were set up to write to me every day that summer to help me stay strong in a nonmember family.

"You have a church home," my father told me my first week home, on a Friday afternoon in July.

I'd spent the month of June in an Armstrong summer intensive—a graduate-level class that toured New England literary historical sites. I'd been to Louisa Mae Alcott's home. Seen hundred–year-old etchings that were referred to in a classic I'd loved as a child. I'd stood in Longfellow's home and stared at the staircase that was the central point in a poem my mother had recited to me from the time I was a toddler. I'd been to Yale. Seen Hawthorne's home. I'd walked the streets where the Scarlet Woman had walked. Imagined how she'd felt.

Because I'd been scarlet, too. But I'd been forgiven. My new faith assured me of that.

And my father thought I was going to turn my back on that?

"I want you to come back to church with us."

"I can't."

His lips tightened. I tensed. And I stood my ground. I wasn't a little girl anymore. I'd made mistakes. I'd lived through a broken heart. Broken dreams. But I was redeemed.

"You're hurting your mother."

I couldn't help that. This was my soul we were talking about. My mother, in her seeming refusal to allow me the freedom of religion that my country allowed, was hurting me.

My father didn't stand. He didn't even sit up straight. In a quiet but very determined voice, he said, "Your mother and I have talked, and it's either your church or your home, young lady."

I'd already lost my heart. My love. I couldn't lose my God.

"Then I choose my church."

⁓

James was the first person I saw when I got back to Alabama that summer. I was early. I'd flown in instead of catching a ride. I was the first of the girls I was rooming with to show up. We had an apartment, campus housing for seniors, out by the railroad tracks.

Running from the silence, from the fact that I'd spent the summer staying with the woman I worked for, from the fact that my mother and father were still estranged from me, I went for a walk along the railroad tracks.

"Hi!" The lilt in James's voice was nice. Familiar. Welcoming. Here was someone who was glad to see me.

"Hi." I was glad to see him, too. He was easy to be with. We liked each other.

"How was your summer."

"Rough. How about you?"

"Worked like a dog, but it was good. I saved a lot of money. What was wrong with yours?"

"My folks kicked me out for joining the church."

We were walking then, side by side along the tracks. He didn't touch me. His hands were in his pockets. I liked that.

"You're kidding."

"Nope."

"I'm sorry."

"Yeah, me, too."

"You okay?"

"I guess."

"You want me to call them? Maybe if I talk to them . . ."

"No!" They'd never even heard of James. And anyone from the church calling them would probably set off a major explosion. They'd still sent me to school. Paid for my plane fare. Were paying my tuition. They still cared at least a little bit.

I couldn't take the chance of losing what little bit of them I had left.

"They'll come around."

"I hope so."

"They will. They love you."

"I'm not so sure."

"Well you aren't alone. You know that."

"I guess."

"Hey," he stopped me, took me by the shoulders, and looked me in the eye. "You always have me. I love you. I mean that."

He loved me? He was talking about the love in Christ that was so freely expressed on campus. Part of me knew that. But we weren't even dating, and he'd told me he loved me.

"We're friends. You can come to me anytime."

Tears filled my eyes, I nodded, and we walked on.

He was still seeing Emily. His heart was in it. Almost all the way. As much as his heart could be into any woman.

The first cut was the deepest, and he'd been cut. Bad.

His little blonde girl was gone, but she was not forgotten. He'd accepted the fact that a part of him would always yearn for her.

"Hi, Cowboy, you ready to go?" Emily was a couple of years older than him. A teacher in the local elementary school. He'd gone to school with her brother.

"Yep. Got your helmet?" She'd bought it when he'd bought the Suzuki 250—the motorcycle he'd had his eye on for more than a year.

"Of course." She pulled it out of the trunk of her new little Pacer. Emily wasn't the most beautiful woman in town with her ordinary brown hair and lack of fashion sense, but she had a pretty face, a great figure, and most important, she was like him. She'd grown up in Eaton. Liked country music. And didn't need expensive things to be happy.

She was grounded. Had a steady income.

She fastened the shiny red helmet under her chin and leaned toward him for a kiss.

Tim held his lips against hers for a long time. Enjoyed her taste.

He mounted the bike, already feeling the power between his legs. She climbed on behind him, wrapping her arms around his waist. He gunned the engine and sped off into the sunset.

Thanksgiving 1979 was a strange time.

"I can't believe your folks still aren't talking to you," James said a couple of days before students began leaving campus for the four-day holiday break. Some, the ones who had too far to travel, were going to stay with friends. Most were going home. Shuttles were scheduled for the students who had to make it to Little Rock to catch a flight out.

"My dad wrote," I told him. We were sitting in a white picket fence-type swing extended from one of the trees on the huge grassy quad in the middle of campus. Dressed in white shorts and a long-sleeve white T-shirt, James had just come from a scrimmage tennis match. I was supposed to have made it out to watch him, but I'd been writing a paper that was due the next day.

His piercing brown eyes pinned me, his dark bushy brows coming together as he frowned. "He did?"

"Yeah." I should have told him. But . . .

Rubbing my hands along the jeans I'd changed into after class, I hugged my arms, wishing I'd added a jacket to the orange and beige sweater.

"When?"

"I don't know. A week or two ago." Make that three or four. The letter had come shortly after Mom's almost daily notes had stopped.

"He wants me to come home for Thanksgiving."

"What about the church?"

"He didn't say anything about it."

"He didn't apologize? Didn't say he was wrong?"

"No."

"Did he tell you that you could go to church while you were there?"

"No." Dad hadn't mentioned church. He'd talked about love and family and duty and nothing about the rift between us. Which made me nervous.

"So he isn't backing down."

"I don't know."

"Do you think if you go it'll be like agreeing to his dictates from the summer? Like you'll be agreeing to choose your family over your God?"

The question irritated me. "I don't know."

"What are you going to do?"

I wanted to go home so badly. And yet . . . my faith in God, and in my church, had sustained me through the worst year of my life. It was only with God's help that I could endure the loss of Tim and still be happy.

"I don't think I can go home. Not until I know that I don't have to give up my God to do so. Besides I haven't heard a word from my mom in weeks. If she wanted me home, she'd have written. My dad only deals with me when I'm in trouble, which has been about once in my whole life. It's always Mom and me who arrange everything."

"What are you going to do then?"

"Rachel asked me to go with her. She's going to her grandma's in Mississippi. Her mom and little brother are meeting her there."

Rachel Bowman was in my social club. We'd been friends since my first week on campus the year before.

"You can come home with me. It's going to be just me most of the time. My mom's babysitting all weekend. But we'd have fun."

"I really want to go with Rachel. She's my best friend. And I like her mom a lot." I'd met Mrs. Bowman, a divorced mother who I respected, on campus when she'd brought Rachel to school, but I'd also been to their house for a weekend visit once.

"Do you guys have a ride yet?"

"I don't know. Rachel was going to check with some kids going to Florida to see if they could drop us off."

"I'll drop you off."

"You?"

"Yeah. I'm going to Atlanta. I can take you."

"You're sure it's not too far out of your way?"

"I'm sure." He smiled and my heart warmed. We'd been dating on and off all semester. James wasn't like the other boys at school. He hadn't grown up in the church, either. He was a convert like me.

And he'd suffered. He understood heartache.

"You really don't have to take me to the family gathering," Emily said, climbing in Tim's car on Thanksgiving morning. "I'm perfectly fine here with my mom and dad."

She'd asked him to join them, but Tim always spent the family holiday at his older brother Mike's house. Two years ago he'd taken Tara.

Emily had that look in her eye again. One he'd seen a lot lately. Like she was hurting. They'd been sleeping together for a while, and he knew she wanted more.

So did he. He wanted a wife. A home. Kids.

He just didn't want to get married.

Running his fingers through her hair, he cupped the back of her neck. "I want you there," he said, and kissed her softly. When they broke apart, Tim looked her straight in the eye. "I really do," he said.

And meant it.

Rachel had a meltdown on Thanksgiving Day. Torn between the man she loved with all her heart—a reprobate who'd sinned and left the church—and the man who loved her with all of his heart—a law student whose parents held ranking in the church—she needed some time alone with her family. Time alone with her mother and grandmother.

Sitting in the back bedroom of her grandmother's home where I'd slept the night before, I tried not to think of my family at home, my mother busy in the kitchen doing four things at once, my father carving the turkey. My brother Scott picking all of the cucumbers out of the salad and eating them before the bowl ever made it to the table. Chum's wife sitting silently, saying nothing. And Chum lying on the floor chewing on a pen while he watched football.

I missed them all so much.

I'd never felt more alone in my life.

And I thought of James, all alone on Thanksgiving Day. Not for the first time in his almost twenty-one years of living.

Mom and Dad knew where I was. They hadn't called.

I picked up the phone on the table by the bed. Dialed a number.

"This is collect from Tara," I said when the operator came on the line.

James picked up on the second ring. "Will you accept a collect call from Tara?"

"Of course!" His voice sounded good. He really cared about me. And I cared about him, too. I didn't want him there all alone. "Hi, Sweetie Pie. I didn't expect you to call."

He'd asked her to, though.

"I know."

"What's wrong?"

"Nothing. I just . . . you said you'd come get me . . ." He'd told her when he'd dropped them off the afternoon before that if she needed him, she should call. He could make it back to Rachel's in Mississippi in no time.

"You want to come here?"

"If you really don't mind driving all the way back."

"Are you kidding? I'd love to have you here."

"What about your mom?"

"She's not going to be here—she's babysitting on the other side of town—but she'll be thrilled to know you are. I've told her all about you. She wants to meet you."

I'd be alone with him in the two-bedroom apartment he shared with his mother, who was currently a student at a local community college. But James was a good man. A member of the church. Spiritual leader to my social club. He'd never do anything to get either of us kicked out of school.

He cared about me. Respected me.

We didn't do physical things. We'd kissed maybe ten times since I'd known him.

The thoughts chased themselves around my mind. Colliding with emotions that were quickly escalating out of control. Thoughts of past Thanksgivings. With my family. And with Tim.

I had to get out of there.

"Okay, come get me."

⁓

"I love your family." Emily's voice was soft, husky. Still full from the huge Thanksgiving buffet his sister-in-law had put on, Tim had suggested a drive out to Houston Dam. They'd walked a bit and were lounging along the backseat of his car, his arm around her, her head on his shoulder.

Tim was content to sleep off the beer he'd consumed with his brothers.

"They're so different from mine," she continued talking, and he tried to stay alert to what she was saying. "At my house it's always just been me and my brother and Mom and Dad. Dad and John would watch sports and Mom would read, or sit with Dad and doze, and while I liked the peace and quiet of the day, I see now that we missed a lot. There was so much life there today. You're so lucky you have such a big family."

He had a lot of family members who gathered for holidays, but at home it was just him and Jeff and their mother. Except for the time Harry had been there, too. Harry, the man Tim's mom had married when Tim and Jeff had reached puberty and were presenting more of a challenge than a fifty-five-year old woman felt she could handle alone.

They hadn't been married long.

"Do you guys always go downstairs like that?" He'd left Emily upstairs with the women while he went downstairs with his brothers to play poker.

"Yeah."

"The women, I couldn't keep up with them, but . . ."

He tried to listen. He really did. The air was cool but not yet cold. His stomach was full of good food and equally good beer, and Emily's weight against him coaxed him into a state of relaxation that he couldn't resist . . .

I watched for James's car from the front window. And I wondered about the weekend ahead. The choice I'd made. I fully trusted that nothing untoward would happen. But I couldn't help comparing the time ahead with time in the past. And I wished that it was Tim I was going to spend the weekend with. I would spend the entire weekend in bed with him.

And be thankful.

The thought brought shame, and I asked God for forgiveness.

I thought of Tim's family, all gathered together at his brother's house. And I wondered if he'd taken Emily there with him. If they were still together. And when tears pricked the backs of my eyelids, I quit thinking about Tim.

Alone in Rachel's grandmother's living room, I stared at my watch. And when I saw the gold Honda pull up in front of the house, I ran out the front door.

James had his arms open by the time I reached him. I threw myself against him. Right then he was as close as I got to family, and I was falling apart.

He held my hand as he drove. A new thing. It was nice, though. I needed the connection. I needed a place to belong. And I loved how happy I made him just by being there. I was glad I'd called him.

"Mom wants us to stop over there tonight."

"Oh, good." His mother's approval made what we were doing that much more appropriate. I relaxed more, trying not to feel as though I were leaving purgatory for hell. I was going to spend the weekend alone in an apartment with a man.

But he was a man I could trust.

And the place had two bedrooms.

We chatted some more. I asked him if he'd had any turkey. He hadn't. But he didn't much care. I gathered that a big dinner on the table for

Thanksgiving hadn't been a common occurrence for him growing up. I felt sorry for him. And wanted to change that for him.

I wasn't sure how I'd go about doing that. I didn't have a family to invite him home to anymore. But maybe by next year I would.

By next year, I'd be graduated from college and probably wouldn't ever see James again. He was from Atlanta. I was from Ohio. And he had another year of college to complete.

"I want to talk to you." His words were kind of ominous, but they needn't have been. His tone was as gentle as always.

"Sure." I turned to face him. Thankful that he'd come all that way to get me. I didn't deserve such loyalty. While James had been spending his holiday alone on the road, coming to get me, I'd been thinking of Tim. Yearning for Tim.

"I was thinking . . . you and I . . . we're a lot alike. We're both converts to the church. We like the same things . . ."

We did? I wasn't sure what those were. We were both involved in the same social clubs, and those obligations and activities kept us busy, but . . .

"We've been dating for a while now and, with you graduating in the spring and having nowhere to go . . ."

I had nowhere to go? I'd be a college graduate. I'd get a job. And a place of my own and . . .

I was graduating with a degree in English because I was going to write for Harlequin someday. I hadn't certified to teach. I hadn't minored in anything that could sustain me.

Where on earth was I going to find a writing job in enough time to support me the second I had to move out of student housing the day after graduation?

James had been talking. I'd missed what he said. But I tuned back in time to hear, "So I was thinking we should get married."

Married.

"I love you, Sweetie Pie, so much. I want to spend the rest of my life with you."

I'd just had a proposal of marriage.

Once, a long time ago, I'd wanted nothing else.

"Just think about it," James said, his voice filled with excitement. "You don't have to answer me right now, but think about it. We could get married next summer. We could go back to Armstrong next year, live in married housing, and you could get one of the jobs on campus that they save for wives of students."

An office job.

But I'd be at Armstrong. Could still attend the college church. And would have plenty of time to write.

"And you'd be married in the church," he added, tapping into another of my worries. At Armstrong we were encouraged, voraciously it seemed to me, to pick a mate because once we got out into the real world, into the work world, the secular world, our chances of meeting an eligible member of the church diminished greatly.

I was a convert. I already didn't have family in the church. I couldn't bear the thought of a mixed marriage as well.

Nor could I bear the thought of living my life all alone. Heck, I couldn't even seem to survive Thanksgiving alone.

Marrying James would solve a lot of problems.

But did I love him enough to marry him? I cared about him.

I remembered how happy I was to see him.

How, at Rachel's grandmother's house, I'd been certain that spending the weekend with James was the right thing to do.

James was kind. Gentle. Soft spoken. He was going to be a chemical engineer. And maybe a part-time preacher.

I did what he told me to do. I thought about his request all weekend.

He woke up to the sound of tears. Or maybe to the soft jerks that accompanied Emily's sobs. She was sitting upright on the opposite side of the backseat, looking out the window.

He'd screwed up.

"Hey," Tim said softly, pulling her back to him. "I'm sorry about that."

She held herself stiffly, resisting him. "I was talking to you."

"I know."

"I was pouring my heart out." Obviously he'd been asleep longer than she knew.

"I know, Teach, and I feel the same way, I swear . . ." He loved her. That was all that mattered. "I just . . . the feel of you against me, listening to your voice, it just felt so . . . you know, like we were married and . . ."

"Married?" The stiffness left her body. She leaned against him.

"Not now, or anything, but I've been thinking about it. Someday."

"You want us to get married?"

"Someday."

"I love you, Cowboy."

"I love you, too, Teach."

And before she could launch into a rehash of whatever heart outpouring he'd missed during his nap, providing more chances for him to make a mess of things, he turned her face up to his and kissed her. They were in a secluded part of the park.

And lovemaking always seemed to get rid of Emily's insecurities where he was concerned.

"Have you thought about my question?" It was Saturday afternoon, and James and I were driving back from the home where his mother was spending the long weekend, babysitting for a couple of cute kids whose parents had opted to spend the holiday alone together rather than with their kids.

James's mother had felt as sorry for the kids as I had. She'd made a Thanksgiving dinner, of sorts. She'd made me feel more welcome than I could ever have imagined.

She also made it clear that she would be more than thrilled to have me for a daughter.

"Did you tell your mother you were going to ask me?"

"I mentioned that I might. You're staying at the apartment. She'd have guessed anyway."

The apartment. We were heading back there. I liked the place. It was small but very well kept. Clean. Decorated. Lots of plants. It felt open and calm and welcoming and safe.

I was sleeping in James's room, in one of the two twin beds. He'd slept in his mother's double bed in the room next door.

"I've thought about it."

"And?"

"I . . ."

I was twenty years old and other than Tim, James was the only man I'd ever even thought about spending a lifetime with. I could make him happy. I had no doubts about that. And I enjoyed being with him.

He'd be a good provider. A good protector.

"I . . . guess."

He stopped the car and stared, his mouth open. "You mean it?" You'd think the man was hard up for women, rather than the target of more than half of the girls in our social club.

I thought about what I was doing, scared to death. I thought about the boys I'd known, the few I'd dated since Tim. I thought about Tim choosing the safety of Emily rather than trusting me to be there for him for the rest of our lives. "Yes," I said.

I was going to get married.

Excitement flooded me.

And I felt like crying.

Thirteen

"WHAT DO YOU THINK? SHOULD THE PICTURE HANG HERE or over there?" Dressed in jeans and a loose fitting button-down shirt, Emily stood on the hearth of the fireplace in the hundred–year-old home she'd rented from her grandparents. She was holding a picture Tim's mom had painted. It was one of Tim's favorites. The covered bridge brought back memories of childhood freedom and a world filled with nothing but opportunities.

"There," he said, grabbing the cement nails and hammer. It was early spring. Birds were back from their winter getaways, buds were starting to pop out on the trees. He'd seen his first flowers of the season the night before on the way home from the gas station where he'd worked his usual four-hour evening shift.

And instead of being out on his bike, he was spending this glorious Saturday helping Emily move. He'd taken the day off for this.

"Come on," she said, taking his hand as soon as he'd hung the picture. "Let's go put the bed together."

She knew him well.

And half an hour later, when he had the slats in place, the mattress and box springs she'd been using since she was in junior high placed on top of them, he helped her put on the sheets and quilt her grandmother had made for her when she graduated from high school. Pillow cases were next.

Emily threw the pillows toward the headboard and then sat down. "Come here, Cowboy." She grabbed his hand and spread her knees, pulling him between them. "You want to take a break?" She glanced at the fly of his jeans.

He wanted to want to. Usually he wanted to.

Must be the weather. The bike that had been cooped up under a cover all winter calling out to him.

"We have to christen the place." Emily's smile would probably have shocked the people who saw her every day at school.

Why was he hesitating? Her having a place of her own was a godsend to them. No more timing their lovemaking when his mom was out or her parents were gone. No more frustrating sessions in the car.

They were adults. And free. And . . .

"What's wrong?" That hurt look was back in her eyes. He hated that look. His Emily was so sweet. Everything he'd ever wanted, really. Mostly.

"Nothing," he said, pushing thoughts of his motorcycle to the back of his mind. "Just . . . it's just kind of . . ."

She sat back, her expression guarded. "What?"

Tim sat beside her. He loved her. He really did. There was just something missing. In him. "It's all me," he said.

Her lips started to tremble. "You're breaking up with me."

"No! It's nothing like that." Emily needed a ring. She needed forever. And he wanted that, too.

Someday.

Probably.

"I love you, Teach, you know that." He grinned his best grin. The kind that usually had her melting for him.

"Then what?" She played with a couple of his fingers.

"I just . . . I'm not ready to . . . live together." The words were a relief. Yeah, that's all that was bothering him. "You're all settled. You've got your degree, your career, but I'm still in school. I've got another year before I graduate." He'd lost a little time when he'd left Wright State to transfer to an engineering school in Dayton.

She didn't say a word. But she was listening.

"I'm not ready to take on the financial responsibility of a home. It takes pretty much all I make to help Mom keep up with hers."

"Hey, Cowboy?" Her voice was soft as she ran her fingers lightly along the jeans encasing his thigh.

"Yeah." Her touch was nice.

"I haven't asked you to move in with me. I just asked you to help move me in."

He should probably be embarrassed. Relief took precedence.

"I love you, Cowboy." Emily's words floated around him, holding them in their sweetness. "I know you have things to do before you'll be thinking about setting up house . . ."

She did? He was a tad bit curious about what "things" she thought he had to do. But not enough to risk asking.

"I do, too," she said.

"What things?"

"I need some time on my own. My whole life I've had to answer to my parents. Commuting to UC saved a lot of money, but it meant that I never had time in a dorm, finding my freedom like other kids did. This is my time."

His elation was simmering down. "You planning to hold wild parties?" Inviting other guys over?

"Of course not," she smiled, her hand moving up a little higher on his thigh. "I'm planning to eat what I want when I want without anyone to know or worry about me. I'm planning to leave my clothes on the floor if I want, or pick them up if I want. I'm planning to put the milk on the refrigerator door because I want it there, and to set my makeup on the counter like I've always wanted to. I'm planning to play what music I want, when I want, as loud or soft as I want. And . . ," her hand

READER RESPONSE CARD

TVA

We care about your opinions! Please take a moment to fill out our Reader Survey online at **http://survey.hcibooks.com**. To show our appreciation, we'll give you an **instant discount coupon** for future book purchases, as well as a special gift available only online.

If you prefer, you may mail this survey card back to us and receive a discount coupon by mail. All answers are confidential.

(PLEASE PRINT IN ALL CAPS)

First Name _____ Last Name _____

Address _____

City _____ State _____ Zip _____ Email _____

1. Gender
❏ Female ❏ Male

2. Age
❏ Under 20
❏ 21-30 ❏ 31-40
❏ 41-50 ❏ 51-60
❏ Over 60

3. Marital Status
❏ Married ❏ Single

4. How you did get this book?
❏ Received as gift
❏ Bought for myself
❏ Borrowed from a friend
❏ Borrowed from my library

5. If bought for yourself, how did you find out about it?
❏ Recommendation
❏ Store Display
❏ Read about it on a Website
❏ Email message or e-newsletter
❏ Book review or author interview

6. How many books do you read a year, excluding educational material?
❏ 4 or less ❏ 5-8
❏ 9-12 ❏ 12 or more

7. Do you have children under the age of 18 at home?
❏ Yes ❏ No

8. What type of romance do you enjoy most?
❏ Contemporary
❏ Historical
❏ Paranormal
❏ Erotic
❏ All types

9. What are your sensuality preferences?
❏ Wild and erotic
❏ Steamy but moderate
❏ Sweet and sensual
❏ Doesn't matter as long as it fits the story

10. Where do you usually buy books?
❏ Online (amazon.com, etc.)
❏ Bookstore chain (Borders, B&N...)
❏ Independent/local bookstore
❏ Big Box store (Target, Wal-Mart...)
❏ Drug Store or Supermarket

11. How often do you read romance novels?
❏ Every now and then
❏ Several times a year
❏ Constantly

FOLD HERE

12. What influences you most when purchasing a book?
(Rank each from 1 to 5 with 1 being the top)

Author	1	2	3	4	5
Price	1	2	3	4	5
Title	1	2	3	4	5
Reviews	1	2	3	4	5
Cover Design	1	2	3	4	5
Series/Publisher	1	2	3	4	5
Recommendation	1	2	3	4	5

13. Annual household income
☐ Under $25,000
☐ $25,000–$40,000
☐ $41,000–$50,000
☐ $51,000–$75,000
☐ Over $75,000

14. How long have you been reading romance novels?
☐ 1–2 years   ☐ 3–5 years
☐ More than 5 years

15. What other topics do you enjoy reading?
Non-Fiction
☐ Family/parenting
☐ Relationships
☐ Addictions/Recovery
☐ Health/nutrition
☐ Cooking
☐ Religious
☐ Spirituality
☐ Inspiration/affirmations
☐ Self-improvement
☐ Sports
☐ Pets
☐ Memoirs
☐ True Crime
Fiction
☐ Mystery
☐ Chick-lit
☐ Historical
☐ Paranormal

Comments

brushed against the seam that joined the legs of his jeans, "I'm planning to entertain the man I love."

Bingo.

⁓

"Come on, Sweetie Pie. You can do this. We're engaged. I'm going to be your husband. But that's not for a couple of years, and you've got me so tied up in knots I'm going crazy."

I looked out the window of the car. The farmer's fields that stretched for miles on either side of us had just been freshly plowed. I'd seen the fresh tractor marks and newly disturbed dirt in the car's headlights as we'd driven down the long deserted road. I wasn't sure what farmers did in April, but I prayed that one would need to check his dirt at night.

"I have to be pure when I get married." I repeated the words I'd said countless times before. To Tim. And to James, too. The first time he'd pressured me to let him have sex with me was the weekend I'd stayed with him in Atlanta over Thanksgiving. The night I'd agreed to marry him. After we'd told his mom. And my best childhood friend. And, at her behest, bit the bullet and called my folks and told them, too.

That night he'd crawled into the twin bed I was using in his room and told me about a man's needs and how only his woman could satisfy them. I'd told him, quite gently and with love, that I'd be fine with that after we were married. He'd coaxed. Cajoled. Gently. And when I'd started to get upset, he'd conceded that I was right and it would be even better if we waited. He'd slept in the room with me that night, though. In the other twin bed.

For months after that, he'd been as he'd been in the beginning. Satisfied to hold my hand and bestow his chaste kisses on me. But there'd been a time or two—once over spring break—when he'd pressured me to undo my clothes for him. To let him touch private places.

I said no.

I didn't want to do that. I didn't want him to do that.

And that unsettled me. Would I want it when we got married? I told myself I would. That once I let him actually touch me I'd feel things again. For now, my lack of temptation made it easy to stick to my principles this time around. Sometimes I thought that maybe, because I'd repented, God was helping me to be a good girl by taking away the temptation that had consumed me during my relationship with Tim.

Sometimes I worried that I would never ever feel those feelings again because they were meant for one man only—Tim.

The one thing I knew for certain was that I was not going to be physically intimate without marriage.

And now here I was, on a dark country road, miles from any sign of civilization, more than an hour from campus with a man who wanted to have sex.

He'd said he wanted time alone with me. That he wanted to talk about us.

He'd been feeling insecure. And I felt guilty about that. So I agreed to the talk.

I hadn't agreed to more than that.

"Tara, it's your job to do this."

"Not now it's not. We aren't married yet." With Tim, lovemaking had been a mutual give and take. Not one person doing it for the other.

"But I'm a man and men need, you know, release. And the only way I can get that, in a way that God approves, is if I do it with you. We love each other. You're wearing my ring. We're getting married. Do you really think God's going to care about an earthly piece of paper? What he cares about is that we're committed to each other. That it will only ever be me and you."

James had been chosen to give us our social club messages that semester, in addition to leading our prayers. I'd heard leaders talk about his Bible study and his level of faith and commitment.

"That's baloney," I said. "If all God cared about was our emotional commitment, or our intention to stay together, then he wouldn't require marriage at all."

The Bible clearly said a man and a woman were to marry before making love. I'd been taught that my whole life.

"Would it be okay with you if we just sit close?" He ran his hand along my neck. "It'll help if you just put a little pressure on . . . it. Just sit with me."

We'd been taught my first semester at Armstrong that girls were not to sit on boys' laps. We'd be kicked out of dormitory living if we were caught sitting that way.

I wasn't a new student in the dorm anymore, but I didn't want to break the rules. And I told him so.

"Please, Sweetie Pie? You love me, don't you?"

"Yeah." I thought I did. I wasn't really sure what love was. He'd spilled a Coke on himself and I'd cared. I'd hated to see him humiliated and uncomfortable. I'd wanted to make it better for him. That meant I loved him, didn't it?

I still didn't want to sit on his lap.

"Do you understand about men?"

"Yeah." They got hard. And wanted to put it in women.

"You know that it brings a man physical pain to be turned on and not get release?"

No. And I didn't want to know.

Had it hurt Tim? He'd never let on. And why was I thinking of him now?

It was wrong. Futile. And suddenly all I could think about was my Tim. About being on a country road with him.

In the backseat of his car with his fingers between my legs, touching me in places only he had touched. His places.

God, give me that country road again. Please, God.

Wait. I stopped myself. God, please forgive my sinful thoughts.

Tim didn't want me. He hadn't offered to marry me. James had. I was engaged to marry James. I was going to spend my life as his wife.

It wasn't fair to him that I was thinking about another man when all James wanted to do was love me. I was not a good and faithful woman. The Bible said that if our thoughts were impure, it was kin to impure actions.

"Please, Sweetie Pie? Please just sit on my lap for a bit. Let me hold you."

My chest was so tight it hurt. "Okay. But only that. Nothing else. I have to be pure when we get married."

I wasn't budging on that one. I'd paid a very dear price the one and only time I'd let my morals slip. I'd lost the man I loved more than anything else on earth. Because I'd been too easy. I'd lost my heart and all of the magic it had contained. Because I'd given too much too soon. And I'd spent two long years gaining back my self-respect with faithful service to God. I'd lost my family to put God first—to be forgiven and regain my pureness.

James moved. There was a console between us. "Your seat will work better," he said, his tall frame looming big in the car as he moved toward me. "The steering wheel is in the way here."

I didn't say a word. He was never going to fit in my seat. Where was I going to go as he climbed over?

"Put your seat back."

I did as I was told.

And before I had my next thought, he'd picked me up and was sitting underneath me.

"That's it, just sit," I said, feeling stupid. And dirty. And wanting to go home.

I also wanted to be a good wife to the man I was going to spend the rest of my life beside. I wanted to be a good girl. I wanted to make him happy.

I wanted to be capable of wanting him.

So I sat there.

He moved. And I sat. He moved again. I sat.

He reached down. I couldn't see what he was doing in the dark of the car, but he wasn't touching me, just like he'd promised.

"I know of something we can do to help me and you'll still be a virgin," he said then, sounding . . . odd, and out of breath. There was no softness in his voice. No gentleness. He sounded like he was talking to another guy, not to the sweet girl he was going to marry.

I had no idea what he was talking about, but I figured he was going to tell me.

He was a good man. I knew his heart. And I trusted him.

"As long as I'm pure when we get married . . ." I wouldn't look. I would let him do what he needed to do and not speak of it again.

He moved again, displacing me. His hands were between our bodies, but he wasn't rubbing anything. He was fidgeting with something. His fingers were bunched. I heard clothes move. Heard his zipper. And my heart started to pound. The door was locked. He was holding me on a sideways angle.

"I want to go back."

He didn't say a word. But he was breathing hard. I didn't like what was going on. At all. But I still trusted him. Mostly.

I trusted him right until I felt his hands on the front of my jeans. My hands met his there, stifling his attempt to get my pants unfastened. I held on, trying to still his fingers. But they were beneath mine. And stronger than mine.

As was the arm that held me around the middle as he moved me once again and got my jeans partially down, exposing my backside to the cool night air—and the roughness of his jeans. My legs were pinned between his and the dash of the car. His arm around me was like a brace, holding my arms down. His other hand was moving on my bottom, pulling me over. I started to fight and felt his push at the same time.

With one shove he'd forced himself up inside the part of me he'd exposed.

Pain held me frozen. I fought back nausea.

I couldn't think at all.

In the space of a few seconds, the girl I'd been, the woman I'd hoped to be, died an excruciating death.

———

"You were a very good girl tonight. My girl. You know how to take care of your man."

We were still in the car. My clothes were in place. So were James's. His expression was calm as he drove down the highway back to school.

"It's your fault, you know." I could hear him talking. I just couldn't respond. I didn't exist. I was a body that hurt. "I've never been like this before. You do it to me."

I wanted to deny the accusation. But I couldn't. I'd done it to Tim, too. There was something immoral about me.

Lights appeared in the distance. Town. I was going to have to get out of the car. Stand. I was afraid there'd be blood on my backside.

I was afraid that my pure and innocent roommates would notice the difference in me straight off. Notice and be horrified.

I was going to be kicked out of school a few weeks before graduation. I wouldn't get the degree I'd earned.

"You have to marry me now," James continued to talk. "No other man will have you."

I wasn't surprised to hear that.

"You have a problem, Sweetie Pie. You're a tease. You drive men crazy. But I know you can't help it. And it doesn't change my love for you. We'll deal with it together."

I couldn't speak.

"I still want to marry you. You're my good girl. I don't care that it was your fault. I don't blame you."

I blamed me. I'd agreed to sit on his lap. I didn't fight. Not until it was too late.

I'd trusted to the point of stupidity. He'd tried to tell me of his desperate state. He'd needed me to be strong. To guide us to safety.

And I sat on his lap.

"You aren't going to tell anyone are you?"

I stared straight ahead.

"You'd get kicked out of school."

I hadn't even known physical things could happen that way. I sure as hell hadn't wanted it to happen. But who would believe me?

James would tell them it was my fault. I'd gone with him willingly. I'd agreed to sit on his lap. I didn't tell him no at that last point.

I hadn't known what was going to happen. I hadn't been able to speak.

I was fear. Not afraid. Just . . . fear. I *was* fear.

"You can't tell anyone, Sweetie Pie."

I could tell someone. Though I couldn't think of who that would be. Mom and I didn't talk about such things. I'd never told her about the things I'd done with Tim. But she knew our dates had lasted until 4:00 AM more often than not.

I could tell Rachel. She'd be shocked. I'd be judged as a convert. One from the outside. I was worse than a whore, worse than a fallen woman. My vagina hadn't been penetrated, but I was no longer pure. Not even a little bit. I'd never even heard of that happening to a girl before, and I was certain she hadn't either.

She knew I'd gone with James. She knew him, too, just like I did. Everyone loved him. So many girls were jealous that I had him.

She'd find me as disgusting as I found myself.

Everyone would.

We were in front of the student-housing apartment I shared with Rachel and three other girls.

"Just remember, Sweetie Pie. Even though tonight was your fault, I still love you. I'll always love you. You're my girl. You're my good girl. And you're still a virgin."

Technically, I wasn't. Tim had taken care of that medical proof.

The lights were on in every room. It was curfew time. Everyone would be there, and I was going to have to get out of James's car and walk up that long sidewalk to the front door.

I wasn't sure my violated body would let me walk. I couldn't get out of the car.

With a frown, James watched me and then slowly got out. He came around to my side of the car. Opened my door, just like he always did. He reached in with tender hands and helped me out.

He supported my weight as I stood. "You can't tell anyone, Sweetie Pie," he said again, his voice laced with concern. Compassion.

I nodded.

Tilting my chin he looked me straight in the eye. "Promise me? It's our secret. Part of our love."

I nodded again.

He kissed me—a normal, chaste kiss—and I almost cracked open right then and there. Two things occurred to me in that second.

There would never, ever be anything chaste about me again.

And . . . the entire time we were on that dark country road, James had never kissed me. Not once.

With an arm around me, holding me to him, James walked me up that path. I felt what he'd done to me with every step I took. I pictured the bathroom in the back of the apartment. I had to get to it.

I had to take care of me.

I might be lost. Changed. Different. Scared to death and confused. But one thing was very clear to me. For the rest of my life I had to take care of me. There would never, ever be anyone else I would trust to do that.

Fourteen

By THE SUMMER OF 1980, EVERYTHING ABOUT TIM'S life was settling into place nicely. He and Emily were a couple, invited to each other's family events. School was fine; he was on track to graduate in a year. So why was he thinking about Tara so much? It had been a year since Emily had given him the ultimatum—go see Tara for lunch and we're done. He hadn't heard from or contacted Tara since. And he couldn't get her out of his mind.

I was home for the summer. I hadn't seen James since classes let out in May. I missed him. He was the only one who knew the real me, now.

I loved living at home again—being welcome there. A member of my family. Being back with my mom.

And I felt like such a fraud. No one had guessed what had happened on that dark country road that night in April by looking at me. And I wasn't talking about it.

But it was there with me every second of every day. I'd graduated. With honors. My folks were there for that, too.

James hadn't touched me again, other than to hold my hand. And give me chaste kisses.

"I'm okay now," he'd said once. "You were a good girl and took care of the problem you'd created. I can withstand the temptation of you now until we get married."

He could withstand it for two more years?

And after we were married, then what? Would I like sex any better? We could do it normally then. But every time I thought about any man ever touching me again, I wanted to die.

I'd get over it. I knew I would. I had to. I wanted children. A family. James loved me. Really loved me. He'd stood by me. He would stand by me through anything.

He still wanted me.

No other man ever would.

He'd been incredibly kind, attentive since those minutes when everything had changed. He worshipped me. Spoiled me.

And I really did make him happy. That meant a lot. It might take a while before I felt real joy again. But at least being with me made him happy. That was huge—to be able to make someone happy just by being around them.

That meant I was worth something.

⁓

As Tim and Emily got closer to a time when they might seriously think about getting married, he thought more and more of Tara. Was it ego because she'd asked for her ring back and he had some perverse male need to prove that Tara still wanted him? He'd like to think so. But the truth was probably a lot more simple. He was still in love with her.

She defined him, made him feel things that he'd never felt before or since. And when she'd written *I love ya* in those letters from Armstrong, she'd been feeling the same way, too. He had a couple of years of growing up behind him. A year in a relationship with another woman. He'd learned a lot.

How could he have been so blind? So closed off?

And how could he be with Emily, have her waiting for marriage, if he had a chance with Tara?

He had to call Tara. To set the past straight before he could move on to his future. She should have graduated in May. Chances were she was back living with her parents. School was only twenty minutes from her house. Maybe they could meet. Talk. Resolve things between them once and for all.

The phone only rang a couple of times, but his heart was still pounding as he stood at a pay phone in Dayton.

"Hello?" Her mom answered.

"Mrs. Gumser? This is Tim Barney."

"Hi!"

"I'm not sure you remember me, but . . ."

"Of course I remember you! How are you? Did you graduate from college?"

"Not yet. I have one more year. I don't want to bother you, but is Tara there?"

"Yes . . ." Her tone got more hesitant.

"May I speak with her?"

"Yes, just a moment."

He had no idea how many seconds passed, probably not nearly as many as it seemed. The light on the corner turned red, and cars started to line up beside him.

"Hello?"

He started to breathe again. "What's up?"

"Not much. How are you?"

"Good. I'm good. I'm going to be in the area and wondered if I could stop by. Just to say hi."

"I don't think that would be a good idea."

"Why not?" he pressed her. He wasn't taking no for an answer, not this time. It wouldn't be right.

"I just want to catch up on your life, Tara. I promise, no funny stuff."

"I'm engaged."

Wow. He hadn't seen that coming.

He should check his pulse to see if his heart was still beating. He could hardly breathe enough to get the next words out, and he remembered hearing that when someone is faced with an event of catastrophic proportion, something inside him takes over and his heart is no longer in control. Instead, the brain compensates, leaving him on autopilot.

That's where he was when he said, "Really, Tara, all I want to do is talk. This might be the last time we ever see each before we both start our new lives."

"I don't know . . ."

"I won't stay long. I'd just like to say hi."

"Okay."

"I'll be there in twenty minutes." He hung up before she could change her mind.

I wouldn't be able to go on if Tim ever found out what I'd become. I'd been his Tara. His sweet girl. Innocent. And hungry. He'd been the only man who'd ever touched me. Ever. Anywhere.

What would he think of me now? A woman who'd been . . . a woman who teased men to the point of that?

A woman who couldn't bear the thought of a man's body part? Who was afraid of sex?

A woman who'd been penetrated in the most hideous way.

I couldn't bear the thought of the disgust I'd see in his eyes. If Tim knew what James had done, it would turn Tim off completely.

I couldn't bear to have Tim be as disgusted with me as I was with myself.

But he'd called me.

He wanted to see me.

Maybe God hadn't completely forgotten me.

I turned and saw my mother standing there.

"He's coming over to say hi."

She nodded. "I gathered." There was no judgment in her gaze. Concern, but no judgment.

As I went up to my room to change clothes and fix my hair, I imagined Tim walking up to my front door, lifting me up against that chest that made me feel so safe, so secure, putting me in his car and driving me away to a place where I could wipe out the past three months, the past two years, and go back to being Tim's girl.

But I knew, even as I lived in my imaginary world, that my fantasy could never happen. Some things just couldn't be undone.

He was a mess. Excited to see Tara again, and betraying Emily because she didn't know about the meeting with Tara. She'd disapprove for sure.

Driving in Huber Heights, he was filled with a sense of familiarity. He'd made the drive so many times before—during the happiest time of his life. He saw his road a block away, turned left, and followed it to Drywood.

He was in Huber Heights to see his Baby. No, that was the past. He was there to say hello and get on with the rest of his life.

Wasn't he?

Could he see Tara again, knowing he loved her, and say nothing?

He pulled the car in the driveway and sat for a moment, nervous as hell, trying to regain his composure.

I was watching for him. The Le Mans pulled into my driveway exactly twenty minutes after we'd hung up. Tim's car. His face behind the wheel. They were so familiar. So right. Like coming home. He got out of the car, and I choked up with tears.

I couldn't be this way. I was going to be another man's wife. Had to be another man's wife. Tim wouldn't have me if he knew what James had done. No man would.

What man would call a woman his own after another man had known her in such a . . . personal . . . way?

Stopping short of the front door, I waited for Tim to ring the bell. Even if a miracle had happened and he wanted us to get back together, I couldn't do it. I couldn't be with him. He'd find out what had happened. And he wouldn't want me anymore.

And I didn't want sex. Ever again.

I might look the same on the surface, but I'd changed. In the deepest way possible.

And Tim wasn't going to know that. Ever.

I couldn't have him, but we could have our memories. I could have our memories to hold in my heart for as long as I lived, as long as he still saw me as the girl he'd known.

I opened the front door with a big smile on my face—and tears in my heart.

———

There she stood, his Tara, wearing three-quarter-length green khaki pants with a yellow polo top, her blonde hair, blue eyes, and her girlish smile greeting him. She looked exactly the same. And yet, something was different about this girl. The smile wasn't the same. She wasn't the same.

She invited him in, and he stepped by her into the house he'd spent so many hours in—and that felt different, too. Like he was an intruder.

He'd been selfish thinking of only what he wanted and needed. Something was wrong.

This wasn't his Tara. There was a disconnect between them. Something that hadn't been there even when they'd had that disastrous meeting at Christmas the year before.

She'd tried to tell him he shouldn't stop by.

An awkward tension fell between them as they stood there, saying nothing.

Was it because she was nervous about him being there when she was engaged to another man?

"When's the wedding?"

She shrugged. "Two years. Or so. He has to finish school."

Had their love been snuffed out by her new man? Had the guy given her the conversation that she so desperately needed?

But that didn't feel right, either. Something else was wrong. Something out of place. Her expression was old. Mature.

She didn't look happy.

"Is something wrong?" he asked.

"No!" Her voice was cheerful. "I'm fine. How about you? You're looking good!"

"You seem far away."

"I'm just settling back in after graduation, figuring out what to do with my life for the next two years. Let's go sit down so we can talk."

He went into the kitchen with her. Sat at the same table they'd been at so many times before.

In the past they'd been holding hands—except that last Christmas. Then he'd only wanted to hold her hand.

He wanted to now, too.

She asked about his classes. About his job. About Eaton and his mom and Steve, his old carpool buddy.

She didn't ask about Emily, and he didn't bring her up.

"Sure seems like a long time since the old Wright State days," he finally said, looking for a way in to his Tara.

She shrugged. "Do you have any idea what you want to do when you graduate?"

"Something in auto parts. How about you and your writing? Remember that night I went with you to the Vandalia city council meeting?"

"Yeah. Why auto parts?"

"Good job opportunity."

She didn't ask why he'd switched his major from geology. Didn't talk about Wright State, or ask why he'd stood her up. She didn't bring up the past at all.

The old Tara would have asked. He was crushed. He didn't know this woman.

"I guess I should probably get going," he finally said, when nothing he said got through to her. It was as though the relationship he remembered, the intense love he'd shared, had been in another lifetime. With another woman. Tara didn't seem able to connect to it at all. To remember him. Or them.

"Thanks for seeing me." He stood. "You look great."

She led him through the foyer out to the front porch and stopped there, toe to toe with him. It was the closest they'd been all day.

And then, out of the blue, with no notice at all, she threw her arms around his neck, hugging him as though she'd never let him go.

Her body was pressed tightly against his, and without thinking his arms were around her, too.

He wasn't sure who moved first, but before he knew what was happening their lips were locked together. The feel of her tongue against his shocked him. He returned the kiss for all he was worth. And then it was over.

Tara turned back toward the door, not saying a word. She stepped inside. Completely shocked, Tim told her good-bye and left.

The drive home was pure hell. Why had a woman who was engaged to another man kissed him like he was her lover? Her man?

And then turned her back on him?

He'd lost her forever. To another man who she must love more than she'd loved him.

So why had she kissed him like that?

What was he lacking that she needed? He could feel tears forming in his eyes and thought how crazy it all was. He had Emily. She tended to him. Cared for him.

And he was sad because Tara had moved on.

⌒

In July of 1981 I agreed to spend the night with James. We'd been engaged for almost two years, and other than the one night he'd lost control because of my teasing, he'd never once treated me with anything but decorum and respect. He still hadn't graduated from college. He'd changed his major instead. And transferred to a university close enough to my folks' house that we could see each other on a regular basis.

He'd said being apart from me was killing him. I was glad that I still made him happy.

I'd left the church. So much for my great faith. It couldn't withstand me feeling dirty every time I went to service. I was a seductress who drove men crazy. Not a good little church girl.

And maybe, just maybe, I was a tad bit angry at the God who'd allowed that night on the country road to happen. To James. And to me.

Anyway, getting on with my life, I enrolled in classes, too. I was certifying to teach so that I could make a living until I could earn money with my writing. I figured I'd start out with magazine articles or something. Until I could write my Harlequin romance. Until my heart could feel the romance again.

I was hoping that sleeping with James would not only relieve some of his pressures so he could study and get good grades instead of being distracted by me all the time, but would also bring back my heart. My desire.

We were going to Columbus for the weekend. Just the two of us. I packed my bag. I said good-bye to my folks, who knew we were going to Columbus for the weekend and hadn't said a word, and climbed back into the car where James had lost control that night eighteen months before.

I didn't want to go with him. I didn't want to sleep with him.

But I loved him. Not like I'd loved Tim. Not with that all-encompassing, stop-the-world magic. A girl got that kind of love once in a lifetime. If she was lucky.

I'd been lucky.

And now I was with a man who was good to me. And who was happy with me. A man who I enjoyed. Who was a good companion. An entertaining conversationalist. A man who liked the same things I liked. Who wanted the same things I wanted.

A man who, in spite of my shortcomings, believed in me. James believed I really would sell a book to Harlequin someday.

He hadn't said a word since I'd gotten in the car. We were on the highway, speeding toward Columbus, and we hadn't even kissed hello.

"Are you having second thoughts?" I asked. Because I was and it would be a whole lot easier if he was, too.

"No!" He glanced at me, took one hand off the wheel to hold mine. "Of course not. I've been looking forward to this day for three long years."

I'd been looking forward to a wedding, first. But while James was in school, he could still be on his mother's health insurance, and we couldn't afford to get our own.

I was working at a fast-food joint at night, in management, that provided mine.

"It's going to be great," James said now.

And I had to be honest with him. We were partners now. "I'm not sure I'm ready."

"What?" He glanced my way again, frowning now. "What do you mean?"

"I don't know. I'm just . . . I don't feel . . . it." I'd been raised not to talk about such things.

"Well, thanks," he said, his voice grumpy. "Do you have any idea how that makes me feel?"

I'd hurt him.

"I'm sorry," I said. "It's not that I don't want you. I'm just . . . scared, I guess."

"Oh," he relaxed back against the seat and sent me the sweet smile I was more used to seeing on his face. "Well, that's understandable. The first time's usually not as good for girls as it is for guys. But I'll go slowly. I promise. And then the second time, you'll like it as much as I do. You'll see."

I didn't see. But I was going to be his wife. I was going to have to sleep with him at some point. It might as well be now.

Funny, I thought, forty-five silent minutes later as James pulled into the parking lot of the hotel we'd chosen. I was a girl who exuded to the point of making guys crazy with desire, but I felt nothing at all.

James carried in our bags—two duffels—and I about died of shame and embarrassment as he set them on the floor of the lobby and checked us in. I was certain the two women behind the desk were watching us with knowing eyes. Knowing what we were going to be doing in that room.

If James hadn't picked up the bags and motioned me to follow him, I'd have bolted.

The key in the lock opened the door on the first try. The door swung open, revealing a generic hotel room like thousands of others like them in the city. Two queen beds. Clean, blue commercial carpet. A built-in dresser with a TV on top.

The door swung shut. James set our bags down and clicked the security chain into place.

I was hot. And cold. Panicked. I wanted to call my mother. Reached for the phone.

And James came around the bed, grabbing my arm before I could get to the receiver.

He pulled—harder than necessary—and I was flat on my back on the bed, staring up at him while he pulled at the dress slacks

I'd worn for the dinner we'd talked about having.

"What are you doing?"

"It's best just to get this over with," he said. "You aren't going to like it anyway. And this way we can get on to the second time, which will be better for you. Besides, I've waited long enough."

"No," I tried to sit up. He pushed me back down.

"I want to eat first. We said we were going to dinner . . ."

"We will." He had his pants undone and yanked mine off, and before I'd even realized his intention, he was forcing himself inside of me. There was no touching, no attempt at lovemaking.

It was done in a matter of seconds. I burned between my legs. I was dead in my heart.

And sick to my stomach.

Racing for the bathroom, I threw up.

Fifteen

In August of 1981, Tim Barney graduated with a degree in electrical engineering. With a job lined up, he was on top of the world as Emily met him after graduation. They were going camping for the weekend before he started work on Monday.

Emily loved camping as much as he did, and they had the site set up, using a tent until he could afford the pop-up camper he had his eye on. While he chopped up the wood he'd brought for the fire and got the thing burning, she cut up potatoes and put them in foil with butter and onions and salt.

He'd bought T-bone steaks to celebrate.

And a twelve-pack of beer.

"To you, Cowboy," Emily said later that night, as, dinner done, they were sitting by the fire with fresh beers. She tipped her bottle and drank.

"To you, too, Teach. I couldn't have done it without you."

She hadn't helped with the studying. He'd managed that fine on his own. But when he'd had a run-in with a professor who'd tried to tell him that credits weren't going to transfer as he'd been told and he'd been ready to quit school altogether, she'd calmed him down and convinced him to hang in there.

He was glad she had.

They were sitting side by side in camping chairs, and Tim pulled her closer to him, putting his arm around her and pulling her into his chest.

"A campfire, a full stomach, a beer, and sharing it all with the woman I love," he said softly. "It doesn't get any better than this."

Her silence fit the campground that had quieted as families put their children to bed and husbands and wives moved like shadows in the darkness.

"It does get better, Cowboy," Emily said. It took him a minute to figure out what she was referring to. He'd had an Eagles song running through his head. "Take It Easy . . ."

He took another long swig of beer. Taking it easy.

"It gets better when we're a family, too," she said, motioning toward the camper next to them—a couple not much older than them with a two-year-old son. They'd met them earlier that night when the boy had thrown a big plastic ball their way.

Tim had thrown it back and started an impromptu game of catch with a two-year-old that lasted fifteen minutes.

The swig of beer got stuck on the way down.

Now Emily wanted kids? They weren't even married yet. And . . .

"You're graduated now," she said.

Yeah, well, college graduation was one hell of a long way from fatherhood. He didn't have his camper yet. And everyone knew you couldn't take babies camping in a tent.

Didn't they?

He'd never seen anyone with a baby in a tent.

Not that he'd looked, but . . .

"When I moved into the house you said . . ."

When her voice faded off, he thought back. And remembered saying something about not wanting to move in with her while he was still in college.

And she'd remembered.

Of course.

"We were talking about living together."

"No, you were talking about living together. I don't want to do that.

I don't want to live with you until you're my husband. I want to know, when I get in the bed with you every night, that it's forever."

That didn't surprise him.

"I get that. And I agree." In theory. "I just don't want to run off and do something before we're ready."

"We've been dating for two years, Tim. We've been lovers for most of that time. And you don't know yet if you want to marry me?"

Her tone was his clue. "Of course I know I want to marry you," he said quickly. What he knew was that he didn't want to lose her.

He didn't want to hurt her.

And he didn't want to lie to her, either.

"I just . . . give me a little time to get settled in my job, first. I'm not big on the idea of being a kept husband. Nor do I want to go into this dependent on you. I need to be bringing home money, too."

"You will be starting Monday."

"We have no idea if I'll even like the job once I get in there."

Emily sat forward, and his arm fell back to his side. "Look, Cowboy," she said, her arms on her knees as she stared toward the fire. "I bought it when you said you wanted to wait until graduation. But now that's here and you're just making more excuses . . ."

"No," he interrupted before she could issue the ultimatum he heard coming. He didn't deal well with ultimatums. Especially ones he couldn't comply with.

"It's not like that at all. I'm only twenty-two, Em. Once we're married I take on my share of the financial obligations. I need to know that I'll have the money to make good on that. I want to marry you. Hell . . ."

He got down on one knee, his beer bottle still in his hand when he grabbed her hand and cupped it between his—with the beer an awkward guest. "Emily, will you marry me?"

"Stop it, Tim. Don't make fun of . . ."

"I'm not making fun, Emily. I swear it. I'm asking you to marry me.

I just want to wait to set the date until my probationary period is up at work and I have benefits and job security."

"How long is that?" Her look was skeptical, but she hadn't pulled her hand away. And her lips had softened into a half smile.

"Ten months." When he felt the beginning of a jerk on the hand he held, he added, "But I'll buy you a ring, now. Well, when I get my first paycheck. Assuming it's enough to cover my expenses. But if it's not, I'll get it as soon as I've saved enough. Hell, now that I'm employed full time I should be able to get a credit card. Not that I want to rack up debt, but . . ."

Her finger on his lips stopped the humiliating babbling. "It's okay, Cowboy. We're really engaged? Officially?"

"We will be as soon as you answer my question. Assuming your answer is yes."

"Of course it's yes, you idiot," she said, pulling him up on his feet and throwing her arms around him before planting a wet one on him.

His feeling of dread was just a result of the very natural fear of change.

He was happy. He loved Emily.

Everything else would work itself out.

⁓

I tried to like sex. Thankfully James didn't ask for it often during the fall of '81 and spring of '82. But the couple of times he did ask, I didn't refuse him. I wasn't a virgin anymore. I didn't have anything to hold out for. I was willing to serve his needs. Because, other than the sex, I really liked being with him.

I was safe with James. He knew me better than anyone. And he didn't try to change me. Nor did he criticize my shortcomings. He just accepted me, loved me, as I was. He continued to encourage me to write. To start my Harlequin romance. And I would have if I hadn't been working two jobs to help supplement his living expenses so that he didn't have to work and could concentrate on his upper-level physics classes and get done with school.

He was due to graduate in August of '82, and we were going to be married the following week. Mom and I had found my dress. It was being altered. We had a reception hall, a band, and flowers all picked out. I'd received my teaching certificate and had a job lined up for the fall as a substitute teacher in a suburb of Columbus.

I was living in an apartment in the city, across the hall from Chum and only a few miles from James's place.

On the second Friday in June of 1982, James invited me over for a cookout at his apartment complex. He had a studio unit, paid for by student loans and me, and had become friends with a couple of fellow chemistry students who lived in the same building. He wanted me to meet them.

I thoroughly enjoyed the evening. The three of them talked about their classes, making fun of themselves as much as of their professor. James was the wittiest of the three and, I thought, the most perceptive. I couldn't remember a time I'd laughed so hard.

And for the first time in forever, I was happy. The future was going to hold a lot more nights like that one. It was going to be good.

The guys left around eleven, and I turned to ask James if he wanted to sit out on the balcony a bit longer.

He'd locked the door and was coming toward me, a strange look on his face.

"You liked them, didn't you?"

"Of course I did. They were nice guys. But I expected them to be. They're your friends."

"No, I mean, you really liked them."

He couldn't mean what I thought he meant. "Don't be ridiculous."

"You're a whore, Tara. You just can't turn it off. And if you want it that badly, then I'll be the one to give it to you."

When he lifted me to the card table that served as his dining room, I knew what was coming.

"No!" I squirmed and pushed. "No, James. Not again."

"You want this. You know you do."

"No! I don't!"

"Of course you do. You want it this way. That's why you act like you do. You're a whore."

I fought him, but it did no good. He was much bigger, much stronger than I was.

As soon as he finished, James softened. Became the gentle, caring man I knew him to be. He invited me to lie with him.

Without a word I went into the bathroom and locked the door. I spent a good part of that night crying—the first real tears I'd cried since the first time James had defiled me.

He'd just done it for the last time.

I pulled off my engagement ring.

I was done with him.

Whether another man would ever have me or not didn't matter to me anymore. Because I didn't want another man.

Ever.

Ten months after he graduated, Tim met Denise Denton. He'd been in his office, going over a work schedule for a first shift line, when she'd appeared in the doorway with a stack of forms in her hand.

His heart skipped a beat when he first saw her, and he did a double take. No. She didn't look anything like Tara. It was just the hair. Same color. Almost same style.

Turned out she worked in human resources.

He'd made it through his probationary period with flying colors. She was there with his insurance forms.

Probation was done already? He stared at the forms, knowing that they meant it was time for him to ante up.

Time to marry Emily.

"Why haven't I seen you around here before?" She smiled, and again he thought of Tara.

"I was supervisor on second shift until yesterday."

"Oh."

"How long have you been here?" He was engaged. Sort of. He'd never bought the ring he'd promised Emily that night after his graduation. They'd been saving for a camper. And a bike for her.

Well, he was doing that. She was saving for their wedding. Her dad had lost his job, and her parents weren't going to be able to help.

"A couple of years." She smiled directly at him, looking him in the eye like she was talking to him, and then her bravado slipped a bit and he saw her insecurity. Tara, again.

He had to go get Emily a ring. His probation was up.

"What's your name?" He smiled back at her.

"Denise. You want to have a drink or something? After work, maybe?"

Emily had junior-high cheerleading practice that evening. And every other night that week. Summers weren't time off anymore like they used to be.

"Okay, Denise, one drink. After work." Just to show himself that the girl was nothing at all like Tara Gumser.

One drink. That was all it was going to be.

Until one drink turned into drinks every night that week.

And that weekend, he told Emily he couldn't marry her. He told her that there was someone else.

And he hated himself for all the hurt he'd caused her. For not being able to love her enough. God knew he'd tried.

Her parting words didn't make him feel any better.

"You really did me a favor, you know."

"How's that?"

"You saved me from going through my whole life feeling like I'm second best."

On July 4, 1982, Chum was killed. The car he was in was hit head-on by a kid coming up over the hill on the wrong side of the road. The kid was high on acid. I'd insisted he take my car instead of his motorcycle because I'd been afraid it might rain. My car was totaled. And I was the last person ever to see him alive.

The blockbuster movie *ET* had just come out that summer, and Chum and I had a date to go see it the day after he was killed. I went alone. And when Neil Diamond came to town, my parents and I went to see him. I sat through the concert with my eyes closed, hearing my brother's voice instead of Neil's, and mostly unaware of the tears streaming down my face.

Completely alone in Columbus, I spent the following year on a collision course with death. I drank too much. When I slept, which wasn't much, it was on the couch in my apartment. I had a bed, but didn't get in it. I took up cigarettes. When I wasn't partying, I was crying.

I honestly didn't care if I lived or died.

Neil Diamond came out with a new song, "Turn On Your Heart Light," about the movie *ET*. I figured Chum was telling me something, but I was too lost to listen to his message.

I quit my teaching job and started selling furniture. And ice cream cones.

And then, eighteen months after my big brother's death, while on vacation in Albuquerque, I met a man. He was calm. Stable. He had dark hair and a mustache, just like Tim's, but was much taller. He was a banker. And he asked me to the movies.

Three months later, after weekend trips back and forth to Ohio, he asked me to live with him. There was no fire in his kisses, no tingle in his touch, but I didn't expect there to be. James had killed any chance I'd ever feel those things again. I knew that now.

Chris didn't mind. He was happy with our love life. He said I was everything he wanted and needed. I wanted to make a home for him. Raise his kids. And I knew how to dress, how to act, when he had clients to entertain. My keep-up-appearances upbringing fit him perfectly.

He was what I thought I needed, too. He was steady. Reliable. And loyal. He liked to work. And he was happy to support me while I wrote my Harlequin romance and tried to sell it.

He thought I was a lady. Not a slut. He treated me like a lady.

And in 1985 I married him.

Sixteen

"THANK YOU FOR ATTENDING THE 1998 SEMINAR ON hydraulic press specifications."

No, thank you for letting me attend, Tim thought sarcastically. How many of these things did a guy have to sit through in a lifetime?

And why did they always seem to hold the damned things in September? Thinking of the school busses and their new routes, the parents lining up to pick up kids, all the traffic he had to fight to get out of the city at 3:00 PM before he could start the long drive home wasn't improving his mood any.

He'd better call Denise and let her know that he'd be later than he'd expected. Chicago at rush hour wasn't going to be easy. And he had another six hours after that before he was back in Eaton.

As soon as he was on the open road, Tim started to relax. He'd forgotten about the best part of the damned seminars he was required to attend. They gave him time alone on the road, listening to the radio and thinking about life. Time out to reacquaint himself with who he was and what he wanted. To put things into perspective. They also gave him a chance to have the radio blaring—something Denise complained about.

Just then a familiar song came on, and Tim cranked the volume up full blast.

"Hot August Night." A Neil Diamond tune.

And he was back in Tara's kitchen, holding her hand. Listening to Chum playing his guitar. Tim pictured Tara's brother, sitting with the guitar perched on his knee, head back, eyes closed, and singing like he was in concert.

He wondered how Tara was doing. It had been eighteen years since he'd seen her. Was she still in the area? Had she become a journalist?

Did she have kids?

He thought about one of the letters she'd sent from Armstong. She'd gone on and on about two orphan girls she'd visited. She'd loved kids. His guess was that she had at least two of her own. And a houseful of poodles, too.

Tara was still on his mind when Tim rolled into the Dayton area later that night. He'd spent the whole trip with her. On a lark, he made a slight detour.

Once again, he made that familiar drive: Brandt Pike left to Brandt Vista and then right on Drywood. It was probably a good thing it was dark outside. He was nuts, some kind of crazy stalker, a thirty-eight-year-old man driving by an old girlfriend's house so many years after the fact.

What was the matter with him? Why couldn't he let go of the memory of his little blonde girl from Wright State?

The house looked the same: same brick, same driveway; the pine trees out front that Tara's father had planted were much taller.

He sat for a bit. Remembering. And then put the Buick in gear.

Well, Gumser, he thought, *Never say that I didn't stop and say hi.*

~~~

"Dammit woman, can't you get anything right? Look at this counter. I work all day. I expect things put away when I get home."

I'd set the notebook on the kitchen counter while I made a stop in the bathroom. He'd arrived while I was incapacitated. I grabbed up the binder—my *2004 Policy and Procedure Manual.* I was president of a multimillion-dollar international writers organization that had more than 9,600 members.

"You'd think, after nineteen years of marriage, you'd at least be able to get a simple thing, like picking up after yourself, right."

Had his nose always been that thin? His eyes that beady? Where had the pretty blue gone? I didn't see any color in them now at all.

"Dammit," he said again, slamming his hand against the counter. "I take care of you. Why can't you take care of me? I don't ask for much."

I didn't say anything. It would only anger him further.

You parked with the wheels turned again. Do I have to do everything for you?

You're a writer, not a business person. You aren't good with numbers. I'll take care of the finances. You worry about getting that book written.

Just wait for me to take you to the grocery. Lifting the bags isn't good for your back.

Let me make the phone calls. You're good at writing, not so with real conversation. I understand, though, it's because you spend all day alone with the people in your head, how could you be expected to carry on normal conversation?

Other conversations replayed themselves in my mind while Chris got himself a drink—the Cognac he had every single night as soon as he got home. It was expensive. But he didn't have many extravagances.

I waited until he'd had a couple of sips and then said, "Remember, I have a writer's meeting tonight."

It was more than that. We were having a three-day board meeting in Albuquerque. I'd been in meetings all day and had rushed home on dinner break to put the casserole in the oven for Chris and to make certain that I was there to greet him as he expected.

We'd never had children—my fault, I'd never been able to conceive—and Chris was right. He really did ask for very little. A clean house. Dinner at night. His wife home when he got there.

And available when he needed her. But he didn't complain about all of my traveling as long as I had meals planned and ready for him to reheat while I was gone. And he hadn't complained about the seven years it had taken me to get published, either. The years he'd supported me while I sought to make my dreams come true.

He'd been my rock six years before when my father died.

"How late are you going to be?"

"I'm not sure. The advent of e-books might change the publishing world in the very near future, and we're already being challenged to look at our definitions of publishing. Tonight's a special brainstorming session on . . ."

I'd have said more but Chris was reading the paper he'd picked up from the bin by his chair. I placed it there every evening before he got home.

I walked over and gave him a quick kiss on the cheek. "Dinner's ready. It's in the oven on warm. There's salad in the fridge. Leave the dishes. I'll take care of them when I get home."

He nodded. Glanced my way and smiled. "Be very, very careful. You're a small woman. And gorgeous. Which makes you prey to all the creeps out there."

Hating the reminder that because I was a woman I was vulnerable, I nodded. "I will. See you tonight." I probably wouldn't. He'd be asleep before I returned, and we'd had separate bedrooms for more than ten years—ever since he'd found out I couldn't conceive.

I don't think he heard me, anyway.

I don't think he'd heard a word I'd said in years. I'd published more than thirty books in twelve years and Chris hadn't read a word of them. He didn't really know what I was capable of. Or didn't want to know.

My writing friends had pointed it all out to me. After one of them overheard a particularly bad phone conversation between Chris and me. I'd been in New York, meeting with my new agent. I'd been wined and dined. And he'd let me know that I'd made a bad decision taking on the agent I had. He'd said I had no business sense. I knew words, not numbers.

What made my friends mad was that I agreed with him. I will never forget hanging up from that call to face the woman I respected more than anyone else in the world. Her lips were pursed, her cheeks red, and she said to me, "You're responsible for a multimillion-dollar organization that is growing in amazing numbers and you think you have no business sense?"

I understood. Chris felt threatened by my success. Like my ability to sell books would somehow make him less valuable. So he had to make certain that I saw less value in myself than I saw in him.

He was afraid I was going to leave him.

He needn't have worried. I'd given him my word to be with him until death parted us, and I was going to remain loyal to him. Just because I had a successful career didn't mean that I was a better person. Nor did I let my success go to my head. My business, as any business, was fickle. As a writer I was only as good as my latest book.

Besides, I knew full well, had always known, that life wasn't about money and career. It was about family. Chris was my husband. And he'd been good to me.

The summer of 2006 was mild in Ohio. Warm, but not too hot. Humid, but not wet. The last day in June Tim drove home from the auto parts engineering job he'd had for twenty-five years, looking forward to the July 4th holiday ahead.

Four days of no work, no paperwork, no shop to worry about, no technicians and line workers to oversee. Four whole days of campfires, beer, and Denise.

Her little red sports car was parked in the drive when he rounded the corner and the house they'd been sharing for the past twenty years—one he'd purchased and almost had paid off—came into view.

The RV was not there. She was supposed to have picked it up from the storage lot after work. They'd been planning to leave for southeastern Ohio within minutes of his arrival.

She was sitting at the dining room table when he walked in, her blonde hair hanging down, rather than up in the pony tail she always wore camping. She still had on the black slacks and white blouse she'd worn to work that morning. "Hey, Dee Dee, what's wrong?"

Was she sick? Had someone died? Her hands were clenched on the top of the table.

"We need to talk."

His heart sank. Not those words again. It had been almost thirty years, but he still remembered them with dread. Tara's words.

Right before she'd asked for her ring back.

"What?" Pulling out the chair opposite her, he sank down, noticing a black grease stain on his jeans. Denise would get it out. She always did. She'd probably bitch a bit about the way he, an engineering manager, had to crawl around on the factory floor fixing machines that the technicians who'd been hired to fix them couldn't fix.

He'd been in such a hurry to get out of work, he'd forgotten to change out his steel-toed shoes.

Glancing back up, he caught Denise staring at him, a look in her eyes he'd never seen before. Like she was in pain, only not the physical kind.

"What's wrong?" Had she had a miscarriage or something equally tragic? She hadn't said she was pregnant, but stranger things had happened.

That brief thought—of a child, a real family—gave him a twinge. And he moved on. He liked their life together. It was pretty much perfect.

"I'm not going camping."

He was disappointed, of course, but . . .

"Okay." If that's all this was about, no problem. If he hadn't been so worried, he might have gotten angry. But hey, beers and fireworks could happen anywhere, right?

"Aren't you going to ask why?"

"I figured you were going to tell me." Mentally shifting, he thought about the steak they'd bought the night before during their grocery shopping expedition. He could grill that tonight. Sit out by the pool. Listen to tunes. And have Denise close . . .

"I'm leaving you, Tim."

Sit out by the pool. Grill steak. Yeah, that was it. Listen to tunes. And . . .

"Did you hear me?"

"What?" He glanced at her. Sort of. He glanced her way. "Yeah."

"Aren't you going to say something?"

What? Hell no, he wasn't going to say anything. If she walked out that door she better not ever think about coming back and . . .

"Tim?" She had tears in her eyes. He'd seen them before. Many, many times. Every time she got it in her head that he didn't love her because they weren't getting married.

"What?" Steak. Grill. Pool. Tunes.

"I said I'm leaving you."

The words stabbed him. "I heard you." He needed a beer. There was no reason to fear what she was saying. He owned the home. And everything in it. He could more than afford to pay the bills.

He had the RV. He could go camping anytime he wanted. Anywhere he wanted.

He felt kind of panicky just the same.

"That's it, then? You have nothing to say?"

He tried to meet her gaze. Those blue eyes pissed him off. They said she cared. And clearly she didn't.

"What do you want me to say?"

"I don't know. Ask me to stay. Ask me why. Something."

Possibility walked back in the door. "If I asked you to stay, would you?" They were in foreign territory. He wasn't going to just put it right out there.

"No."

That pissed him off all over again. What kind of game was she playing with him now?

"I've met someone else."

She should have just slapped him or something.

"Then why are you still here?" A guy could only take so much.

"Because we've been together for more than twenty years. I didn't think it was right to just walk out without a word."

"But it's okay to see someone else behind my back?" She'd slept in his bed the night before, and how many nights before that while she was seeing another man?

"It wasn't like that."

He didn't want to hear any more.

"I didn't mean to, Tim. I . . . he's a sales guy from work and for a long time we just talked when he came in."

She was still in human relations, with a medical supply firm.

"How long's a long time?" He stared at her then. Pinning her like a bug to a wall. He hoped.

She glanced away, and he really just wanted to go get the RV and get on the road. Except then he'd have to come back home. To an empty house. "I don't know. A year maybe."

A year. They'd gone to Florida just a few months ago. Had a honeymoon-like vacation. She'd said so herself.

"How often does he 'come in'?"

"About once a week. He lives in Indiana but has several clients in the Dayton area."

And how many other women did the bastard screw on his route?

"Is he married?"

"No."

"You sure about that?"

Her softly spoken "Yes" convinced him of far more than he was asking, and he knew.

"You've been to his house."

"Yes."

"You've slept with him."

"Yes."

"How many times?"

"Twice."

Tim stood. "Get your things and get out."

"I've already packed."

His gaze immediately sought the top of his mother's hutch—a piece he'd inherited when she'd passed away about five years after he and Denise had moved in together. Denise's thimble collection wasn't there.

He'd teased her about the damned thing enough times. Complained about it the time or two she'd coaxed him into using a dust cloth. He should be glad to see it gone.

Turning, he glanced behind him. The family room was equally bare. No dried flowers. No china figurines. She'd even taken the blanket that she kept on the back of her chair.

She'd left the chair. But then, he'd purchased it.

He hadn't noticed anything missing until now.

"Like I said, why are you still here?" The coldness in his voice was in direct contrast to the anger raging through him. Anger because he was scared to death.

She'd played him for a fool. He'd given her everything he had and . . .

"I'm here because I want you to know why I'm leaving," she said, still sitting at his table. Like it was her table, too.

It wasn't. Not anymore.

And that chair? The one she'd occupied every day—sitting at the table with his brothers and their wives and kids, taking her place as a member of his family—for twenty years, wasn't hers anymore either.

"Because you're an unfaithful hag."

"Tim, please sit down."

He recognized the obstinate tone in her voice. She wasn't budging. And he wanted her gone. He sat. But he wouldn't listen to a word she said. She was a lying witch.

"I love you."

Try again.

"I've always loved you. But I need to be loved, too."

"I loved you." The words were defensive. Nothing more.

"I know you did." The soft tone got to him. And he ordered it not to. She was after something. And what more was there to take? If she thought she was getting money out of him . . .

He wasn't listening.

"Just not enough," she said. "I don't know what it is with you. You're such a great guy. Kind and funny and smart and . . ."

Shut the hell up. That's what he wanted to say to her.

"But you can't seem to give your whole heart. All these years, I kept hoping that you'd get over your aversion to marriage, but . . ."

For a second there, he relaxed. That's what this was about. Marriage. Again. They'd been through it a dozen times or more. And they got through it each time.

And then he remembered about the bastard who'd slept with his woman. Correction, his ex-woman.

"I'm forty-three, Tim. If I don't try to have a baby in the next year or so I'll have lost any chance . . ."

He'd wanted children. He'd told her so. She wouldn't consider bringing a child into the world without marriage.

"This guy, what's-his-name-salesperson slime, he's going to marry you and give you children?"

"Yes."

Tim stood up again, blood boiling. "He's a medical supply salesperson for Christ's sake, Denise. He makes enough money to support you?"

"No. I'll have to work. But I don't care. Money was never important to me. You know that. I loved you with everything I had, but it wasn't enough. I wasn't enough. Now I am."

It was like there was an echo in the room. Emily's voice come back to haunt him. *You saved me from living my life as second best.* Or some such thing.

What was it with women? What did they want? To crawl inside of his skin and take root? Did they want his every thought? He gave Denise his home. His money. His love. And that wasn't enough?

"I think you should go," he said quietly. Calmly.

She dropped some keys on the table. Her key to his truck. To the RV. And her house keys. She'd been holding them in her clenched hand all that time.

Without a word Tim pulled his keys out of the pocket of the work jacket he'd yet to shed, disengaged her car key, and handed it to her.

He brushed her palm with his finger as she took it, and took pleasure in the way she pulled back, in the stark look in her eyes. He still had his touch. His ability to get to her. Maybe he was a bastard to let her know that, to let her see that he knew it, but he didn't really give a rat's ass one way or another at the moment.

Her steps sounded loudly against the wood floor as she walked to the door. It opened. Quietly swished shut behind her. The click as it latched was like a gunshot in the room.

She hit her mark.

Only thing was, she'd missed his heart.

And that's when Tim understood what she'd been trying to tell him all along.

Seventeen

AN OLD HIGH-SCHOOL AND CHURCH FRIEND CAUGHT ME at a low moment during December of 2006. Chris and I, both consumed by our careers, hardly spoke anymore. I provided dinner. He ate. And we kissed each other on the cheek when we left the house in the morning.

I owed Chris. He'd been a good provider, just as he'd said he'd be. He'd understood when I could no longer tolerate his touch—any touch—sexually speaking. He didn't know about James. He just thought I was frigid. But he'd stood by me, hadn't asked for a divorce.

Still, I was lonely. All I'd ever wanted, besides publishing with Harlequin, was to love and be loved.

I wasn't sure Chris and I loved each other at all anymore.

When I got the e-mail from Lois Schneider, my old church friend, asking me to attend my thirty-year high-school reunion, I actually thought about doing so. Maybe it wasn't too late to form friendships. Maybe I could bond with the kids I'd hardly known.

But when I realized I couldn't remember five names from my graduating class, I came to my senses. Attending my high-school reunion would be a futile effort that would only reinforce my sense of isolation.

Still, Lois persisted. I'd made something of myself. People would be interested. At least, she urged, sign up for Classmates.com so people from the class could see that I was there.

Tara Taylor Quinn (I'd had my name legally changed to my pen name after the terrorist attacks of September 11, 2001) didn't put personal information anywhere. It wasn't safe. I'd had too many letters from lonely guys in prison to feel safe being exposed.

My phone was unlisted. My address was a P.O. Box.

And James was still out there, someplace. I didn't want him to find me. Ever.

But Tara Taylor Quinn also protected me. No one knew that Tara Gumser wrote books. I could sign up with Classmates.com under my maiden name and be as anonymous as ever.

Lois had been a loyal friend to me all of our adult years. We weren't close. Weren't in touch all that often—particularly living a country apart. But she was the only person from my high-school days, my church youth-group days, who even acknowledged that I existed. She wrote to me every time I had a book out—telling me what she thought of it. Not always complimentary, but always honest.

I'd always liked her. She was one of the few kids back in the late seventies who'd had the courage to walk by the convictions of her own beliefs. A kindred soul, I'd always thought. Only back then, Lois had had the courage to walk boldly while I'd hidden behind the covers of my Harlequin romances.

I signed up for Classmates.com.

And that very same day was served divorce papers. I didn't blame Chris. Our lives were empty. But still . . . in December? Without talking to me first?

Maybe there was something we could do. We were family. That stood for a lot.

And yet, what was there that we hadn't already tried? Except the counseling that he'd opted not to participate in?

"Can't we at least talk about this?" I asked him that night when he got home from work. I handed him the Cognac I'd poured for him when I'd heard the garage door go up, signaling his arrival. I had the papers I'd been served in my left hand.

He sipped, and looked at me over the rim of his glass.

"You know as well as I do that this is no way to live."

"But . . ."

"Look, it's going to be painless for both of us," he said. "We agree to a sixty/forty split—I'm giving you the sixty in lieu of spousal support— you sign the papers you were served today, and in thirty days it's done."

"What about the house?"

"I'm buying you out of it. It's all in the papers." He spoke as though I were a child, assuming I hadn't read the papers.

He was right, of course. I'd been too shocked. Too hurt. And I'd had pages to write. I was on deadline. I had the second book of a suspense trilogy I was doing for MIRA books due in February, and two weeks later, also in February, I had a book due to Harlequin Superromance— the launch book for a five-author continuity series.

Chris knew about both projects. Or he should have. I'd been talking about little else for weeks. His timing couldn't have been worse.

That night, with the door to my bedroom suite shut tight, I drew a bubble bath in my garden tub, poured a glass of wine from the carafe I'd carried up with me, lit a candle, turned on some soft classical music, laid back in the hot water, and cried.

The next day, I called a lawyer friend. She advised me not to sign the papers until she'd had a chance to go over them. I'd read them. They were more than fair.

Still, was this the right decision? I'd married "for better or worse, in sickness and health, 'til death do you part."

Chris couldn't do anything more without my signature. Unless he wanted to sue me for divorce.

I needed time to think.

Was there more I could do to make Chris happier? What would a divorce do to my mother? And what family would Chris have without mine? His parents were both gone. His siblings, two sisters and a brother, called about once a year. Maybe.

Was this the only way? Had we really passed the point of no return?

I had my answer on January 21, 2007, when I came home to find a woman in bed with Chris. It was Sunday afternoon. I'd said I was going to be out with an unpublished writer I was mentoring. She'd had a family crisis and couldn't make our meeting.

I'd come home to work. And was intending to let Chris know I was there.

"What the hell are you doing, you stupid bitch?" Chris jumped up when I opened his bedroom door to see his naked butt moving on top of a female body.

Standing there naked, with a hard-on protruding out in front of him, he didn't even attempt decency as he came toward me. "Get out," he growled out the words, shoving me, as he slammed the door in my face.

I stumbled across the upstairs foyer to my suite and started packing.

All of the clothes from my dresser were in the two suitcases I'd had in my walk-in closet by the time I heard Chris's door open twenty minutes later. A minute after that the front door closed, and then a car started up down at the street. Must have been the Mustang I'd passed as I'd pulled in our driveway. It had been parked on the side of the road in front of our house, and I'd surmised that it belonged to someone visiting next door.

"What the *hell* do you think you were doing barging in like that?"

I swung around, my heart pounding as the door to my bedroom flew open and slammed so hard that the knob left an indentation in the drywall behind it.

"I . . ."

"You stupid bitch . . ." Chris was wearing jeans and nothing else.

He'd called me that only once before. Half an hour earlier.

I was not a stupid bitch.

"You stayed there and finished," I said, though I had no idea why. It's not like I cared anymore. It's not like I really thought Chris had been celibate for ten years. But he'd been discreet. He'd never brought his sexual exploits to our home. Because he respected me.

Or so I'd thought.

"Of course I finished," his voice raised a couple of octaves as he approached me. I backed up a step. "Jenny drove all the way over here from Santa Fe. And we were right in the middle of things."

Right, and God knew, Chris wouldn't stop once he'd started. He just hurried up and finished. Or rather, I knew. A long-ago memory surfaced. And then faded.

"Did you pay her?"

"That's none of your goddamned business."

His pupils were pinpoints of anger. And I was the one who'd walked in on my spouse, in our home, while he was having sex with someone else. The dichotomy struck a note someplace that preserved me.

"You are the most selfish, insensitive woman I have ever met." He took another step forward. "What in the hell is the matter with you?"

I didn't know. But I agreed with him. Something was definitely wrong with me. I drove men to hate me.

"Why are you trying so hard to hurt me?" He screamed. "Just because you're an unhappy person, you have to drag me down with you? You have to make me miserable, too? You can't even let me have an hour's worth of pleasure?"

He advanced another step. I backed up again.

And met the wall.

"I'm done with you, do you hear me?" He was yelling so loudly I was afraid the neighbors across the street would hear. "I don't even want to be friends with you. I don't ever want to have to see your face or hear your voice again, do you understand? You make me sick." I nodded, hoping my acquiescence would calm him.

I knew for certain that if I spoke, it would just incite him further.

"I never thought it was possible to hate a person. But I hate you. Do you get that?" His chest jutting forward, he came right up to me, his fists clenched and down at his sides.

I nodded again.

"You're nothing, Tara. Nothing. You'll never be anything. I pity any man who ever comes into your life. You don't know how to be a woman. You don't know how to love. You're worthless. You couldn't even do a simple thing like get pregnant. I can't believe I wasted twenty-two years of my life with you."

He was up against me. Holding me to the wall. I raised my hands up, ready to cover my face, only then noticing the little angel figurine I held. One from the collection on my nightstand.

Chris had never hit me. I didn't really think he would now. But I was scared.

He grabbed the angel, cutting my finger with the force of his yank. I heard the helpless little figure shatter against the wall to my right. I didn't look at it. I couldn't.

Chris did, though. And the sight did something to him. Still clearly angry, he stepped back, turned, and strode from the room, closing the door softly behind him.

I sank to a shaking puddle on the floor, sobbing. Wondering how my life had become such a confusing mess when all I'd ever wanted was to love and be loved. And be a good person.

My tears finally subsided. All I felt was an exhausted numbness. I started to move mechanically. I had my alter ego, Tara Taylor Quinn, now. As I stood there in my bedroom, facing the rest of my life, she was there, taking over where Tara Gumser could not. She put one foot in front of the other. She opened drawers and made choices.

I finished packing what I could gather up that night. With Chris sitting in his chair in front of a football game, I carried everything out to my car, one step at a time, drove to a hotel out by the highway, and checked into a room.

I had no plan. No sense of what I was going to do, other than to take a couple of aspirin and go to sleep.

I'd left my signed divorce papers in the middle of Chris's unmade bed.

Tim hated Sunday nights. They were too quiet, especially now that he was the only person in the house. That third Sunday in January of 2007 was one of the worst. He'd run into an old friend at the department store in town that afternoon—and heard that Denise was having a son.

It was frigid outside. He was restless and lonely and avoiding regrets. Why he went to the attic, he had no idea, or at least he wasn't owning up to it. He knew the box he wanted. It was rectangular. Tin. Locked. And had multiple BB holes through it.

Opening the box he saw two things that put a smile on his face: the pink yarn Tara had left on his class ring, and the glass-horse earrings that she'd left in his bedroom on Maple Street almost thirty years before.

He wondered what she was doing. Where she was living. Hell, she could still be in Huber Heights, less than an hour away.

He had time. A computer. And in the past few years the Internet had made it possible to find just about anyone.

After a couple of hours of an exhausting searching that led absolutely nowhere, he thought of Classmates.com. He knew Tara had gone to Wayne High School. And that she'd graduated in 1977. He typed in her maiden name, expecting another dead-end.

"I'll be damned," he said out loud. He couldn't believe it. Tara Gumser. The name was right there. She'd registered with Classmates.com. Which meant that she was out there somewhere. Or that she had been somewhat recently.

He could even send her a message.

If he registered with Classmates.com. So he would. A little thing like filling in a few blanks wasn't going to slow him down. He was on a mission now.

He'd hurt two women because he hadn't been able to let go of Tara enough to love another fully. And he'd never told Tara how he felt about her. He had to rectify that.

He registered. He was in. And he started typing.

> *January 21, 2007*
> *Wow! I can't believe I actually found you . . .*

On Sunday night I slept like a baby. I had no idea where my life was going, but I'd reached a place of total honesty that brought a measure of peace. Of total acceptance. And when I woke up Monday morning, I lay in the bed, completely alone, and realized something: I was who I was. And, overall, I liked me. I knew my heart, my intentions. I knew that I really cared about other people and wanted to make a positive difference in the world. I knew that I gave my all. I tried my best—always. I meant well. Deep inside, away from the things I'd done and the things that had happened to me, I was still the young woman who'd driven to Wright State University in the fall of 1977 with conviction in her heart.

I was a good person. I really believed that.

It didn't matter anymore if anyone else did.

At least, it didn't matter then.

I realized, as I lay in the bed that next morning, staring at the generic painting of a colorful garden on the wall across from the bed, that I'd been moving toward this point for a long time. And in the end, it had only taken hours to get here.

Chris hadn't been happy with me. But I hadn't been happy with him, either.

My happiness mattered.

I waited for the guilt to descend, to spread over me, consume me. *You're the most selfish individual I've ever known.* Chris's words played in my brain.

I don't know whether it was the hotel, or if I'd really come through a thirty-year storm into the sunlight, but I seemed to have landed in a guilt-free zone.

You're an incredible, giving, caring woman, Tara. Your readers relate to you because you get life. You get what matters. You're loyal and honest. And a great friend.

Words from one of my writer friends came to visit me as I lay there. And I knew she'd be proud of me if she could see me right then.

I thought about calling her. But knew now wasn't the time. I wasn't calling my mother, either. This moment was for me. I had to get through it on my own.

I wasn't quite as needy and helpless as I'd believed for so long. With TTQ's help I'd somehow become the strong, capable woman who'd first walked into geology class. One who'd had experience that had brought understanding. And, I hoped, compassion.

And if I wasn't, I could be. I would be.

Chris might be right. Maybe I was just selfish beyond belief. James had said I do things to men. I bring out the worst in them. Maybe they were both right.

And maybe not.

Maybe I had something to offer the world that neither one of them saw. I used to believe that I had plenty to offer. I used to be excited about the idea of contributing to the betterment of the world.

I was up, showered, and back in my car by seven. I had work to do. A book to finish. But as I drove, I thought about the past ten years of living virtually on my own. Emotionally isolated.

And I thought about what I knew about myself. My bottom-line goal. I wanted to love and be loved.

That hadn't changed. But I added a caveat that morning. I'd rather live alone than live with someone who didn't love me. To live with someone I couldn't love with all of my heart.

Like I'd loved Tim.

Slowing, I pulled into an alcove on the side of the mountain community where Chris and I had settled on the outskirts of Albuquerque.

Tears flooded my eyes as I saw myself, my life, from the outside in. In a sense, James and Chris were both right. I'd let them both down. Because I hadn't been able to love either one of them as I'd loved Tim.

I'd given them everything I had. But it hadn't been enough because I hadn't been able to give them my whole heart.

I wondered if either one of them had ever known that.

Maybe, if James hadn't done what he'd done . . .

No. Closing my mind to all thoughts of James—as I'd been doing since that last night I'd seen him—I reached the house Chris and I shared, forgoing the front door for the side gate and out to the separately keyed office that had been our deciding factor on purchasing the house several years before.

And thoughts of James protruded again. Had his actions that night on the country road ruined me for everyone who would come after, just as he'd said? But not in the way he'd said? Not morally, but emotionally? And physically?

Just as I was incapable of feeling sexual desire, was I also incapable of loving completely?

Unlocking the door, I stepped inside, taking in the solid oak desk, the love seat with Raggedy Ann quilts and pillows and dolls that faced me every day as I wrote, to the wall of shelves and drawers that held my supplies. In the back, through another door, was a very small but perfectly fine lavatory.

The office was exactly the same as I'd left it the day before. Papers strewn across my desk. The chair pushed back.

It seemed more open. Like there was more air in the room.

My marriage had ended years before. I knew that. I didn't want to let go, to admit defeat. I didn't want to be a failure.

I didn't want to be someone who let my husband down.

I didn't want to believe that trying hard, giving everything I had, just wasn't enough.

And I didn't want to waste another minute trying to be something I was not. Trying to compensate for my past. I'd spent twenty-seven years of my life trying to be enough, and here I was, forty-seven years old and all alone. And what I suddenly understood was that I *was* enough. Why a prostitute in my ex-husband's bed had brought it all home to me I didn't know, but I didn't really care, either. I was who I was. And that was okay.

What wasn't okay was being dead alive.

Eighteen

T<small>IM GOT UP AT HIS NORMAL TIME, MADE COFFEE,</small> grabbed a bowl of cereal, and turned on the TV for some sitcom rerun company before hitting the shower. It was another cold January day. Monday. A good day because it was a new one. He'd made it through a not-good Sunday. One of those rare days in a guy's life that asked more questions than it answered. Questions for which there were no answers.

He was ready to tackle the world by the time he was in his truck and heading out to the plant. If life was missing something, he'd find it. He was a wild spirit. A man who had to be able to get up and go. Before long he was going to quit his job and head out to see what the world had to offer. Maybe he'd drive a semi.

Or get his real estate license, buy cheap homes, fix them up, and sell them for a profit.

There was only opportunity ahead.

A brief thought of the night before intruded. Would the message he'd left on Classmates.com ever find Tara, or would it be lost in cyberspace forever? She was someone he'd known and loved. Sad to think that he might never hear from or see her again.

Still, life was changing and he was going to change right along with it. That decision made, he sipped from his coffee, upped the volume on the radio, turned at the next corner, and took a different route to work.

I sat in my chair just like I did every morning. I clicked on my media player, choosing Grady Soine's *Beautiful* album, with which I started every single workday.

And I opened my e-mail program. I'd go through the messages so they wouldn't be calling out to me, and then close the program and give myself over to writing for the rest of the day. I had a system. It worked for me.

I saw the name and thought it was one of those eye tricks. The kind that showed you a puddle of water ahead when you were lost in the desert. My stomach was tumbling, my heart pounding, and I looked again.

Tim Barney.

In the subject column. Couldn't be the same Tim Barney. I took myself in hand as I stared at the name. Tim was a common name. Barney probably was, too, though I hadn't personally run across it ever again in my life.

What had it been? Twenty-seven years? I was forty-seven. Tim would be, too.

Tim Barney.

It wasn't him. Glancing over the other e-mails awaiting my attention, I kept seeing that name.

I was going to open it, of course. I had to. Just in case. But I'd clear out my inbox first. I'd be practical and take care of business. Then, just before I started work, I'd bother to look at the e-mail just to make sure it was someone trying to sell me something.

Maybe a top spot on search engines for the TTQ website.

Or maybe it was one of those *Dearly Beloveds,* as I called them. The ones where someone had left me a fortune and I just had to give up all my personal information to collect my funds. Or someone was dying and wanted to send me their money for safekeeping.

Maybe it was . . .

I clicked. Before I'd looked at a single other e-mail.

And I came up blank. The message was from Classmates.com. It told me that someone I knew, someone from my past, a Tim Barney, had sent me a message.

Tim Barney had sent me a message, but it wasn't there for me to see it? Was this some kind of joke?

A really sick one?

And then I remembered registering Tara Gumser at Classmates. com just the month before. I'd listed my e-mail address for Classmates. com to send me private messages but not to share with anyone else.

They'd just sent me a message.

I had to retrieve it. It had to be my Tim. What other Tim Barney would have sent Tara Gumser a message?

With shaking fingers I clicked on the URL in the message, which took me to the Classmates.com website. I quickly filled in my username and password. My stomach was in knots.

My Tim was only seconds away. He'd contacted me. He remembered me.

The screen changed and . . .

The message wasn't there. Another one was, from Classmates. com. I'd only completed their free registration. If I wanted to receive messages through them I had to join their club. I had to pay $15. But more than that, I had to share more personal information than I could share.

"Damn." I said aloud. And right clicked on Tim's name. I searched for him on Classmates.com. I went out on the Internet and ran a search for him. I was pretty computer savvy. I'd find him. One way or another.

Or not.

Two hours later, writing time passed with zero pages to show for it, I was back on the Classmates.com website, typing in my personal information. I paid my fifteen dollars. With shaking hands, and a stomach that was now doing flip-flops, I waited.

The screen changed.

And . . .

> *WOW! I can't believe that I actually found you. I was going thru some of my old stuff today and ran across some of your letters and started wondering how you were doing. I'm still in the Dayton area and doing pretty good. I would love to hear from you and hear about your life. Are you a famous reporter yet??*
>
> *Please feel free to e-mail me. If I don't hear from you, I understand. Talk soon.*
>
> *P.S. I guess I just assume that you remember who I am. I was that crazy long-haired guy from Eaton that went to Wright State with you back in 1970 something. You broke my heart and ran away to Alabama to go to college to be a famous news-paper writer (haha). Seriously, it would be nice to hear from you if that's okay.*
>
> *Tim Barney*

If I remembered him?

It was Tim Barney. *My* Tim Barney.

I sat. I stared. I turned up the music. Turned it off. I couldn't believe it.

I had to move. To work off excess energy. I must have had too much diet cola. I had to use the restroom. Urgently.

I had to call someone.

Who would I call?

For so long the only person I reported to, good or bad, had been Chris. He didn't like to spread our information around. He said people judged. And didn't forget.

Back in front of my computer screen, I read the note again. I had to answer Tim. I had to tell him I hadn't broken his heart. He'd broken mine. More than once.

I hit reply.

No, that didn't work. It was going back to Classmates.com.

I read again what he'd written.

He'd given me his private e-mail address.

I had a book due. Two of them. I had hundreds of pages to write in a matter of weeks.

I had business e-mail to tend to.

I copied that e-mail address, opened another post window, and pasted. I addressed an e-mail to Tim Barney.

Sitting back, I couldn't quit grinning. At that moment, I didn't care that I was forty-seven years old. I didn't feel forty-seven. I felt like I was eighteen again. And fully alive.

Really, truly alive.

Like I hadn't been since that night on the country road with James.

The memory might have stopped me, before. It had stopped me the last time I'd seen Tim, that day in the summer of 1980 when he'd come to see me.

But I was Tara Taylor Quinn now. A woman who'd learned that she could take care of herself just fine. A woman with friends who cared about her. A woman of worth.

Old history was just that—old. I'd left it behind. As of this morning. I'd heard from Tim the very same day I'd broken from my old life and was finally seeing myself honestly. The timing was not a mistake. It urged me on.

Tim wasn't in the past. He was saying hello now. And I wanted to answer him.

I had to answer him.

I scrolled down and started typing.

Coming in from the factory floor where he'd been supervising the trial of a machine he'd designed to mold plastic to go around a windshield, Tim stopped at his desk in the engineering office to check his e-mail and see what fires he had to put out there before he could start on the design waiting for him.

The engineering portion of his job he enjoyed. The managerial bull was usually a huge time waste.

Tara Taylor Quinn.

Who in the hell was that? Some toolmaker trolling for business? Didn't sound like a toolmaker. Probably just junk mail.

He clicked.

And skimmed what was there. Wait. Was this his Tara?

Skipping down to the bottom of the e-mail, Tim read the signature. Sure enough. It was Tara.

His heart was racing, and he could feel the grin stretching across his face. Sounds around him faded. Everything faded. He was in another world as he kept reading.

> *Tim,*
>
> *I finally got in to get the message. It kept sending me to different places.*
>
> *Of course I remember you! You were my first love—my first boyfriend. My mother and I were talking about you not long ago.*
>
> *I was just in Ohio in October on book tour and drove by the Eaton exit and was telling my traveling companion about you.*
>
> *No, not a famous reporter, but I'm a* USA Today *best-selling author, believe it or not!*

There was more. Her mother was widowed and in Arizona. Tara was living in Albuquerque. Chum was dead.

*And, about breaking your heart, I hope not. I was a kid
breaking free of the binds my chauvinist father put on me, and
you got caught in the backlash. I always cared about you, and
the way I remember feeling, I would have come back in the
end—I just didn't know how to communicate that. I also wasn't
ever confident that you really loved me. My issue, not yours.*

I'm looking forward to hearing from you.

Tara

Of course I remember you, she'd written. Deep down he'd known
she would. She wouldn't forget him. How could she after all the things
they'd done together?

Now he had to come up with some witty response. Could he keep
her attention? He had to know details. Like, was she married? Did she
have kids? Was she married? When was she traveling to his part of the
country again? Was she married?

Was she happy without him?

He was going through a rough time. But just because he'd realized
that most of his life's unhappiness was tied up in his loss of her didn't
mean that she'd suffered similarly. She could be happily married.

But she'd said, *I look forward to hearing from you.* He read the words
again.

I look forward to hearing from you. She must want him to write her
back.

He hit reply and typed. There was so much to tell her. So much he
had to say.

Whether she was happily married or not.

I didn't close my e-mail program.

I grabbed up the three-hundred-page line-edited manuscript I had
to make it through that day. I stared at all the scrawled handwriting,

the changes my editor had made. And the notes she'd made in the margins—all issues I had to tend to. And I watched the e-mail icon in the bar at the bottom of my computer screen. Was a message coming in?

He could have had my message in seconds. And have had it read in another minute or two. Could be typing a reply . . .

Or he could be away from his desk.

I got up. Went into the bathroom. Came back out. Stepped outside the office for some warm desert sunshine on the cool January day.

I was forty-seven, not eighteen. I had a life. Had to think about where I wanted to live for the next month or so—I already knew where I going to settle. I was going to move to Phoenix where my mother was.

I visited her several times a year and loved it there. Even more than I loved Albuquerque.

I just had to figure out logistics. And I'd been away from my computer long enough.

Still nothing.

He might have read my reply and moved on. His having searched for me didn't have to mean anything. With all of the social media available these days, people were commonly looking up old acquaintances, saying hi for old times' sake, and moving on.

Just because they could.

Tim had been that once-in-a-lifetime spark for me. That didn't mean I'd been that for him.

Or that it mattered, now. I was a very different woman from the girl he'd known.

I'd walked through hell and come out on the other side.

I'd found and accessed my inner strength.

And I had no interest in sex.

I sat. Clicked on the album for the current work in progress and forced myself to sink into the world that I'd created.

Until 12:57 PM. 2:57 PM his time. My icon popped up, followed by a flash of the message that had just come in.

It was dated January 22, 2007.

> *Tara: I can tell you're a writer (haha). Your life sounds great, I'm very proud of you. I'm at work right now. I will send you an e-mail later tonight to catch you up. Note my cell #. I would love to hear your voice.*
> *Talk later, Tim*

I stared at the number at the bottom of the page. He told me to note it. So I did. I memorized it. But I wasn't calling him.

I had no idea what he wanted from me. Or what I could give him. But my heart was pounding. What would his letter say? How much of himself was he going to share with me?

I wanted to know it all.

Twenty-seven years had passed since I'd heard from him, and with one e-mail I was right back where I'd been at twenty.

Aching for him.

Chapter Nineteen

THE AFTERNOON WAS LONG. I DIDN'T HEAR FROM CHRIS, but I hadn't expected to. He was done with me. I understood that. I got through about 100 pages of changes. And when 3:00 PM arrived, 5:00 PM for Tim in Ohio, quitting time I surmised, I started to watch the computer again. Each time a new e-mail popped up my stomach jumped.

His name popped up at 3:46 PM my time. Forty-six minutes after he'd gotten off work.

I clicked on the post. And stopped once again. There was no letter. Just a note saying the letter was coming. But he'd attached a song. He asked me to listen to it.

"Hot August Night."

I clicked to play the song and closed my eyes, as I always did when I listened to Neil Diamond sing, and heard my big brother's voice.

And I knew that him sending me that song was a sign to me, from my brother, or from the universe, that talking to Tim was the right thing to do.

There was something else, too, which I told Tim in the e-mail I quickly sent back to him.

I know every word of the song—as well as every other song Neil Diamond sings. I've seen him live more times than I can count.

*And how ironic is this? I spent the day doing line edits
on a book that I wrote several months ago. It takes place in
Ohio—with the whole catalyst of the mystery revolving around
something that happened at Wright State University twenty-
one years ago.*

Tim and I had happened there, too, more than twenty years before.

I knew that the cascading events—me signing up for Classmates.
com, the events the day before with Chris, the Neil Diamond song,
and the book connection—were more than coincidence. I was being
hit over the head with signs that what was happening was meant to be
for some reason.

I couldn't have stayed away from Tim if I'd had to—not even to save
my life.

I couldn't leave the office, either. Not until I'd read the letter he was
sending. It came in a long hour later. I looked at the signature first, and
froze. He'd signed *Lots of Love, Tim.*

Oh my God. I read those words. I read them again. My insides
danced. And then clenched with fear. I ordered myself to calm down.
And I just kept looking at those words.

Lots of Love. My signature from so many years ago.

We weren't kids anymore.

I wasn't Tara Gumser anymore. I couldn't feel attraction or desire.
Tara Taylor Quinn didn't need them. She was a writer, and the only sex
in her life was in her books. My books. Tara Taylor Quinn had writer
friends and professional associations. She did not have sex.

That's when I remembered that I still didn't know if he was free.

I saw the lights come on in the house. Chris was home and I hadn't
made dinner. Or poured Cognac. I hadn't been in the house at all. I'd
booked my hotel room for one more night.

And then Tim's words obliterated all other thought.

Tara:

I just want you to know that I'm so happy to hear from you. I never had any doubts that you would be famous someday. I remember your older brother. We were at your house and sitting at the dining room table. I can still remember to this day that he played "Hot August Night" by Neil Diamond. Whenever I hear that song I always think of that day and you.

I never married but was in a relationship for the past twenty some years until about six months ago when she left me for another man. One who would marry her. They got married this past fall and she's pregnant already.

He caught me up on his life then. His mother was gone. And his brother Mike, too, who had died suddenly of a heart attack on Thanksgiving a few years before.

He mentioned my dad, too, telling me that he knew my father had never liked him.

Tara, the one thing that I want you to know is that I was very much in love with you. I know our relationship seemed physical all the time, but at that time I didn't really know how to express my true feelings. To this day I regret how I treated you and made you feel. So, please don't ever doubt how I felt about you. The biggest regret I have is when I let you walk away from me that day in the hall when you asked for your ring back. I didn't want you to know how much that hurt. I should have gone after you. I'm sorry for that. I don't mean to be too sentimental about the past, but it does bother me that things ended so suddenly and without any emotions on my part. Every now and then I catch myself thinking back to that cold and rainy Oct. day when this cute little blonde haired girl from my geology class talked to me. You had me from that

*moment. I can remember that next Monday trying to find you
everywhere on campus. I even had Steve looking for you, and
then there you and Ann were outside the library.*

*Whenever I meet someone, I always judge my feelings about
them based on that good feeling I had when I met you at
October Daze. Oh, by the way I would have taken you back in
a heartbeat.*

*Let's talk soon. You know it's very intimidating writing a let-
ter to an accomplished writer such as yourself!*

Lots of Love to You!!!

Tim

I finished the letter, and my blurred gaze went immediately back to
the top of the page. "Tara, the one thing that I want you to know . . ."

I was sobbing by the time I got through that paragraph a second
time. He couldn't possibly have known, but Tim had just given me
back a piece of myself.

For all these years, I'd felt like I'd given Tim something precious and
he'd just used me. I'd felt like the whore that James had called me. Like
maybe James had been right and I had something wrong with me—
something that called out to men, inviting them to do bad things to me.
And it hadn't been that way at all. I'd given myself to a man I adored. A
man who'd loved me, too. A man who'd still been boy enough to fumble
at communicating his feelings. It hadn't been lust that had driven Tim's
behavior, but the love I'd believed in.

I read the letter a couple of times more, slowly, taking it all in. Maybe
this was why Tim had found me now, right at the time I was coming to
terms with myself and taking control of my life. Was he there to set me
fully and completely free from the binds of my past?

From the belief that I was somehow bad?

My face was still wet with tears as I read the closing over and over.
Lots of Love. The exact words I'd used all those years ago when I'd

needed to tell him I loved him, but couldn't come right out and say the words without him having done so first.

My fingers flew on the keyboard.

Tim,

I'm leaving my office and I have plans this evening but I've got much to say about your letter. The universe has been active today and I am very thankful. More on that tomorrow.

Send me your address and I'll send you a book to read.

Sleep well.

Tara

Sleep well. It was warm. Loving. Without committing to any more than a re-connection between old friends.

Still, with a smile on my face, and a huge weight lifted from my life, I locked up the office, walked out to my car, and went to meet a local writer friend I'd called earlier in the day. She was divorced, had a huge house, and was struggling to make ends meet. By evening's end we'd agreed that, as of the next day, I was her new boarder.

⁓

The next morning, after a night's sleep filled with dreams of Tim, I checked out of the hotel, drove through a local fast-food place for a diet cola, and headed straight for my office. My head was spinning with things to say to Tim.

I had two critical deadlines pressing down on me. I'd just signed papers to end my marriage. And I was walking with a lilt in my step.

I didn't even notice if Chris was still in the house as I took the paved path around back. I couldn't get to my desk fast enough.

I bypassed my usual morning album, and seconds after I was inside the room, Neil Diamond's voice filled the space. I felt like it was a hot August night.

There was another message from Tim.

You are a true mystery writer Miss Tara: "I have much to
say about your letter! More tomorrow."

His address followed and then . . .

Lots of love
Tim

Lots of love. Again. He was putting something out there. I had to
find out what it was. The fact that I was no longer capable of fully
engaging in a relationship wasn't even enough to stop me. We were
a continent apart. A full relationship was out of the question anyway.

And as I scrolled through my inbox, I saw that he'd written to me
later that night as well.

Tara: Just a quick note. I just realized that there
was a link in your signature attached to your website.
I went to it and was very impressed! Tim

He'd read up on me. And now he knew I was successful. That I'd
made something of my life. There was a picture of Chris and me on
my website.

And Tim was backing up. He'd signed the post, simply, Tim. No love
anywhere. Not even a *Have a nice day*.

I panicked.

I wasn't going to lose him again.

Lose him? I didn't have him. Couldn't have him. I wasn't a
complete woman anymore. I was TTQ, a successful, two-dimensional
stand-in for the person Tara had been. I was being totally honest now.
No more hiding or pretending. A part of me had died that night with
James on the country road. TTQ was the person who'd emerged from
the darkness. She was my protection. And my strength.

And Tim's hints of love were threatening TTQ's stability.

But apparently parts of Tara had survived. And apparently that girl had more of a say over my life than I realized.

And so I began what turned out to be a flurry of e-mails over the next twenty-four hours.

> *Tim,*
>
> *I was very touched about your memory of my brother and Neil Diamond. Out of the blue you write that—without knowing that Neil is the connection we all keep to him.*
>
> *I'm so sorry to hear about your brother. I remember him. I loved being at his house; it felt safe and full of love and family.*
>
> *I don't remember that my father didn't like you. I actually can't ever remember the two of you being in the same room! Wonder why I blocked that? Maybe because I was blocking him so I could breathe. What I do remember is how much my mother adored you. She was always after me to be good to you and encouraged me to spend time with you.*
>
> *Do you still lift weights?*

I deleted the line. And then put it back in. And then TTQ took over again, philosophizing because that's what she did. Life had taught her a lot. She talked to him about finding perfect moments amid the cacophony of life. She talked to him about her writer friends. And about how hard the public aspects of her job used to be for her. I wanted him to know and understand TTQ. To know that I was TTQ. And then Tara popped up again.

> *That's what's so nice about you. You just know me—without all the trappings—and you're reminding me of who I really am, the person inside. You wrote to me without knowing or caring anything about my career.*

It's nice. Very nice. Sometimes I lose track of the girl I used to be and I miss her a lot.

I've thought about you a lot over the years and want to hear about your life.

Thanks for listening. It's done my heart very good to meet up with you again.

A wave of fear passed over me and TTQ swooped in.

I'm out of here for today. I'm on deadline and this week is going to have some late nights, but if I start this early in the week, I'll be in trouble by the end. So . . . until tomorrow . . .
Tara

Tim was at home alone, pushing himself to the limit on the treadmill that night. In twenty-four hours his entire life had turned upside down. Tara was there! And yet . . . she wasn't. She was answering him. But her letters were so formal. Because she was blowing him off?

When he heard the new message alert on his computer on the other side of the spare bedroom that was both workout room and office, he flipped the treadmill off and went to see what she'd written.

Parts of the post didn't sound like his Tara. But other parts did.

And as he read her exposition of her life, he started to understand a bit better.

Out of everything she'd written, those lines stood out. He read them again. And wrote back immediately.

I'd left the office, but I didn't leave Tim behind. I pulled up my e-mail on my smartphone and watched for a reply to my post. My stomach was in knots. His name popped up while I was in my car in the parking lot of a pizza place. I was taking dinner home to my new landlord and her kid.

Okay, I needed that. I had no idea what I was walking into. I just kept thinking that I was pouring out my heart to you and telling you how much you mean to me now and in past years, and all you were giving me was this journalist view of your life. I never even once thought of you as this person who received fan mail and dealt with all the other stuff that goes with being out in the public. Again, my view of you is this cute little blonde girl who broke my heart at Wright State. I can now understand why you were so matter of fact in your conversations—duh, I get it now. Forgive me, I was only thinking of myself and my emotions and not taking yours into account. Please just feel safe with me. I HAVE NO HIDDEN MOTIVE, only want to reconnect after a lot of years and catch up.

I want to find out more about your past and listen to your feelings. I'm good at reading between the lines, and I feel and hear a lot of pain. We can share that later if you want. Mostly I want you to know I will always listen if you need. Talk later.

P.S. You really sounded like you need a hug today.

Tim

I hit reply, but couldn't see the small keyboard on my phone through my tears. I took the pizza home. I went to bed. And wished that I could lay my head on Tim's chest and go to sleep.

Twenty

THE NEXT MORNING WHEN I OPENED MY E-MAIL, THERE
was another message from Tim in my inbox. And I opened the post
with mixed emotions. I needed Tim so desperately. And I couldn't be
the other half of his whole.

Tara,

*I thought about you a lot over the years and always won-
dered how you were doing, and what you were doing. Do you
remember when I came to see you in the summer of 1980 after
we had broken up? You were engaged to some guy named
James. And you were different. I've always wondered why.*

*The other day I was reading the letters you wrote to me from
Armstrong. They were cute, and I loved them. I'm going to scan
them and send them to you, to remind you of who you were,
in case you have forgotten. Because the truth is, no matter how
famous you get I just can't see you that way. I will always see
you as my October Daze girl. Oh, by the way I have a newspaper clipping of the article you wrote for the Dayton Daily News
about the commissioner's race. That was the night you shushed
me when I was trying to talk to you.*

*Tara, I'm really sad to see that you have such thick walls. I
understand why, but you have to let some people in your life.*

I know it can be difficult to let people see your heart because
they can easily break it, but a broken heart is just like anything
else broken—it can be put back together with the right glue and
touch.

I really like talking with you and hearing about your life. I
don't want you to worry about saying or doing the right thing,
just let it out and be yourself. I like that.

Well, October, I've got to go. I'm killing my spell check and
grammar check (I've never seen so many red and green lines).

Take Care of Yourself.

Love you,

Tim

Oh, God. He was doing it to me again. Pulling me into him. Just like
he had in geology class all those years ago. I had to say no. Even if we
didn't live a country apart, I couldn't give him anything but friendship.
I couldn't do this—couldn't let him consume my life. Couldn't let
something build between us.

My heart didn't listen to me. It listened to him.

It was almost impossible to believe that only two days had passed
since I'd first heard from Classmates.com. My entire universe had
tilted.

I wrote back to him first thing. Or, rather, TTQ did.

Okay, I have to say, I love the part about red and green
lines! I feel for your spell check! Those lines are some of my best
friends, you know, so watch how you treat them!

And I'd love to see the letters I sent from Armstrong. I have
such mixed emotions about that time in my life. That's where I
met James. So much for safety and security at this little clois-
tered church school!

I remember that day you came to the house. I remember

being so confused and feeling trapped by everything. Everyone
wanted something from me, expected things from me, and I
was so lost. I was struggling to put one foot in front of the other.
I was trying so hard to do what I thought was right. I think the
fact that I agreed to see you was very telling.

I'm very very sorry I hurt you. It was not knowingly. I had
no idea how much you honestly cared. I wish I'd known. I
really thought you were prompted by a part of your anatomy
a little farther down than the heart. If it gives you any sense of
justice, I suffered hugely. The universe didn't let me hurt some-
one and run off into the sunset.
Tara

And as soon as I finished the note to Tim, I sent out an S.O.S. to my
two closest writer friends.

"I'm in over my head," I wrote to them. I told them about Tim.
About the past two days. And I asked them if I was making a mistake.
If I was doing something wrong. If I was being selfish. After all, Chris
and I had just signed divorce papers. I wasn't even moved out of his
house yet.

In just moments I heard back.

Tara,
You are separated. You should be divorced. But you ARE
definitely separated. You can do any damn thing you want to
do, including having conversations with an old college friend.

That definitely does NOT make you selfish. You have stuck
with Chris far longer than he deserves, and he has abused and
misused you emotionally. You deserve to feel special . . .

And in the same batch of mail was a one-line note from Tim.

> *Finally, Tara has arrived! Welcome, glad you could join me.*
> *Tim*

He was pushing me. I was tense. Scared. And so driven to connect with him that I couldn't listen to reason. I didn't answer him, either. And a couple of hours later, I heard from him again.

> *Okay, you're in the pool with no life preserver. Start swim-*
> *ming! I finally got to look a little deeper inside your life. Can I*
> *hear more about your relationship with James? Did you guys*
> *have any good moments?*
> *Tim*

Tim didn't really want to hear about James. He wanted to know her, and he was frustrated as hell. The epistles she was sending him were a smokescreen. One that was easy for him to see through.

There were things she wasn't telling him, and if they were going to have half a hope of making it this time, he had to know what those things were.

Making it this time?

Was he really considering the idea that he and Tara had a future together?

Tim asked the question, but he already knew the answer. He'd lost twenty-seven years of his life for needing this woman. He couldn't let her just slip away again.

And it wasn't just his own need that drove him. He could feel Tara's pain between the lines of her letters. He had to help.

But first he had to get her to tell him what he was helping with.

He watched for her response to his challenge. And read it as soon as it came through.

I don't speak about James. He's never mentioned in my pres-
ence. Ever. Not by anyone. My mother and I have never spoken
about him since the whole thing happened. Even my husband,
Chris, never knew a thing about him. If there's something spe-
cific you'd like to know about him, ask. I can't just brainstorm
him. I suppose there must have been good moments. I can't
remember any.
Tara

It wasn't enough. Not nearly. His fingers tripped over themselves as
he typed.

What the hell? Her husband?

Okay, you're floating, not swimming! Put your head under
the water and get wet all over! First of all, I thought you and
James were married. I didn't realize that there was someone
else! Can you talk about that? Also, what is your situation
now???????????? I'm confused. I've been waiting for you to tell me
all this.
Tim

He went to work as soon as he hit send. If Tara was married, he'd
best get a grip on his heart. And the best anecdote to a man's bleeding
heart was diversion.

He didn't see her response until much later that night.

Don't get frustrated with me. I don't do well with tension.
I'm writing this from my phone. So it's going to look and sound
weird. And u have no idea how far for me my head is under
water. I don't generally talk about Tara in a private sense. U
already know more than most of my closest friends. The deal is
u ask I'll try to answer. U get mad at me I stop.

I'll have to explain my husband tomorrow when I can really type. For now can u just relax and be content that we're talking at all?

Tim didn't sleep much that night.

⁓

Thursday morning I held my breath as I opened my e-mail client. Would there be a note from Tim? Or had I pushed him away again?

I told myself either way it would be okay, but I knew it wouldn't be okay. Either way. I couldn't bear to lose Tim again.

And we'd never be a couple again, either.

I saw his name in my inbox and didn't even pretend to notice other mail.

Sometimes I have to prime the pump a little to get any water, but you're doing fine. You are finally starting to sound like someone I knew before.
Tim

I paced my office. And when the walls were too confining, I went outside to walk along the edge of the desert behind the house that had been my home for so many empty years.

I hadn't seen or heard from Chris since Sunday night. At some point we had to make arrangements for me to get the rest of my things out of the house. To get my share of the furniture, though all I really wanted was my family heirlooms and my kitchen. The dishes and pots and pans and utensils were all my personal choices.

I'd paid my friend for a month's rent. Hopefully the dissolution paperwork would be done by then. I could pack a moving truck and head to Phoenix. And sometime between now and then, I had to call my mother and let her know what was going on.

And I had to make a decision about Tim. He wasn't accepting Tara Taylor Quinn. He wanted Tara.

Could I give her to him?

And be strong enough to recover when he moved on?

My answer came in the form of another question: Can you live with yourself if you don't at least try?

I sat down to write what was probably going to be the hardest letter of my life.

⁓

Tim slept to escape. He'd been headlong on a course to live a miracle and Tara apparently had a husband. Or used to. He hoped. He'd been pushing her to give him her intimate confessions, her innermost thoughts, and he'd been out of place doing so if she was married.

Was that why she was so newsy and standoffish? So distant? Because she'd only been connecting with an old friend while he'd been running off into the sunset with her?

Clearly she was it for Tim. He'd wasted years of two women's lives. Hurt two women by his inability to love wholly and completely.

There was nothing new on his computer when he hauled his ass out of bed just after six the next morning. But then, there wouldn't have been. It was only 4:00 AM her time.

Out in the shop most of the morning, he didn't get to his e-mail at work right away, either. And that had been his choice. At least partially. They'd had a machine break down. But one of the technicians could probably have handled it.

By lunchtime, he couldn't hold himself off any longer. As she'd promised, Tara had e-mailed him. He wasn't sure he wanted to read what she'd sent.

He had to know.

Tim,

I didn't sleep much last night. My husband's name is
Chris . . .

The office bustled around him, engineers talking, phones ringing,
people walking by—all buffers to his imminent crash and burn. Tara
gave him a very brief overview of a marriage that sounded as though it
was empty at best, and Tim was jealous anyway.

I signed the divorce papers on Sunday. I haven't seen or
spoken with Chris since, and don't expect to do so. I'm renting a
suite of rooms from a friend.

I'm guessing you don't realize it, but you've scored tremen-
dously this week. I'm telling you because I want you to know
you mattered. I rarely leave the protection of Tara Taylor
Quinn. She's how I've survived. Tara is in hiding a good bit of
the time. I guess it sounds schizophrenic, but I've come to learn
that it's really quite normal. Especially when you have to be in
the public eye.

Over the years, TTQ slowly overtook the majority of my
persona. I know she can handle anything. She's the one who
told Chris, after ten years of marriage, that I could only be his
friend, nothing more. I moved my things out of our room and
into the second master suite twelve years ago.

You think I was deliberately withholding stuff, making you
drag it out, and yet I was putting more out there than I ever do.
I just don't want you to think I was being disrespectful to you or
demeaning you in any way. Whenever I write to anyone—with
the exception of two or three people, my posts are signed TTQ.
Always. That's me. You got Tara right from the start.

She didn't sign her name.

I didn't pretend to work while I waited for his response. I dusted the bookshelves. Took a walk in the desert. Drove to the store for more diet cola.

And when Tim's letter came, I accepted that I was in way over my head and, heart pounding in my chest, sat down to read.

> *Tara:*
>
> *Just for the record I'm not trying to score points or keep score, but explain what the meaning of "you've scored tremendously." I don't scare easily, so be assured of that. You made my day, when you said "you mattered" and by letting me know I had your special signature. I'm sitting at my desk smiling. By the way, I want to give you some emotional homework for this weekend. Go and rent the movie* The Notebook *and watch it and tell me about it afterward. Talk to you tonight.*
> *Tim*

The sun was shining brighter again, like we'd weathered the storm. I wrote right back to him.

> *Tim,*
>
> *I own the movie* The Notebook. *Just saw it again about a month ago. My feeling afterward . . . I screwed up. I'm never going to have that. Followed by, it's just a movie. And then, damn that was good storytelling. And then, okay . . . I think that's the most important thing on earth—to share a love that deep. And that made me sad. At which time I turned on* Without a Trace. *And then* Mary Poppins.
>
> *Scored tremendously, didn't mean as in keeping score, but scoring something, as in obtaining something.*

It's good to picture you smiling. You had the greatest smile. I think it's only fair that since you've seen my website—and therefore a recent picture of me—you should send me one of you.

And something else I want you to know is that I've only, to this day, dated three guys more than once. One was Chris. One was James. And the third was you.

Tara,

Ok, here is a picture of me at the finish line of a marathon I ran in Oct. Be warned, I'm showing some leg!!!!!!!!!!!!

Tim,

You aren't smiling. And I can't see your eyes. But you still sweat as much as you used to! You're in great shape!

Tara,

I'm not smiling because that is when I hurt my leg. . . . Send me a recent of yourself, but send to my home e-mail.

I don't want my work monitor to catch on fire!

Tim was flirting with me. And I'd responded. I felt guilty, there was no doubt about that. In twenty-two years of marriage I hadn't given Chris a single innuendo. I was leading Tim to think I could give him something I wasn't capable of giving.

And the repartee felt damned good.

We'd come twenty-seven years into the future, and yet we hadn't traveled a step. He wanted me. I was bone-deep in love with him. And I wasn't going to be able to sleep with him.

He'd mentioned fire. Like he knew I was sitting in it. Needing him there. And I knew better than to trust anyone to be there. Except me.

He'd asked me to call him.

I couldn't.

But I wanted to talk to him. So badly. I wanted to hear his voice—to know if these past three days had any basis in reality at all.

I was in too deep. Already.

Truth was, I'd been in too deep from the very first post. I just couldn't do casual, or confident and mature, with Tim Barney.

I knew his number. I could call him.

And I started to shake, just thinking about doing so.

Tim didn't even have his coat off before he was at the computer in his home office on Thursday, signing on to see if Tara had sent him a picture. He was embarking on the rest of his life—finally starting his life—and all of the emotions of the eighteen-year-old who'd needed her so badly were comingling with the very mature needs and desires of a forty-seven-year-old man and burning him alive.

The extent to which he was losing it was evident by the sudden jerk of his heart when he saw her name in his inbox. He opened the attachment first—and was instantly hard. He couldn't stop staring.

Tara was sitting at a slot machine. Her hair was a little longer, a bit more expensive looking, but those eyes were the same. So was the smile.

Eventually he made it to her words.

Tim,

This was taken in Las Vegas in September during an all-girl getaway. I'd just won a jackpot. And I was freezing in the casino, which explains the cape. TTQ is very TTQish. She wears tight jeans, tank tops, and lots of fur, black leather, and fringe. Unless she's making public appearances; then it's always suits. But always, even on days when she's slumming, she wears gorgeous jewelry. Please note the purse that she got from an art

gallery in New Orleans after coveting it for three days. She's a
bag lady on the side and this is one of her prized possessions.
She usually only carries it when it matches her outfit, but this
was an extreme circumstance.
Tara

He looked at the picture again, typed a quick message, and left the room. He had to do something, to stay busy. And remind himself that he was forty-seven, not eighteen. He was not going to embarrass himself.

Taking off his coat, he threw it over a chair and went into the kitchen to see about dinner. To feed at least one of his appetites.

I looked at the clock. He'd be home from work. Probably making dinner. I already knew his schedule. His habits. I should always have known them.

He was in my blood. In my soul. And I was a stranger to his life.

I picked up my phone. Looked at the keypad, visually punching out his number. I could hardly breathe just doing that much. I'd never be able to talk if I actually got up the guts to call.

"What are you afraid of?" I asked aloud, just to hear a voice outside my head.

I wish I had an answer to give me. I wasn't afraid of Tim. I wasn't afraid of the call going bad—that would free me from this craziness, right? Put me out of my sweet torture.

So was I afraid of the call going well? Because, in the end, it would be as empty as my marriage?

Tim was already frustrated with TTQ. I loved and needed her.

In the end, I pushed the numbers—in a text box. And quickly typed my message.

Can you get txt?

I put my phone down. Tried to focus on the cursor in front of me. A woman had just been raped on the page of my current work in progress. I couldn't think about her.

Jumping up, I paced to the other side of my office. Halfway there, I heard my phone announce an incoming txt.

I hit my hip on the corner of my desk as I raced to get the phone. And then I fumbled that, dropping a very expensive PDA on the floor.

The text message survived.

Yes. Who's this?

Who's this? Come on, I thought. He has to know. The number had a New Mexico exchange.

And now he had my number.

Would he call?

I hadn't invited him to do so.

Sick to my stomach, I paced again, clutching my phone to my chest. I just couldn't do this. It was time to get my life together, not fall apart. I'd promised myself I'd face my challenges head on.

How was I doing?

An e-mail had just come in. Thankful for the distraction, I went to see who'd contacted me. Please let it be one of my writer friends. Someone with a message for TTQ. Someone who would inadvertently bring TTQ rushing to Tara's rescue.

It was junk mail.

And I glanced at the text message on my phone.

Wow, my computer has smoke rolling out of it! Do you
IM? This may be easier for talking. Txt is not so good
for me—man fingers!

My fingers flew over the tiny keyboard on my phone.

> *Yes I IM. And if you're screwing with me and you really grew up to be some lascivious jerk who runs around out to get what you can get, then I'm really going to hate you.*

I hit send and regretted the action the second I'd pushed the button. I was scared to death. An eighteen-year-old nerd who'd never had a date.

I signed onto IM on my computer.

And had an e-mail from Tim.

> *Ouch! You will say anything to break my heart again! K, I'm signed on to my IM . . . Now what?*

He was right there, in real time—not an e-mail on the computer when I happened to get to it. Or he did.

I didn't want to type sentences back and forth like teenagers. I didn't have the patience for game playing. He'd asked me to call several times. It was obvious he wasn't going to be presumptuous and call me. He was letting me make the choice.

Biting my lip to help control the trembling, I dialed the number I'd been silently reciting for three days, left my seat, and paced. I wasn't going to be able to hear him if he answered. My heart was pumping blood so fast, the roaring was deafening.

"Hello?"

Oh my God. My whole body went weak. I almost dropped the phone again.

This wasn't some strange man on the phone. Or on the other end of e-mails. It was a voice I completely recognized.

"Hi."

"I can't believe you actually called."

"I know. I can't believe it either." I was shaking. Blinking back tears. And grinning. Hugely.

"What's going on?"

"Not much. Just taking a break from the writing."

"How's that going today?"

"Okay. Tough. What are you doing?"

"Making dinner."

Around my desk again, I pushed aside my chair, slid down to the floor and underneath my desk, leaning back against the inside wood. There was only so much exposure a girl like me could take.

Twenty-One

FORTY-FIVE MINUTES LATER, TIM AND I HAD NOT YET hung up. And there was still so much to say. Everything to talk about. I wanted to know the color of his socks.

And he wanted to know something else.

"What happened to you?"

I'd come out from under my desk and was lounging back in my chair. I straightened at the question, my chest tightening.

We'd been talking about the old days. College. Our time together.

"What do you mean?"

"You changed. Why?"

"I'm thirty years older! Of course I've changed. Life happened." TTQ came naturally to my rescue with a lighthearted tone.

"Not now. Then. When I came to see you the summer of 1980. You were different."

I didn't say anything. I couldn't. Everything was careening out of control. Sliding back under my desk, I willed my strength, my calm and confident resolve to find its way front and center.

"What happened is all I'm asking."

I was too raw. He was too new.

"That's not something I talk about. Ever. So, what's this thing you called a carry-in?"

He was having a carry-in at work the next day.

"Uh uh. What happened?"

"Tim, I'm not kidding. I don't talk about it. Period."

"Then we might as well hang up right now."

He didn't mean that. "You're being ridiculous!"

"I'm being serious. I mean it."

"Why?"

"Because if you're going to keep secrets, this doesn't work for me. I can't go back, or forward for that matter, if we aren't going to be completely open and honest with each other. If you were anyone else, okay, maybe, but not you. Not me and you."

My eyes filled with tears again. "You're asking the impossible."

"I don't think so."

"You have no idea."

"What's so hard about opening your mouth and speaking?"

"I open my mouth and no words come out."

"I don't buy that. Just say what's on your mind."

How could I get him to understand?

"On that topic, my mind goes blank. I open my mouth and all thoughts flee. I notice the carpet. A smudge on the windows . . ."

"Tara, what happened?"

"Tim, I swear, if I could talk about it I would. But I can't. I never have. Not to anyone. Ever."

"Then it's time."

"Please don't do this."

"I have to."

Strange as it was, I understood that. Some part of me recognized the truth of what he'd just said. He had to push me.

I felt trapped. Panicky. And didn't want to leave the safe enclosure of my desk.

"Can you at least give me some time? This is the first time we've talked in almost thirty years. Can't we just take things as they come for a bit?"

"You're going to tell me what happened."

"If I can." He'd be disgusted. Hate me for what I'd allowed to happen when I hadn't let him . . . He wouldn't want me. What man would? James had been right about that. But then, I didn't want him to want me. I couldn't give him what he'd need if he wanted me.

"You can."

I wasn't innocent. Or sweet. Even after all these years, I was still defiled. I knew what bad stuff felt like. What James had done to me was a part of me.

It was something I would never, ever forget.

Or get over.

Even if Tim could get by the incident, he wouldn't want a Tara who couldn't make love with him.

"I'll do my best, Tim, but, please, just leave it for now?" I just wanted to love him long-distance for a while. Because I did love him. With all of my heart. But I knew that once anything more was asked of me, I was going to freeze up.

I hadn't had a sexual reaction since the night James had taken me for a drive on a country road.

Tim and I talked for a while longer, about all kinds of things, and by the time we hung up it was clear to both of us that we were something to each other. Something big. But with severe limitations.

I was his. I'd always been his. And he had no idea that I was turned off by even the thought of a penis.

⁓

Tim was so jazzed up he couldn't sit. Couldn't watch television or get to work painting the living room—or do anything that took any real focus. He'd had no idea that coming back to life after a twenty-seven-year hibernation would be so painful.

Or so fantastic, either.

But he had to play it cool. This was all or nothing for him. And Tara was struggling. He couldn't risk scaring her off.

For either of their sakes.

When he gave up trying to get any real sleep and got up and ready for work, he wrote the e-mail quickly, without overthinking it.

Tara,

> *Good morning, I didn't sleep a wink all night. Hope you got some rest. I wanted to take a few and say hi and tell you I really enjoyed our conversation last night. Let's keep it real, no games, okay . . . Time will tell what will happen. Now get to work!!!!!!!!! You have deadlines, and I don't want to be the cause of you missing them. Have a great day.*

Tim

I woke up on top of the world. I was still me. Incredibly conflicted. But a long-ago wave of happiness was filtering through me, too. Something was completely right with my world.

Lying in bed, I read Tim's e-mail on my phone. I answered him from my phone, too.

Tim,

> *No games. Thanks for the "good morning."*
> *I'd love a recent picture where I can actually see your eyes. And your smile.*

Tara

And when he called midmorning, I answered on the first ring. But I was deep into the book. Into darkness. A darkness that I had taken on as my own. Or maybe the story was coming from my own.

I wasn't sure anymore.

I felt exposed. Afraid Tim would tell someone something I'd told him. My business was my own. It had always been my own. There was safety in that.

I was short with Tim. And then texted him to apologize. I was a nervous wreck. The host of a battle that was raging inside of myself. Just like I'd been in 1977. I couldn't do this again.

I wasn't going to get any closer to Tim.

I'd made up my mind. Was resolute. Calm.

Right up until Tim's e-mail came in late that afternoon.

Good evening, Sunshine:

Let's get some things straight. First of all, I told you that I'm your safe place and that means whatever you send or tell me is completely between us.

So, calm yourself down and take a deep breath, concentrate on your work at hand, and rest assured that I will be near. Okay?

P.S. Also, my favorite snack is chocolate milk and peanut butter and I'm enjoying that right now.

Tim

The last line made me smile.

And that was my Tim—making me feel good even when I felt horrible.

On Saturday, I had us all figured out. Tim and I were going to be long-distance best friends. There for each other, but with our own separate lives. Something about the idea bothered me. But it fit. My mother was in Arizona and the Southwest was my home. I suffered from seasonal depression and couldn't tolerate the cold. I communed with mountains and blue skies and sunshine. Tim's career, the home he owned, was in Ohio.

And even if we were in the same state, I couldn't give him the physical relationship he was bound to want.

Feeling like I'd reached a truce between the two sides battling inside me, I opened my e-mail program to get the message I was sure Tim would have waiting for me. He'd attached another song.

Tara,
*   The song that I wanted you to wake up to. Enjoy it,*
Sunshine.
Tim

It was Neil Diamond's "Hello, Again."

Tim called me while I had the tune playing for the fourth time. I'd told him I was going to be in my office working all weekend.

I muted the computer as I grabbed my phone.

"Hi!" I grabbed the chain around my neck, playing with it, wishing he could see the jeans and short-sleeve shirt I was wearing. I wanted him to know I was still cute. Still worth his time.

And then I stopped myself. I had no right wanting Tim to be physically attracted to me. I was completely frigid.

"What's up?"

"Just getting ready to start work."

"Did you work out this morning?"

"Yeah. I don't usually on Saturdays but I missed a couple of days earlier this week and I needed the stress relief." I'd told him about the full gym up at the clubhouse in the private community where I lived. I'd lose membership there as soon as the divorce was final.

"Tim, I need to ask you something."

"Shoot."

"What went wrong with you and Denise?"

"I loved Denise, but with a love that could never fully come out. Partly due to the fact the she was so emotionally tuned in to herself and herself only. She never really seemed to get that even though I was a guy, I had feelings, too. I could tell her what I wanted, emotionally, and she would give me what she wanted me to have. Which I think led to a lot of resentment on both parts. At the same time, I wasn't giving her the one thing I guess she needed more than anything else."

"Marriage?"

"Right. To me, the love, the relationship, the closeness was what mattered. Apparently not to her."

"But you just said your love never fully came out, so even if the closeness was what mattered to her, she didn't really have it."

"Maybe. Anyway, when I was away from her I'd miss her, but when I got home, there was no sharing of mutual feeling between us. She always seemed to be more of a spectator than a participant, no matter what we were doing. Like she was biding her time, waiting for something before we started to really live life. So I guess that's how love turns to hate. Hate for the fact that the person you're trying so hard to love won't, or can't, acknowledge your feelings."

"I'm guessing you could be describing her, too, huh? Since what she needed was for you to love her enough to commit to a lifetime with her." I felt sorry for this woman I'd never met.

"Yeah. Can I ask you something?"

"Of course." That's what we were about, right? Tim and I could tell each other anything.

"If Chris were to ask you to come back to him, would you?"

"No." I tried not to notice the clock, the knots in my stomach over the pages waiting to be written. I could not let my life mess up my career. It was the one thing I'd done completely right. TTQ was my success story.

She was also my sole means of support.

"Are you sure?"

"Yes."

"How can you be so sure?"

I could have said I could because Chris had had a call girl in our home. Or that he'd walked me up to a wall and I was afraid that next time he might break more than a china angel. I told him the reason that far surpassed either of those.

"Because of you."

If I'd learned nothing else in my twenty-seven years of adult living, I'd learned this. I was in love with Tim Barney. Period. He'd been my one and only.

I wasn't going to be with Tim. I knew that. I wasn't ever going to be more than a long-distance and, I hoped, close friend.

And yet, in some strange way, I belonged to him. And knowing that, how could I possibly belong to anyone else?

Someone from Tim's work beeped in and he had to go—he was on call that weekend. The timing was unfortunate.

And I didn't hear from him for the rest of the day. I managed to distract myself with work until evening, but when I got to my friend's house, I found her and her kids out for the evening. I was still working from my laptop, but I couldn't seem to stop my head from playing with me.

I'd been too forward. Said too much. I had too many issues. Was too uptight. And standoffish. I wasn't eighteen anymore. I'd made horrible choices in my life that had led to horrible things.

I texted him. Several times.

You don't have to do this.

And a little while later.

It's not too late to stop.

On my next break I sent another message.

I told you I'm intense.

Later that night my mood had changed yet again.

Where are you?

And when I finished work for the day, I just needed facts.

If you're backtracking, please let me know.

He didn't answer. And when it was past the time he should be home and in bed, I called him. He didn't answer then, either.

By the time Elaine got home, I'd had a couple of glasses of wine and had convinced myself it was all for the best.

My life and Tim's were too dichotomous. I was big city. He was small town. I was warmth and sunshine. He was cold and snow.

I was frigid. He was on fire.

As soon as I got this book done I was going to start planning my move to Phoenix. I had to arrange for a moving company. Find a place to rent.

I had to tell my Mom that Chris and I were through.

Before I went to bed I sent Tim one last text, apologizing for all of the text messages.

⁓

Tim didn't get Tara's text messages until late. Too late. He'd been at a friend's house most of the night playing cards. A time-out.

Tara had been back in his life less than a week and already she was his everything. The thought of her there, not quite divorced, with the man she'd spent twenty-some years with close by had freaked him out.

Or so he told himself.

What really got to him was her. Since she'd broken his heart at eighteen he'd been his own man. In his deepest heart, at least. A part of him had remained emotionally detached. Free.

That small, undetached part of him was his safety valve. He understood that now.

With Tara, there was no safety valve.

But he'd told her he was her safe place. That he'd always be there.

And, instead, he'd been out playing cards.

He owed her the bone-deep truth.

Sitting down at his computer in a still dark house, he put his fingers on the keyboard and began to type:

> *Tara*
>
> *Good morning. Please note the time (6:00 AM, another sleepless night). I have something to explain.*
>
> *First, thanks for the text messages. I'd turned off my phone, which is something I never do, but I did. Anyway, please don't stop texting. I look forward to your messages. They show me that you are thinking about me and you do care about me.*
>
> *Now for the hard part. In my life I have lived with a lot of walls. In the past six months I realized that my walls had shut everyone out. So I set out to change that. I wanted to see the outside world again. Good news is that I have been moderately successful. I can see and feel more clearly than I ever have. That's why I had the courage to get in contact with you.*
>
> *But as usually happens, it's not all that easy or clear. You were my first love, and first loves always own a piece of your heart. But more than that, it's like you have a free pass anytime, anywhere, to walk right into my heart and do as you please. That's a bit tough for a guy like me to take.*
>
> *That's one reason why I've been trying to get to your deepest feelings. Turns out you're even more guarded than I am. I know I want us to move forward.*
>
> *In one of your text messages last night you said it was my choice. But I made my choice last Sunday when I got in touch with you, and I'm sticking to it.*
>
> *Whether we move forward is your choice.*
>
> *Tim*

Tim,

I'm going to try my best to get this out here. Where I am with you. I can't explain why I care about someone I've not heard from in thirty years. Last night I was awake, completely and totally consumed with fear. I'm afraid, because my feelings for you override reason.

I crave our conversations right now. I want to be there for you. It's something I feel, this desire to be there for you. Beyond that, I have no idea.

I hope this all sits well with you.
Tara

Okay, sunshine. Since we're putting it all out there . . .

I know there is something eating away at you. It's standing between us just like I told you it would. There's a secret between us.

Tara, whatever happened to you, to change you, please tell me. This will help you let your demons go once and forever. I know what happens when the sun goes down and the house is quiet. That's when they come out.

When I send you e-mails, you respond to certain aspects of my conversation only, and just kind of flow past other things. You don't tell your life history or inner thoughts to just anyone. I get that. But you can with me. I want you to. I don't want Tara Taylor Quinn. I want Tara.

Hope this helps, and as always, any time day or night, you can call me, for anything.
Tim

Tim,

You're right in that there are many things I don't say. I'm blocked. I didn't do it consciously, and I can't seem to *consciously unblock me, either. Something happened. I know what. I just can't talk about it. Or even think about it.*

And yes, at the moment, I'm all TTQish again. For one thing, I have a couple of business calls to make this morning. And for another, TTQ is very secure, safe, accomplished, and I feel strong when I'm her. People don't walk on her—they respect her. (Except those who hate her, and I'm okay with that.) I want to be her someday.

Oh wait, I am her. The only problem is, she's just the surface me.

Tara

And with that I took myself back. Or at least that's what I told myself as I sank down into the book Monday morning. I was hiding. I knew it. Tim probably knew it, too. I just couldn't stop myself.

I also hadn't considered, for one second, the idea that I'd ever have to visit the James part of my life again. Tim had wanted me to swim in the deep end, but what he didn't understand was that I was in way over my head.

And didn't know how to swim.

Twenty-Two

THAT NEXT WEEK TIM AND I TALKED EVERY DAY, SOME-
times several times in a day. And between phone calls we sent text
messages, e-mailed each other, and got on instant messaging on the
computer whenever we could, too.

We told each other everything about our daily lives. He knew how
many pages I wrote each day. What I had for dinner. And what time I
went to bed at night. He knew if Elaine's kids were home or with their
father. And whether or not she and I had found any time to talk. He
knew when I heard from my writer friends.

He knew I was dreading the phone call to my mother to tell her
about Chris. Mom didn't even know that Chris and I had maintained
separate rooms.

I heard all about the ball games he went to and the buddy he
occasionally had drinks with. I heard about the fence he was fixing,
the tools he was designing, and the living room he was getting ready
to paint. I heard when he washed his truck or needed to clean his
bathroom. And I always knew what he was making for dinner. I even
knew when his clothes were clean.

And I knew that he wanted to have sex with me. Innuendo was
seeping into our conversations. Covertly at first, and then more boldly.

I played along as best I could. What could it hurt? It was only conversation. We were a continent apart. But I felt like a time bomb that was going to explode. I just didn't know when.

What we didn't do was speak of love. Any kind of love.

The following Saturday, one week after we'd had our talk about our exes, I went to the office early, needing to work on *The Baby Gamble*, the romance that was due to Harlequin by the fifteenth of the month.

As I'd come to expect, there was an e-mail from Tim waiting. What I didn't expect was for it to turn me inside out all over again.

> *Tara: Have u ever heard this song? This is exactly how I feel about u.*
>
> *I have been listening to it a lot lately and now want share it with u.*
>
> *Please listen carefully to the words.*
> *Tim*

I listened. And started to cry—the first tears I'd shed all week. The song was about heaven—how he'd found heaven with me in the past, and now again in the present. About holding me in his arms. About how there was nothing that could ever come between us again. I loved this man so much. But I wasn't the girl he'd known. I wasn't capable of the things we'd shared back then.

I had to tell him.

I struggled for two days, pretending that everything was fine. And then, on Tuesday, he sent another message that changed everything yet again.

> *Tara,*
>
> *I may be in Atlanta next week. Any book shows there by chance? I thought you'd said you had something coming up there. Write back or call if you want to talk about it . . . see you.*

That was it. No signature. Nothing. But he'd sent that song on Saturday. He said he listened to it all the time.

That he felt exactly as the song said. It said nothing could take me away from him. It said I was all he wanted. It said he found love in me. It said I was his once in a lifetime.

He was going to Atlanta. He wanted me to meet him there.

We were more completely in each other's lives than either of us had been with the partners we'd lived with, and we hadn't set sight on each other for twenty-seven years.

I wanted to ignore the post.

I hit reply.

> Tim,
>
> As a matter of fact, I did have an invitation for Atlanta from my publicist. It's an invitation from a bookseller there who wants to do an event. Is it worth following up on?
> Tara

What in the hell was I doing? I couldn't see Tim in person. He'd know just how much I'd changed. And he'd know that there was no future for us in the way he was obviously envisioning.

Tim wanted to finish what we'd started thirty years before. He wanted to go all the way.

My body was no longer capable of arousal.

But Tim had asked me to meet him, and I hadn't been able to tell him no. I needed to see him.

Tim had to sit down when he read Tara's email. He'd thrown Atlanta out there as an off chance, built out of his growing urgency to see her in person. He needed to look her in the eye, touch her, to feel her touch to make sure she was real and not some illusion he was building in his dreams. He was beginning to feel as awkward and tied up as he had at eighteen.

She was so skittish, he'd expected excuses. Or an out-and-out negative. Not this tentative yes.

How romantic would it be if they could meet over Valentine's Day? If they could make this Atlanta thing work?

How terrible if they made plans and she got cold feet? He had to keep it casual. Friends only. Until she was ready for more. Until he knew what had hurt his Tara so badly so could help her heal.

His whole heart was on the line here—in a way his whole life was—and one way or another, it was time to take the next step. Even if he had to fly to Albuquerque.

Atlanta would be easier. And quicker. She was considering it. If he pressured her he might blow the whole thing.

He took his time to write her back.

⁓

> I will keep u in the loop on Atlanta . . . I'm waiting on an
> answer from my contact there . . .
> Tim

I read the note Tuesday afternoon and felt like a whore all over again. Here I was considering a flight to Atlanta to see the man of my dreams, considering trusting him with my deepest dark secret, considering giving the stage in my life to Tara for the first time in twenty-seven years, and Tim was waiting on an answer from a contact? Like I was some broad that he'd get his jollies with if we happened to meet up?

And if not, then, no loss?

But he'd sent me that song. He'd been telling me for two weeks that he wanted my all. That I had his deepest heart.

He hadn't sounded the least bit excited about Atlanta.

I fretted for too long. And then did what I had to do.

Tim had just gotten home from work Tuesday, was in from the frigid temperatures for the night, when her e-mail came through.

Tim,

I'm really afraid you're building me into something I'm not. I just keep getting the impression that you're building this fantasy and I'm not going to possibly be able to live up to it and then reality will set in and I'm going to fall harder than I've ever fallen before. I'm forty-seven years old. With a body that's lived forty-seven not-easy years. I take care of it, but I can't help the aging process. These days I'm pretty sure I look better with my clothes on than off. And I can't make the secret between us just disappear. I have no guarantee that it ever will. I can promise to never quit trying, but I can't promise that I ever will get by it.

And what happens when the newness wears off and it's real life and ordinary?

You sent me that song, saying that you listen to it all the time and that's how you feel and it's about being in someone's arms. You don't know yet how that's going to feel, so how can you feel that about me? You think it's going to be heaven, and what if it isn't?

I look really really bad sometimes. I get irritable and tense. And wrinkles are just around the corner. Nothing magic about any of that.

Take a break from me. You deserve it!

Tara

The first time he read the letter he panicked. She was doing it again. Asking for her ring back.

Atlanta had frightened her off, just like he'd thought it might.

He went out to the kitchen. Had a spoonful of peanut butter. Two sips from the open can of soda in the refrigerator.

And went back to read the note again.

She was running scared. Afraid of all the practical realities keeping them apart?

Maybe she'd never wanted anything more than a pen pal.

The things he didn't understand were looming larger and larger between them. He had to know what had happened to her. What had changed her so drastically from the girl he'd known at Wright State to the woman he'd seen in the summer of 1980?

Did she have a child out there, one she'd had with James outside of marriage that last year of college? Had she lost custody of the child? Had James had an affair? Giving her trust issues?

Whatever it was had been bad enough that she never mentioned the guy to anyone. That was pretty damned bad.

Alone in his house, wondering what to do about dinner, Tim didn't want to think about secrets between him and Tara. Whatever it was, they'd get by it. They had to.

Whatever it was, he'd just accept it. Deal with it. Better that than lose her. Everything was under control.

Except her fear. She needed honesty. Bone-deep honesty. The most painful kind.

He'd promised to give it to her.

> *Tara,*
>
> *Trust me, you're safe. You are not just a fantasy, you're a wonderful woman. I want to treat you with respect and ease into this. I know the past is very difficult. Let's work through it together.*
>
> *It may be difficult at times for both of us, but we just have to take deep breaths and hold on and reassure each other.*

My eyes and heart are open and that is what scares me most, because I have never let anyone see this deep inside. There are some barriers and fences to get around. but once you're inside try not to move things too much because they have been in the same place for a long time. Just dust them off, and when things are settled, you can rearrange them to fit you better.

One other thing—sex is important, but if we both can't enjoy it then it really has no meaning. Once we're in the mode of sex, then I probably won't be able to get enough of it, but I've made it this long without it—a little longer won't hurt. No, I'm not trying to build up to some climactic meeting where we fall into each other's arm and we make passionate love and everything is great, but it can happen, even at our age. (Okay, yes, I am building to this.) But right now I'm interested in your heart. Just be yourself.

I don't want you to think that I expect anything from you because we were together years ago. The magic will take care of itself; let's get to know each other. I'm the worrier, remember!
Tim

I read the e-mail on Wednesday morning and picked up the phone and called him.

"Have you heard anything about Atlanta?"

"Not for sure yet, but it looks like I'll be going next Thursday morning. What about you?"

"I heard from my publicist. There's a signing Thursday afternoon. I'd fly in Wednesday night and fly out Friday." I was in my office, my book document open. I was going to work all day and into the night. I had my priorities.

Besides, the book was going well. I could feel the people so clearly, and the words were flying out of me.

I was good at what I did. I needed to focus on that.

"Sounds good."

"I can't believe we're really going to do this."

"It's inevitable."

"I . . . have something to tell you."

"I hope so. I've been waiting."

"But, Tim . . . if I do . . . it's not . . . I've never told anyone . . ." He knew that. I'd already said so. But did he understand the ramifications? How could he?

"Then it's probably time you did."

"You just have to promise . . ." What? "Just . . . I don't want you to think any less of me . . ."

"I'm not going to. Whatever it is, we'll get through it. You just need to tell me. Once that's done, you'll see, it won't be such a big deal. It's just getting things out that's hard."

I knew it was more than that. But understood that he couldn't possibly know.

I left it at that. And tried to believe that we really could make something work.

Twenty-Three

TIM WAS IN TROUBLE. HE MEANT EVERY WORD HE SAID to Tara. He was going to be there for her. He would be her rock in the storm. But he was human, too. And he had issues of his own.

Her reticence was not good. The letter telling him to take a break had scared the shit out of him. Hell, he was a walking mass of paranoia where she was concerned. Any other time in his life, he'd have removed himself from the situation. He couldn't do that with Tara.

He didn't like that fact.

But a man knows what a man knows, and that woman had him by the . . . heart.

> *Tara,*
>
> *I just want to get this down before we see each other. I just can't take you walking out of my life again. I'm trying to be completely honest and show you everything that goes thru my head and my heart. This time you won't have any doubts that I'm telling you everything about what I'm feeling.*
>
> *I have a lot of issues with trust and security. When I feel threatened I shut down and suppress all of my feeling, like I did when you wanted your ring back. I hurt a lot of people doing that. All that I'm asking is be careful with me and make*

damned sure this is what you want. Because I'm already
attached too much to you to go back.

When you talk to me, there is a calm that comes from
that, and I need it more and more.
Tim

I read Tim's post late Wednesday evening. And called him for a second time that day.

His vulnerability sent my heart into overdrive.

"Hey," I said as soon as he picked up. "I hope it's not too late."

"It's never too late for you."

"I got your e-mail. You are what I want, Tim. I have no doubt about that. It's you wanting me when you know everything that worries me."

"Oh, babe, believe me, I want you."

It was almost eleven his time and he sounded groggy. "Were you in bed?"

"Yeah, but I wasn't sleeping yet. I was lying here thinking about you."

I slid down to the floor into my desk alcove and leaned back, too tired to fight issues at the moment. "What about me?"

"What are you wearing?"

"What?"

"What do you have on tonight?"

"Jeans. A yellow shirt. And a jacket that matches them both."

"Anything under them I should know about?"

Oh, God. This was the Tim I knew the best. The man who had sex on his mind and wasn't shy talking about it. This was my Tim from 1977. He was way out of my league now.

"Like what?"

"Stuff I like."

I smiled. "What do you like?"

"You know what I like."

"Tell me." I didn't recognize myself.

"I like a nice playground, and from what I remember, you have a very nice one."

"It's probably not real gentlemanly of you to remind me of that."

"Why not? It's just the two of us here."

"I know, but . . ."

"You asked me what I was doing. I was lying in bed thinking about you. About how it used to be for us. Thinking about touching you like that now."

Atlanta. They might be seeing each other very soon. I was a changed woman. I was going to have to tell him. But I was enjoying the conversation so much I couldn't stop.

He was my Tim. And safely far away.

"I really want to play on your playground."

"You're embarrassing me." But his words were building a curious tension inside of me, too.

"I didn't mean to."

"It's okay."

"It's better than okay. It would be great."

I didn't think so. Thirty years ago, sure, but now . . .

He'd said we'd take our time. That he was interested in my heart.

"How can you be so sure?"

"I just know."

"I haven't been with a man for a lot of years."

"I figured as much when you told me about Chris."

"So . . ." I had no idea why I was engaging in this conversation.

"So I will go slow. Be gentle."

"I like the sound of that." Surprisingly enough, I did. I closed my eyes and was eighteen again. Listening to the sexy, sleepy sound of Tim's voice.

"I'll start out caressing your back. And then your stomach. And as I remember, you liked it when I touched your breasts, too."

"You have a good memory."

"Of you, yes. I have some very, very good memories."

I smiled. I was tired of fighting everything.

"Once you're ready, I'll slide inside you."

"Tim. You promised. No sex."

"Until we're in it together."

"I'm not in it."

I said the words, but something had happened, Down there. He'd just made me wet. Where I'd been nothing but dry since James had defiled me.

———

So much was happening so quickly. I'd gone from being in cold storage for ten years to living in the eye of a hurricane. Some of my tension came from the deadline. I knew that.

And some of the emotional upheaval belonged to Annie and Blake, the hero and heroine in *The Baby Gamble*, the book I was immersed in. Annie was twice divorced, finished with love, and wanting a baby. Blake was a released political captive fighting inner demons that prevented him from loving. I think they were both stealing parts of themselves from me.

I was also beyond myself with excitement over the possibility of seeing my Tim again for the first time in almost thirty years.

And I was scared to death of losing him when he knew that I wasn't coming to him as a complete woman. I could give him sex. After our phone call the other night, I was pretty sure I would if he asked. Tim had made it pretty clear he wanted a future with me. And I wanted one with him, too. I couldn't pretend otherwise. But I knew better than to hope for it. Tim wouldn't settle for one-sided pleasure—even if the side was his.

Friday morning I heard from my publicist that I was set up to sign books in Atlanta the following Thursday. I texted the news to him. He texted back that he was going to be in Atlanta.

He called then, from his desk at work, to find out my travel details. By the time we hung up, my heart was pounding and I had to go outside for some fresh air. I was hot. And cold. And excited. And scared as hell.

I'd done it. I'd committed to meeting Tim in Atlanta. I had my hotel. He had his. I was arriving Wednesday night—Valentine's night. He would be there sometime Thursday.

I was really going to see him. After thirty years . . .

And the what-ifs were deafening.

Tim called Saturday afternoon. He'd been with a buddy of his, watching a local basketball game. I was, as usual, in my office.

"I was thinking about you the whole time I was at the game," Tim confessed. "Thinking about holding you."

That liquid warmth spread through me again. For the second time in twenty-seven years. It whipped from my heart to regions down below in the space of seconds.

"How many pages did you get done?" he continued, while I was busy trying to analyze things that weren't meant to be logically understood. Like how his voice could do physical things to my body, when physical touch left me cold and dry.

"Fifteen," I answered his question. Thankfully the book was still cooperating. "Verne died."

"He did." Tim's voice dropped. "Who's Verne?"

"This guy. He died on the toilet." I started to laugh. And then added, "I'm sorry, that's sick. I didn't plan it that way. It's just . . . someone went into his apartment looking for him and there he was, dead on the toilet." I laughed again.

"Who's Verne?" He sounded odd.

And I realized that I'd left out a key part of my conversation. "An old drunk in the book."

"Ohhhh."

"He's the uncle of a character in the book that follows mine. It's a series of five connected books by five different authors, and I was told to kill him off."

"Got it."

"I have to have the book done before I get on the plane on Wednesday."

"I won't keep you long then."

"No, that's okay. I'll just stay up late tonight." I welcomed the distraction. I wasn't sleeping in my own bed, in my own home. I wasn't sleeping much, period.

"I called because I have something I need to tell you."

My heart sank. He wasn't going to Atlanta. He'd heard from Denise and was getting back with her.

"What?"

"I just want you to know that I have no expectations of having sex next week. As a matter of fact, I'll just say it. We're not going to have sex in Atlanta."

Oh. I wasn't sure what to say. The emotional turmoil that had taken over my life left me pretty much speechless. I was relieved. Of course. So did I thank him?

I wasn't disappointed, was I?

"It's not because I don't want to," he inserted into my silence.

"Okay."

"It's just, I'd never had sex before I met you back in college."

"I wondered. You said you hadn't, but . . ."

"Yeah, well, hopefully that can shed some light on why our relationship was based on my hands and not my heart. I was eighteen. When I met you, I truly was in love with you. I couldn't wait until I saw you, I wanted to be close to you all the time, and it just came out wrong."

"I know."

"It's not going to come out wrong again."

"We've spent weeks talking. It's already completely different. If we'd been able to talk back then even a little bit like we talk now . . ."

"I like sex. A lot." He continued. "I think about having sex with you all the time. I just want you to know that I don't take sex lightly. I'm not one of those guys who can do it and forget it."

I was glad to hear that. I wasn't going to be able to have hot sex with Tim, period. He was letting me off the hook.

I should have been relieved. I was relieved. And I was disappointed, too.

"I guess the truth is, I'm dying to get inside your body," he said, the words coming in gusts of energy that might just blow me away. "I need it too much. And I don't want the sex to get in the away again. I also want you to know that you don't have to justify your past to me. I want to know about your past so I can have a full understanding of your emotions and how you got here, but that's it. I don't know if I ever made that clear."

I didn't know what to say, and he just kept talking.

"We have some really important stuff to do in Atlanta. Things to talk about and deal with, and they come first. If I had sex with you, you wouldn't be allowed out of bed until it was time to catch our flights home, and we wouldn't get a word in edgewise."

He still wanted me. I smiled. "Even you would need a breather." I was getting better at the banter, at least.

"With you? I wouldn't count on it."

"Okay."

"That's it? Just okay? What do you think about having sex with me?"

"I think that I have no idea what we're going to do when we see each other," I told him honestly, embarrassed, looking at the floor. "I figured we'd wait and see what happens when we get there."

"Okay."

"And . . . I know I . . . want you to hold me. I need to feel your arms around me . . ."

More heat between my legs. Heat with empty promises.

"I need that, too."

"Good." I let out the breath I'd been holding. "Then we can hold each other and talk."

"And whatever happens, happens."

Did that mean we might have sex after all? Or that he might try? I got nervous again.

"What about birth control?" I was a responsible woman.

"All taken care of."

So he was prepared to have sex with me. Or just prepared for any eventuality?

"How long has it been for you?"

His question embarrassed me. Chris and I had never talked about sex. Or during it, either, for that matter.

"Twelve years."

"Seriously."

"Yeah. I ended that part of my relationship with Chris. I told you that." It had been the morning after the night he'd woken me up when he got into bed by hauling me over and climbing on top of me. He'd been angry and let me know that he had every right to have sex with his wife.

He'd hurried up and finished that night, too.

And that had been the last time he'd had sex with his wife.

"You said you had separate bedrooms," Tim said. "I didn't know if that meant . . ."

"I haven't had a man inside me in so long, my body probably couldn't even take it . . ."

I'd found a way to warn him, at least.

"Oh, it'd take me. I have no worries about that." His voice had softened. And deepened. My body responded to it.

"How about you?" I asked, to distract me from own confusion. "How long has it been for you?"

"I haven't slept with anyone since Denise left."

"There's been no one?"

"Not even a date."

"Wow." I'd been afraid to ask. Afraid of the answer. "I'm shocked."

"I take that as an insult." He actually sounded a bit put out. "Just because I'm a guy doesn't mean that I don't have standards."

"I know that," I hastened to assure him. "But you're gorgeous, Tim. I can't believe that there weren't women after you the second they knew you were free."

"I hurt two women because I couldn't commit to them," Tim said. "I wasn't about to hurt a third."

God, I loved this man. And I couldn't wait to see him.

Whatever happened.

Twenty-Four

ATLANTA WAS AN OKAY CITY. I LIKED THE SOUTHERN feel. The accents. The trees. It was warm enough.

I'd been there with James.

And here I was, back in the city to admit, for the first time in my life, what I'd suffered because of him.

Unpacking the few things I'd brought took five minutes in the four-star hotel room. Makeup out in the bathroom. The DVD player that traveled with me all set up beside the bed. In less than twelve hours Tim would be there. He landed at 6:00 AM and was stopping by to say hello before his morning meeting.

I had to eat. More accurately, I had to have a drink, and I couldn't drink without getting some food in my stomach. Room service, available through the hotel's fine-dining establishment, was way more than I needed. And far too expensive. But there was a pub downstairs that had salads. And more important, a full bar.

It took another ten minutes for me to make it down there, look over the menu, and order. Leaving me a good eleven hours before Tim.

And then I noticed that I was the only person in the bar who was there alone. And I remembered. It was Valentine's Day.

A day for lovers.

Fitting that I was there alone.

I picked up my phone and dialed.

"Hello?" Pat Potter, my closest writer friend picked up.

"Hi. I need to ask you a favor."

"Of course."

"I'm in Atlanta. To see Tim. I'm due to see him in the morning for the first time in almost thirty years. He could be a mass murderer for all I know . . ." I was rambling. I heard myself. And I couldn't stop.

What was I doing meeting up with Tim like this? I wasn't eighteen any more. I'd learned the hard way that a woman was never safe. And here I was leaving myself wide open for further hurt and humiliation and . . .

"If I don't call you by five o'clock tomorrow, please call the police." I told her where I was staying.

"Okay." Pat took down the numbers. Read them back to me. "You're going to be fine," she added just before we hung up. "You know that, right?"

"Yeah."

"Have fun."

Her words incited another onslaught of excitement and fear that not even the scotch I was drinking could quell. They rang in my mind like a permission slip to do whatever I wanted to do. No matter what that might be.

⁓

He went out to dinner the night before he left for Atlanta—a way to keep himself occupied so minutes wouldn't turn into hours.

The work he was going there to do seemed like a pretense. As far as he was concerned, he was flying to Atlanta to meet up with Tara.

He thought about her all night and called her just before going to bed.

"Hey, Babe," he said, relaxing once he heard her voice. "Are you in your hotel?"

"Yeah. All checked in. The room's nice." He pictured her there. Where he'd be in just a few hours. Interminable hours.

"How are you feeling?"

"Nervous."

"Do you miss me?"

"So much."

"I'm going to have a hard time sleeping tonight knowing you're down there alone and I'm up here alone."

"Me, too."

"I've been thinking about the whole sex thing."

"Yeah?"

"It dominated our relationship the last time. I let it get in the way of the things that were most important. I don't want to make that mistake again."

"I completely agree."

"So we'll take it slow and easy. Conversation first."

"Okay."

There. He'd done it. And he added, "Then if it happens, it does."

Just couldn't let it go. Even now. Twenty-seven years after he'd lost her because he couldn't keep his hands off her long enough to let her know how much he loved her, he was still aching to touch her.

⁓

He was wide awake before the alarm went off. He'd been awake most of the night. The thought of seeing Tara for the first time in almost thirty years had kept him conscious. With Tara in Albuquerque and him in Ohio, creating a two-hour time change, he'd been up until 2:00 AM many times, talking to her after she finished work for the night. And he still had to be up at six to get to work on time.

It was almost déjà vu. Reminiscent of the days when he drove from Huber Heights late at night to clock in late at the grocery story.

This time he was older, but he'd still make it work. There was plenty of time to sleep when you're dead, he thought.

For now, he was living again.

Just before he shut off his phone for the trip, he texted Tara.

Hey, Babe, good morning, heading to the airport.

Her reply was immediate.

Can't wait until you're here. Be safe.

I hadn't slept much. I'd been afraid of oversleeping. Afraid my hair wasn't going to cooperate. I only had the hotel's hair dryer, and it might not give my hair as much body as mine did.

I'd been wide awake already when Tim's text came through telling me that he was on his way.

I flew out of bed and into the shower.

What if my hand were shaking so much I couldn't apply my eyeliner? I thought about the jeans I'd chosen. They were too long—all my pants were, but I had high-heeled boots to wear with them. And the shirt. One of my favorites. It was blue with muted flowers in green and yellow. It had gauze sleeves and sequins and fit me well enough to show Tim that I was thinner now than I'd been at eighteen. The shirt covered the top of my jeans, but only if I didn't raise my arms.

I was doing everything I could not to think about the things I had to tell him. And not to think about his body—wanting my body.

I bathed with extra care, making certain that every part of my body received proper attention. I shaved. I left the conditioner in my hair a little longer. I had to be perfect.

Like I could somehow make up for my sexual imperfections, my inability to feel desire during intercourse, if I could just look good enough.

Not that we were going to have intercourse. We weren't. Yet. But it would come up at some point. I could count on that. This was Tim and me.

Unless, after he'd heard about James, he didn't want to touch me at all.

Hair and makeup application all went as planned. Easily. The

Sorvelli jewelry looked perfect. I had three piercings in each ear. And matching earrings for each. Would he think that I was too over-the-top? Be turned off by that many holes in my ears?

And then I paced. Peered out my window. Watched the clock.

I couldn't believe that in less than an hour I was going to be seeing Tim Barney—and was afraid I'd wake up and find out that the past three weeks had been a very, very cruel dream.

My phone beeped a text.

"Just landed."

I was never going to breathe normally again.

A few minutes later, the phone rang.

"Hello?"

"What's up?"

My heart settled. All fear disappeared as I heard his voice. This was no stranger from thirty years ago. This was Tim. My Tim.

He told me that he was on his way to get the car he'd rented.

Life's tragedies, damaged psyches, worries about difficult conversations all faded away. This was my Tim. And after twenty-seven long, desolate years, I was finally going to be where I'd always belonged.

In Tim Barney's arms again.

Holding on.

And being held.

He pulled into her hotel, parked the car, and went straight to the elevator, pushing the button for the fifth floor, loving the fact that he already knew that Tara didn't like the lower floors in hotels. Something about being up high put her at ease.

He found her room and then dialed her phone.

He'd had this crazy idea that if he surprised her, if she was shocked when she saw him, she wouldn't be so nervous.

He was hoping their first moment together in twenty-seven years would be just her and him. No nerves. No fears.

"Hello?"

"Look outside your door . . ."

"What?"

He heard a rustle and then, "Oh! You're here!"

The door flew open and Tim barely registered that she looked exactly the same as she lunged toward him, grinning and half crying, too.

Her arms were around his neck out in the hall, clutching him as tightly as she ever had. And his flew around her, too, filling them with her, completing him for the first time in thirty years.

She lifted her face as if by instinct, and he met her lips without hesitation. Their tongues touched, entangled, and it wasn't new or strange or different. She felt and tasted exactly like Tara.

He'd flown all the way to Atlanta to come home.

~

"Let's get out of the hallway."

I heard Tim's words, though I was having a hard time holding on to coherent thought. It was like I'd consumed an entire bottle of scotch. Really good scotch. The kind that you could drink in large quantities and not get sick.

He walked right into my room as if he belonged there, taking me with him to the armchair on the other side of the bed. He sat, and pulled me onto his lap. It had been almost thirty years since I'd seen him. He should be a stranger to me.

He wasn't. At all. His brown eyes. His smile. His taste. He was my Tim. Exactly as I'd left him.

I asked about his flight. But couldn't remember his answer five seconds after he'd given it.

We had to talk. He had to know the truth about me. We couldn't go any further, or even think about a future together until he knew what had happened. He might be the same man.

I was not the same woman. I couldn't pretend that I was.

He kissed me again and I fell against him, weak with wanting him. I knew the feeling would leave. Long before we got anywhere near the sex we weren't going to have.

But just like thirty years before, I couldn't stop him. Or myself. I thrust my tongue in his mouth as if I had every right to be there. Because in my heart, I did. I always had.

And when he set me on my feet and moved toward the unmade bed that I'd just vacated a short time before, I went with him willingly. Without thought.

His hands were everywhere on my body, caressing my legs through my jeans. He kissed me again. With a wild hunger that I answered. Kiss for kiss. His lips moved to my neck, and I turned my head to give him better access, feeling the cool sheet against my heated cheek.

I was eighteen again. In the house on Maple Street.

He was suckling my neck as he'd done thirty years before, and the sensations shot from skin, through my body, and down between my legs.

There was nothing to say that wasn't being said. Nothing more important than Tim on top of me, claiming what was his. What had always been his.

My hands were all over his chest. I tore at his clothes, getting them out of the way. I was like a woman possessed. I had to have him. I didn't recognize myself. And I didn't argue with the power driving me.

My shirt was up, over my head and off. I wasn't wearing a bra. And he got rid of my camisole as quickly as he had the shirt.

I felt the cold air of the room on my breasts and didn't freeze up. I was a woman. Beautiful. Sexy. On fire for my man. I was Tara Gumser, and he was Tim Barney.

With his thumb against my nipple, he met my gaze and I thought I might cry. He was doing things to me that I hadn't thought possible. Sending desire from breasts that had been numb for my entire adult life down to my most private places.

I knew it wouldn't last. That if we went any further I was going to dry up and there'd be pain. I thought about warning him. He deserved to know.

But I wasn't going to stop him. Any pain I felt would be worth becoming one with Tim. I'd screwed up thirty years ago when I'd made him stop before we'd completely finished. I had a wrong to fix.

Our shoes fell off. He undid my jeans and tugged at them until they were off, and I undid his pants, pulling them down, too.

I was wet down there. Just like I'd been when he'd talked to me on the phone that night.

Tim lay down on top of me, taking my mouth with his as his naked body came into full contact with mine and I was completely on fire.

I could feel his penis nudging at my womanhood, and I lifted my hips to meet him, to press against him. In some faraway foggy place, I knew that this was where it was going to hurt and I just plain didn't care. I loved him so much. And I felt right, completely right and honest and true for the first time in my life.

I wasn't listening to the words of all those who guided me. Or to books or teachings or anything earthly. I was listening to my heart. Finally. And it had led me where it knew I needed to be all along.

Tim's leg nudged mine, spreading my legs, and I opened to him, welcoming him in. I felt the head of him at my opening just as I had thirty years before. We were on Maple Street. In the downstairs bed again.

Only this time he didn't stop. He nudged gently and that was when I left all sense of self. I was floating in an inexplicable space. Tim was there, sliding inside me. Without effort. My body knew him, recognized him. Greeted him with a moist warmth that guided him home.

There was no pain. No stretching. He fit perfectly. And I knew. My body had been made for him.

Only him.

He pulled back and slid in again, and with each thrust he filled me more, fit me better.

I'd never imagined anything so incredible. Tension was building inside me, but there was no threat. No defense. Just a welcoming of what his occupation would bring.

Belief was suspended. I didn't have to work that hard. Didn't have the option of disbelief. I rode with him, having no idea of what would happen next. Each moment was all there was. And each moment was perfect.

Until the most perfect moment of all. My body was reaching. Toward Tim. And toward a pinnacle it had never reached before. I heard my voice as I cried out and tumbled from one world to the next, pulsating around Tim just seconds before he groaned, and groaned again, emptying himself into me.

As I came back to a sense of where I was, I didn't return to who I'd been. Tim and I . . . we were complete now.

And I was the woman I'd been meant to be.

We untangled, and still there was no awkwardness.

"Okay, Barney," I said, filled with a new confidence, a boldness I'd lost somewhere along the way, "that one I owed you, the next one you will have to earn."

Before he touched me again—and he would touch me again, I was absolutely certain of that fact—he was going to have to promise me some kind of future.

And before that, I had to tell him what he'd be signing on for. Because I didn't kid myself. I knew that all of our encounters wouldn't be as perfect as the one we'd just had.

I had issues. Times when just the feel of a man's hand on my shoulder flipped me out. A form of post-traumatic stress disorder, I'd been told.

I was claustrophobic and had insomnia more often than not. I was high maintenance. And he had some tough choices to make.

Twenty-Five

TIM WENT TO WORK, I WENT TO SIGN BOOKS, AND THE WORLD rejoined our lives. I would be forever thankful for those magical moments in my hotel room, but by the time Tim picked me up that afternoon, life had intruded. I'd had a call from Chris on my cell phone.

He wanted me to have my stuff out of the house by the end of the weekend. And he was going to start charging me rent for the office space starting Monday. I wasn't sure he could do that. But I wasn't sure he couldn't, either.

And the reality hit that my life was in the Southwest. Tim's was in Ohio. I couldn't move that far from my mother. I couldn't tolerate cold and months of gray. And I was going to be strapped for cash for the time it took me to rebuild my life. He couldn't leave a twenty-year career. He owned a home.

We'd come back to his room to have our talk. He was on a business call, and I was dreading the upcoming conversation. My stomach had returned to one huge knot.

I heard the words Tim was saying to his associate, and I stood. I needed to walk. Or take a drive. There was no place to go.

What if Tim didn't understand? What if he judged me? What if James had been right and what had happened had somehow been my fault?

I hadn't told him no.

What if I'd just reunited with Tim, finally owning his heart, giving him my whole heart, only to lose him again?

I wouldn't blame him if he opted out of this one.

Even if he didn't blame me, didn't find me disgusting, just dealing with the fact that it had happened at all was hard. There were so many what-ifs. So many lost chances.

So many things that couldn't be fixed.

We'd lost thirty years that would never be returned.

I had trust issues. Privacy issues.

I heard Tim say good-bye.

Twisting my hands, I turned to face the man I loved with all of my heart, feeling trapped.

He was smiling, his brown eyes twinkling. He pulled me to him and kissed me, opening his mouth and taking me with him into the place where only he and I existed. My tongue met his, and everything else faded away.

"Mmmm." His hungry growl made me hungry, too. "I thought about this all day long."

With his hands at my back, he pulled me against him, fitting his groin to my pelvis. He was hard.

And offering me a respite. Another time out of time. A trip back to fantasy land. I accepted his invitation.

I was in that place again, lying with Tim, floating on clouds of sensation, untouchable. One perfect moment led to another, until . . . it didn't.

Tim's fingers were between my legs, touching me. I could feel the crescendo building, and then, out of nowhere, there was dread. And coldness.

I lost all sensation. And started to panic.

I'd promised myself I never had to have sex again. I'd promised. I didn't have to.

His fingers continued to move against my private parts, and I started to cry and squeezed my eyes shut to hold in the tears. I didn't want to do this. I didn't want . . . It had been so good. And I'd hoped and . . . I didn't want to do this. I'd promised me I didn't have to. Ever again. And . . . I was trapped. I couldn't get out. I had to get out. I had to.

"Hey, Babe!" It was Tim's voice. He was above me. But there was nothing between my legs.

"Babe?"

I opened my eyes.

"Babe, it's me. Tim."

I focused on the voice. And then the face above mine. I looked into his eyes. They called out to me just as they always had. He was right. It was Tim. My Tim.

Reaching for him, I pulled him down to me and held on while I sobbed.

Tara was in the bathroom. She'd calmed down, and they'd gone out for something to eat. He didn't want to push her, but he had to know what was going on. He didn't have a hope in hell of fixing it if he didn't know what it was.

Whether she wanted to talk or not, at this point he needed an explanation at the very least.

The bathroom door opened and she came slowly out into the dimly lit room. Sometime between disaster and dinner, the sun had set.

"I'm sorry."

"For what?"

"This. Me. The day."

"I'm not sorry for any of it. Come sit with me," he said, patting the couch beside him.

She sat down, but no part of her body was touching his. He pulled her over and put his arm around her shoulder.

"Tell me what's going on."

"It's bad."

"I figured that much out."

"You aren't going to like it."

"That's pretty obvious, too. I couldn't possibly like anything that's hurt you this badly."

"You might not like me." She started to cry and then took a deep breath, composing herself.

"I find that highly doubtful."

"James . . . he did something really bad."

Tim thought he was prepared. He'd gone through all of the scenarios—the lost custody thing, the affair possibility. And suddenly something clicked. The afternoon's debacle.

Coupled with James . . .

He wasn't sure he wanted to hear any more. And he knew he had to.

"Tell me."

"We were on a date, and he took me down this deserted country road."

He clenched his teeth. Needing to shut out the sound of her voice. And the pictures in his head.

"And?"

"He . . . he wanted to have sex, and I said no, and he . . ."

"He what?"

"No one knows. He told me never to tell anyone, and I haven't. Ever. Not anyone. Not my mom. Not Chris. I don't talk about it, Tim. Please, can't we just leave it alone? Please?"

"No."

"He put himself up in me, okay?"

He'd figured it out. And was glad for the darkness.

"He had sex with you."

"Not normal sex."

"What does that mean?"

"He didn't go where you went today."

Tim froze. All of him. His heart. His body. And his mind, too. Her words played themselves over him a second time. And a third.

"Where did he . . . go?"

But he knew.

God in heaven, how in the hell could this have happened? To his Tara? She'd been his, dammit. His. Her gifts, they'd been for him.

She'd been so sweet. So innocent. And . . .

"Up my backside."

Calm. Stay calm.

"Did you tell him he could?"

"Of course not! I didn't even know anything like that was anatomically possible."

"He raped you."

Her silence scared him. "Good God, Babe, he didn't just rape you . . . he sodomized you!"

She was crying, softly.

"When did this happen?"

"In April of 1980."

"Before I came to see you in July."

That's why she'd been so different that day. She hadn't been in love with another man. She'd been *worse* than raped.

God damn the fucking bastard to hell.

⌒

"We'll get through this."

I wanted to believe him. It was 3:00 AM and we were lying in bed in Tim's hotel room. We were naked, and he was holding me with my head on his shoulder. We'd been talking all night.

"When did you say you met James?"

"In April of 1979."

"A month after I didn't meet you for lunch."

"Yeah."

"If I'd met you . . ."

I put my finger to his lips. "Don't. The what-ifs will eat us alive if we let them."

They might eat us alive anyway. We'd had so many near misses. So many times when tragedy could have been prevented. If I'd told Tim how I felt instead of asking for my ring back . . .

"We're going to get through this."

"How? You can't even make love to me without danger of me flipping out on you."

"So? If we never made love again, I'd still be happy with you. I love sex, Tara, don't get me wrong, but I love you more."

"But . . ."

"Besides," he grinned at her, the old Tim grin, "I have a lot more faith in my abilities than you do. You had no problem the first time today."

He was right about that. I was still shocked, every time I thought about it. "Because I was eighteen again and . . ."

"Then you'll be eighteen every time until we get you through this."

"And what happens when I have another episode like I had this afternoon?"

"Then we stop."

"You'd stop?" I turned to look at him.

"Of course I'd stop. I did today, didn't I? We go together, Babe, or we don't go at all."

"You'd do that for me?"

"What part of 'I love you' are you not getting?"

So I was a little slow. I was trying as hard as I could to catch up. I was not going to repeat my mistakes and let my life go on without me. One thing I knew for sure. If I had to choose between thirty extra years of life and sharing life with Tim, I'd give up the thirty years of life to have Tim.

"Trust me, Babe, I'm here to stay."

Trust. "That night, after James . . . I decided then and there that I would never, ever trust anyone to take care of me again."

"Care to revise that choice?"

"Yeah."

"Then what's the problem?"

At the moment I couldn't think of one. I was too tired to think. Settling into the crook of Tim's arm, I fell asleep.

Friday afternoon came all too soon. Tim drove the two of them to the airport, returned the car, went with Tara to check her bag, and then walked through security with her.

As elated as he'd been the morning before when he'd flown into Atlanta, he was sad that afternoon. He was on his way back to Ohio and sending Tara back to her life in Albuquerque.

He'd had her in his arms since they'd passed through security forty-five minutes before.

"I don't know how this is going to work, me in Albuquerque and you in Ohio, I just don't see the logistics."

"Tara, don't worry about it. What I know about life is that it will play itself out. An opportunity will present itself, and we'll know what to do. Okay?"

She nodded, but he worried, too.

"Promise me you won't back up on us."

"Okay," she said, as he'd known she would, but he also knew that deep down she was coming apart and he wouldn't be there to help hold her together. He was sending her off alone to deal with the ending of her marriage, finding a home, and trying to deal with all of the memories they'd just brought to the surface, with the aftereffects of what that monster James had done to her. Talking about the incident had brought it out of a thirty-year deep freeze. He didn't kid himself into thinking that there wouldn't be fallout.

"Babe, just remember that I'm only a phone call away and it only takes four hours to fly to Ohio if you start to lose it. I can be out there in that amount of time, too, if you need me. And you can text me any time of the day or night."

His flight was called. He pulled Tara behind some columns and kissed her. Really kissed her. Reminding her who they were and what they had together.

"Good-bye, Babe," she said. "Call me when you land."

"I will."

He turned to go, but turned back. "Tara," he called to her.

"Yeah?"

"I have something to tell you."

She stepped closer with a worried look on her face. "What?"

"I love you. I've loved you since I met you on that cold rainy day in October of 1977. I just didn't know how to get the words out. I just want you to know that. It's always been there, and it always will be there."

"I love you, too."

"We're going to make it."

She nodded and, with tears in her eyes, turned and walked toward her gate.

Leaving her was excruciating. He'd just spent the greatest twenty-four hours of his life since 1977 and he was going home to an empty house and a life without Tara.

I've landed, and miss you like hell. I love you.

He sent the text to her when he landed in Ohio, but he knew it would be hours before she answered because she was on her flight home.

I'm home, Babe. I love you, and miss you more than ever.

Her text came in at four in the morning.

He was lying awake in bed without her. Something was going to have to change. Quickly. He'd already lost thirty years of a life with her. He wasn't going to lose any more.

⁓

Less than a week after he returned from Atlanta, Tim had reached the limit on his patience, waiting for an opportunity to strike. Tara was in Albuquerque alone, dealing with her ex-husband and making plans to move to Phoenix. Her mother had taken the news of the divorce well, and she knew about Tim, too.

Her life was falling into place without him while he drove to work in the cold every day, did the same job he'd been doing for twenty years, and then drove home in the cold to an empty house. The Wednesday after he'd returned from Atlanta, he couldn't face the empty house again.

He went instead to the local pub around the corner. It had been years since he'd been out drinking, and Rick, a fellow engineer from work, had mentioned that he was going to be at the pub. Tim texted Tara and let her know he was out having dinner and a drink with a guy from work.

The first drink went down smooth and tasted good, so he ordered another. And then one more.

About that time, a text came in from Tara.

Hey, Babe, how's dinner going?

He hurried to answer her.

Din good. Be bette ifff u are heee.

"Who are you texting?" Rick asked.

"I've been seeing a lady named Tara, Tara Gumser," Tim said, pouring his heart out to a guy he'd been working with for fifteen years and who'd never even heard of Denise.

"To be exact, she was my first love and probably the reason I haven't married all these years," he continued.

He ordered another drink, not quite numb enough yet. But he was getting close.

His phone signaled another text.

How much have you had to drink, Tim?

Onlu 2 Hoo boit u

He thought that seemed right.

Then why are you misspelling so many words?

He was sure it was the phone messing up, but just to be sure, he paid his tab and headed for home.

An hour later, when Tara texted to tell him goodnight, he wasn't feeling so well. He had no defenses. And no inhibitions, either. It was time to take care of business.

He texted her back.

I love you.

I love you, too, Babe.

And that's when he really let it all fly. He just couldn't pretend anymore. Not to himself. And not to anyone else.

Will you marry me and walk behind me the rest of my life?

He got the whole line out without a single misspelled word.

Are you drunk?

Maybe. Will you marry me?

Will you remember asking me in the morning?

Yes.

Yes, I will marry you, but I won't walk behind you, ever. Or in front of you, either. I'll walk beside you.

Okay

And just to be sure, he texted one more time.

You're going to marry me.

Yes. But you have to ask me again in the morning when you're sober.

Okay. I will.

And he did.

I moved to Ohio in March of 2007 to join Tim in his home until we'd saved enough money for a new life in the Southwest. And early in the afternoon on August 4 of that same year, I finally heard the words I'd waited more than half my life to hear with this man by my side.

"Dearly Beloved, we are gathered here today to join this woman and this man in the bonds of holy matrimony . . ."

I stood there, one of only four people in the room, dressed in a beige and brown sleeveless shift with a lace tie its only adornment, my hair down around my shoulders and wedge sandals on my feet, and faced Tim, who was wearing a pair of beige Dockers and a dark, short-sleeved shirt.

We were in front of a stained-glass window, surrounded by antiques, in the formal living room of a 100-year-old house that had been converted into a bed-and-breakfast. My wedding dress was upstairs. His tuxedo was there, too. Guests would start arriving in a couple of hours. Our formal wedding was scheduled for late that afternoon.

We'd rented the whole house, and some of our guests, my mother and little brother included, would be spending the night.

We had a D.J. coming, a gorgeous cake, a photographer, flowers, a catered dinner, and cases of champagne. But the most important moment of my life was already happening.

Tim and I wanted our family and friends to share our joy with us. We just had to have this moment, this most precious and sacred ceremony, take place with just him and me.

And the owner of the bed-and-breakfast who was our witness, and the minister who was officiating both ceremonies.

And when, after we'd read our own handwritten vows to each other, he pronounced us husband and wife—when I was, in the eyes of God, Mrs. Timothy Lee Barney—I whooped out loud with joy. I'd finally found my own happy ending.

Epilogue

I AM TARA GUMSER. I'M OLDER. I'M TATTERED AND TORN. I'm less naive. The days of my life haven't happened like I'd envisioned them. There are things I can't undo. I have bad spells—times when I struggle to understand, to accept, to remember, and to forget.

And still, I am living proof that the love I write about, the love that is strong enough to heal all hurts, really does exist. Here. In our world. In daily life.

Tim and I have been married for almost four years and are closer now than ever. We've struggled, and through the struggles, we've grown together. He stayed true to his word to remain by my side, to "go together or not at all." Every single day he gives me the privilege of caring for his deepest heart as he cares for mine. And he remains steadfastly adamant that while Tara Taylor Quinn is a welcome visitor in our home, she is not the star of my show.

I am Tara Gumser, and I know two things. I write for Harlequin Books. And I am married to my own Harlequin hero. Finally.

About the Author

THE AUTHOR OF MORE THAN FIFTY ORIGINAL NOVELS in twenty languages, Tara Taylor Quinn is a *USA Today* bestseller with more than six million copies sold. She is known for delivering deeply emotional and psychologically astute novels of suspense and romance. Tara won the 2008 Reader's Choice Award, is a four-time finalist for the RWA Rita Award, a multiple finalist for the Reviewer's Choice Award, the Bookseller's Best Award, the Holt Medallion, and appears regularly on the Waldenbooks bestsellers list. She has appeared on national and local TV across the country, including *CBS Sunday Morning*. When she's not writing or fulfilling speaking engagements, Tara loves to travel with her husband, stopping wherever the spirit takes them. They've been spotted in casinos and quaint little small town antique shops all across the country. Visit the author at www.tarataylorquinn.com.

Submit Your Own True Romance Story

*"The marriage of real-life stories with classic,
fictional romance—an amazing concept."*

—**Peggy Webb**, award-winning author of sixty romance novels

**Do you have the greatest love story never told?
A sexy, steamy, bigger-than-life or just plain
worthwhile love story to tell?**

If so, then here's your chance to share it with us. Your true romance may possibly be selected as the basis for the next book in the TRUE VOWS series, the first-ever Reality-Based Romance™ series.

- Did you meet the love of your life under unusual circumstances that defy the laws of nature and/or have a relationship that flourished against all odds of making it to the altar?

- Did your parents tell you a story so remarkable about themselves that it makes you feel lucky to have ever been born?

- Are you a military wife who stood by her man while he was oceans away, held down the fort at home, then you had to rediscover each other upon his return?

- Did you lose a great love and think you would never survive, only for fate to deliver an embarrassment of riches a second or even third time around?

Story submissions are reviewed by TRUE VOWS editors, who are always on the lookout for the next TRUE VOWS romance.

**Visit www.truevowsbooks.com
to tell us your true romance.**

True Vows. It's Life . . . Romanticized

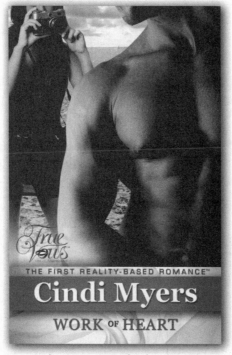

Sexy, Entertaining, Inspiring, and Based on True Romance

Code 5577 • Paperback • $13.95

HelenKay Dimon puts her red-hot pen to paper to tell the breathtaking, sizzling true love story of Victoria Sinclair, lead anchor of Naked News Network, as she finally exposes all: her true identity, the do-tell drama behind the camera, and the whimsical courtship that inspired it all.

www.truevowsbooks.com

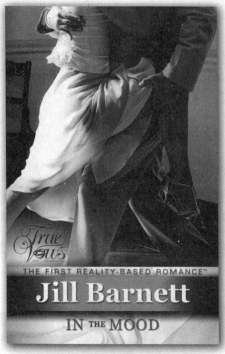

Get Ready to Be Swept Away...
By More *True Vows*™
Reality-Based Romances

Code 5...   ...t $13.95

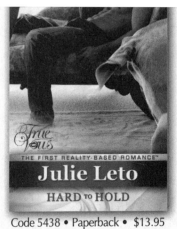

Julie Leto
HARD TO HOLD
Code 5438 • Paperback • $13.95

Available wherever books are sold.
To order direct: Telephone (800) 441-5569 • www.hcibooks.com
Prices do not include shipping and handling. Your response code is TVA.